The Georgetown Cypher

A novel by Kit McKittrick

This book was set in 11.5 point Garamond by Short Run Publishing, Inc.and was published by Short Run Publishing, Inc.. The cover was also printed Short Run Publishing, Inc..

Short Run Publishing, Inc.
5105 N. Ocean Blvd.
Ocean Ridge, FL 33435

All Illustrations, art work and photography found in this book where found in the open domain. The author and publisher would like to thank them for their contribution to this body of work.

ISBN Number for Hard Copy=
978-0-615-41969-5
Library of Congress Control Number:
2010916947

ISBN: 978-0-615-42608-2
(Printed Version)

Library of Congress Control Number: 2010916947

Printed in the United States of America

SHORT RUN PUBLISHING, INC.

Table of Contents

Dedication

This book is dedicated to my beautiful Joan, my sister,

Jeannie and my four daughters.

Dear Mary,

It was so nice to hear about you and your wonderful event. You are the best! I hope you have fun reading this and know the Jesuits will be beating me as you work through it.

My Very Best,

Acknowledgements

There have been many people who have helped me on this nine year journey. I want to thank Phyllis, Nancy, John, Shannon, Laurie, Pat, Edwin and Joe for all of your help and comments.

Message to My Readers

Our fascination with historical mystery, especially in the area of religion is of great interest to readers everywhere. This book is a novel but actual historical events and opinions weigh heavily in its message. There was an alternate interpretation of what it was to be a Christian and its relevance to the early followers, the True Believers. In their Christian practice, The True Believers used special techniques so awe inspiring that legend has Agrippa I creating what eventually became the Freemasons to stop it. Certain meditations and visions have shaped our world for thousands of years. Many attempts have been made to hide or discredit their origin. You will join Ian MacAlester as he travels through guided meditation to unravel this mystery thriller and discover the secret that only in today's modern science is proving what the great prophets tried to share. Thank you for purchasing this book.

Part 1

Chapter 1 - Nathan's

Georgetown, D.C. and the tavern Ian MacAlester found himself was blanketed under a low hanging fog. Inside, Ian cozied up to the bar's TV reading the closed captions. "Today, Assistant District Attorney, Debra Laurie begins her investigation into what can only be described as one of the biggest criminal frauds ever uncovered. The world famous business tycoon, Paul Bailey and others are thought to be involved in masterminding one of the biggest real estate swindles in history. The allegations extend to high-ranking US government officials and the Vatican. We will report more as events unfold."

Reading enough, Ian realigned his stool giving him an unobstructed view of the front door. He had uncovered this plot and it was very dangerous for his health. He tried to hide his six three frame, hunching in the shadows.

Ian called to the bartender,

"OK Steve, I'll have that drink now."

Steve placed the seltzer water down and said with a smile; "After disappearing for 30 years, I see you twice in six-months. What gives?" What Steve really wanted to ask was why Ian didn't order a "stinger on the rocks."

Staring into the seltzer's ice, he answered, "I'm finishing what I started the last time you saw me." Ian internalized Steve's question. It sparked deep emotions as Ian felt the first wave of Thoreauvian quiet desperation coming on, initiated by the usual knot in the stomach followed by a high anxiety adrenaline rush. His thoughts looped to a familiar refrain, I've lost everything; my family, my businesses, my money and my reputation. How am I going to make a living and support my children and what the hell am I doing mixed up in this mess? But he added a new stanza to this mental lament. What irony! Me raised with privilege in Philadelphia society, void of any religious or metaphysical training has ended up chasing sacred elements that added together disclose one of the greatest hidden spiritual truths in human history. It is the last thing I ever would have imagined in how my life would turn out. Ian gazed into the packed bar.

Just inside the front door a man appeared standing in the shadows looking at all the people as they passed. The sight was out of an old film noir. Ian knew the man was looking for him. The combination of the fedora and the turned up collar of his herringbone coat made it impossible to see the man's face.

"Steve, who's the guy standing in the door?"

"Never saw him before! What's with the hat?"

Ian thought; "That guy is part of Bailey's military."

After a short time, the man left.

"I'm just paranoid" as Ian's grip tightened on the cold effervescence. His despair was drifting back when an old friend spotted him.

"I thought we got rid of you months ago." Rosco kidded, as he pulled up an adjacent stool and yelled to Steve for a Heineken.

Ian looked at Rosco and said; "Some things never change, the classic Gucci horse bit loafers, alligator belt, blue oxford cloth button down and white linen pants perfectly creased, not to mention being the best looking guy in the place."

Rosco ignored Ian's line of crap and spoke compassionately. "I just heard about the investigation."

Ian responded. "Yes, it has started. I know I was the catalyst but damn, I wish things had turned out differently."

Rosco, changing the subject, "Are you still writing your book?"

"That's one of the reasons I'm back here. I have to finish my research."

"Months ago when we had dinner at the East India Club, you hooked me."

Ian perked up. "Does that mean you'd buy a copy?"

Rosco winked as he took a pull on the bottle and then asked about Raven.

Ian stared into the bar's mirror and sighed, "Nothing more!"

The two had been friends for so long, Ian's inflections in tone and body language told the rest of the story. Rosco switched the subject again. They talked about the old days, ate dinner at the bar and finished a few nightcaps before Ian headed back to his hotel.

As he got ready for bed he had a sentimental thought, *the time was well spent with an old friend.* This latest hotel stay had given Ian resident status, every concierge and headwaiter knew him by name. After a fitful night's sleep, he put on the hotel's plush terrycloth robe and was finishing his breakfast order when the room service receptionist politely asked him to hold.

"Mr. MacAlester, this is Carl at the concierge desk, sorry for the intrusion but while you were on with room service, a call came in from the District Attorney's office. A Ms. Debra Laurie asked if you would delay your meeting with her until one this afternoon."

"Did she happen to give any explanation?" Ian asked.

"No, sir, she just said; "tell him to be there promptly."

"Thanks for the message, Carl."

Hanging up the phone, Ian could hear Carl yelling into the receiver, he stopped; "Is there something else?"

"A package arrived for you sometime during the night. I will have Gladys bring it up with your breakfast."

"Thank You!"

This time Ian managed to get the receiver to the telephone's base before it started ringing. The call was from one of Ian's consulting clients.

He was on the phone for the next 40 minutes, oblivious to the fact that his breakfast was placed over warmers on a perfectly set mobile dining table. When he finished the call, Ian lifted the silver lids and blew out the flame on the sterno canisters that kept his food warm. He noticed a large white envelope Gladys put on his mahogany night table. He opened it. Ian's eyes flashed in disbelief as his fingers felt the all too familiar tactual luxury of this manuscript's ancient coverlet. His touch mimicked a blind man's as he would recognize brail impressions. The manuscript's outer sheath was identical to one he already had in his possession. Its glorious leather craftsmanship was such a work of art it was hard to imagine there could be something even more beautiful inside.

This isn't possible! Looking through the manuscript's contents, Ian saw the differences from the first one he aptly named "The Grumman." Before finishing his first bite of eggs, he hit the speed dial.

"Carl, can you find out who brought this package to the hotel?"

"I'll work on it, sir and get back to you."

"Thanks, my friend."

After a closer look, Ian put his new treasure into his briefcase and removed his own manuscript. He was nervous about meeting the woman prosecutor. Ms. Laurie had labeled Ian a witness but would make him a target if she could get some mileage out of it. The book he was writing was a work of fiction but there were places, people and events that provided a real time line for what took place. Ian wanted to be accurate in his answers because Laurie's investigation would most assuredly result in criminal indictments based on his deposition.

Turning the pages, he found it hard to believe this story began at his Jesuit orientation dinner at Georgetown University so many years earlier.

Chapter 2 - Orientation

Ian began to read his manuscript which was written in the first person.

"As an incoming freshman, I was invited to an orientation dinner sponsored by the University's Jesuits. As I entered the elegant Federal style Jesuit dining room, I heard a heated discussion in one of its far corners but before I could see what was going on, a priest, dressed in elegant black robes intercepted me and extended his hand. I took it saying,

"Hello, my name is Ian MacAlester."

"Good Evening, I am Father Michael and will be sitting at your table this evening."

After some small talk, we sat down in our seats. The Clarence House upholstered Queen Anne chair wrapped around me as I placed the linen napkin on my lap. The same student who was causing a scene earlier continued baiting our hosts. He said derogatory things about Catholics, in general and Jesuits, specifically. His remarks escalated to the point where he left the dining room claiming some sort of protest.

As things began to quiet down and the group resumed eating, Father Michael turned to me and apologetically said; "I don't recall such intense religious views being expressed by our incoming freshmen." Shifting the conversation to me, I responded, "I don't know much about formal religion and have devoted little time to it. Perhaps my time here at Georgetown will change that." As the words rolled from my mouth, I thought, *where did that come from?* Thank God, the second course was being served, saving me from myself. Then it appeared we had another off the wall comment made at the table, this time by a French Foreign Service School student concerning the Jesuit Suppression and specifically, John Carroll, Georgetown's founder. "Was John Carroll involved with the Freemasons?" No student at the table knew what the Suppression was, let alone could comment on how it related to Freemasonry. *Was this more insult innuendo or a legitimate question?* Not having a clue I just filed it away. The older Jesuits shifted slightly in their seats like the question was an annoyance when one of them changed the subject. The student's question was intentionally never answered.

Later that night heading back to my dorm, a Father Cortez, who was also at the dinner, stopped me saying he couldn't help but overhear the question about the Suppression and asked if I was interested in learning more about it.

He invited me to join him at Copley's Crypt chapel to hear him say Mass and "maybe afterward we could talk further." Since I didn't do Mass but still feeling the need to continue my brown nosing, I nodded yes;

thanked him for making my acquaintance and headed to my dorm. As I walked into the room, I felt elated to be there. The view from my dorm window overlooked Key Bridge and the Potomac River.

After all of those freezing New England boarding school winters, what a welcome change. Mom would have liked this view and Dad will probably never see it. I hope he is feeling better; at least Mom's suffering is over.

I quickly adapted to my new environment. The legal drinking age was 18. My personal drinking preference didn't include beer. It made me feel bloated and took way too long to achieve its desired effects. Philadelphia's favorite color in liquor was "brown." My parents and many of my friend's parents either became severely disabled or died of it. I preferred something sweet and lethal. I drank stingers whenever possible.

Stanley's saloon was close to campus and became my new watering hole. The employees were scions of some of the wealthiest families in the world. They waited tables for sport providing them the perfect cover to pick up women. Many were known to gift Dom Perignon to patrons they liked. It was a continuous cocktail party with the employees often footing the bill. Many of the seniors I met there lived in Copley Hall which also housed "The Crypt" chapel. Father Cortez was always somewhere close by.

One night, two weeks before Thanksgiving, Father Cortez approached me; "Have you come to a decision about joining me in learning more about our heritage?" I told him I was going to pass for the time being but thanked him for remembering. *Damn, I never followed up, finish what you start! Why didn't you get back to him?* As School got more demanding my evening cocktail parties gave way to studying in Riggs Library.

I was there every night, same time and same seat. One evening I was reading Azure Blue's "Comparative Cultures" study notes and heard pacing sounds coming from the cast iron stacks above. I was positive that I was the only one in the Library. I started up the spiral stairs to see who was making the noise. A shadow cast down on my shoes from above. I looked up but saw no one. For some reason I became frightened and chickened back down the stairs, retrieved my books and ran out the door. When I got to my dorm room, a note lay under the door. It looked like a formal invitation with a crimson wax seal guarding its contents. The calligrapher addressed it to Red, my roommate. I put the envelope on his bed. When he came through the door, I pounced asking him about the envelope. He became very defensive; "Forget about it, man!"

I wouldn't let it go, "Is it school related?"

Red said; "No."

I couldn't help myself. I bugged him more; "Does it have some Jesuit significance?" thinking Red would have to say "yes" giving me an opening, but Red said; "Look, it's personal. I don't want to talk about it."

I acquiesced; "OK!"

I tossed and turned most of the night trying to figure out who sent the note and what it said. I thought I would find out something over time but nothing more was ever said about it, time passed and my studying intensified.

There was one bright spot in my otherwise monotonous routine. I began to see a mysterious woman at the entrance of Healy, the building that housed Riggs Library. She seemed to have a purpose in being there. For some reason she intrigued me. Her hair caught the walkway lamp light in such a way that reflected a rainbow you would see in raven's feathers. She remained just far enough away to where I could never get a good look at her. These sightings were intermittent and continued for weeks. They were quickly becoming an obsession. I wanted to know her. Then one night, as I came into the library, I saw her sitting in the seat next to my usual spot. As I came closer, I felt the tension you get in your stomach when you're romantically infatuated but all I could see was her beautiful hair and the straight line of her jaw as she moved away from me at an angle that made it impossible for me to see her face. I glanced at what she was holding; a beautiful black leather coverlet containing what I supposed to be a manuscript of some sort. She wore a full-length black cloak and it took flight. As she passed by me, the scent of night jasmine filled the air. I was utterly spell bound and in complete awe, the magnificent hair, the cloak and a glide gait so fluid it seemed like her feet never touched the floor. I couldn't talk. I finally turned to Izzy Goldberg, my study mate and asked him if he had ever seen that woman before. He answered "What woman?"

"Come on Izz, you must have seen her?"

He was studying hard for an exam and had no time for my interruptions so I stopped talking and tried to study but my mind was out of control. I had to get some air and eventually wound up just going to bed. I went back every night to Riggs at the same time hoping to see her but no return performance.

Christmas break lasted for a month. I was the older of two siblings. My father was infirmed but continued to play golf especially when I could play with him. I tried to do whatever I could to make him happy. My nights after dinner with the family were my own so I attended many debutant parties late courtesy of being part of the Social Register's lucky sperm club. Due to the sheer volume of parties most of the guys had a wardrobe consisting of numerous dinner jackets, five pairs of tux pants, two black tie formals and one "white tie" tuxedo, numerous cummerbunds, formal vests, multiple pairs of patent leather pumps and tie shoes and all of the associated jewelry. The sad news was we were all aware that these parties would be winding down in the future as the Country was in the midst of a great social change. The very debutantes that historically benefited the most from their "coming out" parties questioned the idea that a woman should have to be formally introduced into society. The Lester Lanin Orchestra, the champagne fountains and the grand formality were all becoming a thing of the past.

All of it was being replaced by the British Invasion, "weed" and Hugh Heffner's Philosophy. Women's rights were entering a new phase and the pill helped with leveling the sexual playing field. Philadelphia WASP society did have a few perceived immutables such as maintaining a severe Catholic prejudice. Attending a Catholic university and dating Catholic girls didn't do much for my eligibility status. It did however reinforce my disdain for those affected with "Main Line lock jaw."

After returning to college, my saloon friends asked me why Red was spending so much time at "The Crypt". They told me he had keys to the place. I had no idea what they were talking about. I asked Red about it and got the same annoyed response he gave me regarding the sealed note. My curiosity returned. I followed him one morning and waited 10 minutes in the outer hall before sneaking into the chapel. No one was there. I ran through the door leading outside to the narrow street across from the student bank to see if I could catch a glimpse of Red heading in some direction but I missed him.

The note and the keys suggested that there must be some type of organized involvement. The next day I followed him again but this time, I stayed so close to him that if he'd turned around, he'd have found me in his clothes. Luckily, he didn't and walked directly into the chapel. I hid in the corner and watched as Red's hand pressed something on the right edge of the altar. As he pushed, a stairway in the floor appeared. He descended down and then the floor returned to normal. The molding and the staircase were so expertly crafted that once the trap door was again closed, even knowing where to look there was no evidence of a passageway. I sat down to collect my thoughts when students began arriving for Mass. As I got up to leave, I noticed two priests come in. They stood near the outer entry doors. They wore floor length black gabardine cassocks exquisitely tailored with matching black embroidery on the chest and back plates accentuating both men's excellent physical condition. The cassocks flair at the knee gave them a medieval warrior look. Their demonic appearance scared the hell out of me. Later that day, having a drink with Rufus, a bartender at Clyde's, I asked if he'd ever seen what could only be described as a military order of priests.

He said, "No" as he spun around and grabbed the phone off the wall. He called Joe McGwen, the manager of Chadwick's. He told Joe that I was a new friend and would be down to see him. Rufus said; "if anything weird was happening on campus, Joe would know about it." I walked down to Chadwick's Restaurant to find Joe sitting on a stool next to the window. I introduced myself and we immediately hit it off. I related what I had seen earlier in 'the Crypt" leaving out the part about the trap door. Joe replied; "If Rufus likes you, you're probably OK but my advice is to leave this alone."

I had heard rumors about the University and its extracurricular activities. I thought it best to follow Joe's advice and discontinue pursuing my curiosity. I had to be pragmatic.

I occasionally thought about Red's involvement with the Crypt and even Father Cortez. I really thought I had moved on until one night walking up from the bottom of Wisconsin Ave. toward M street, the smell of jasmine filled the night air. It was too cold for it to be blooming. I looked up and saw my raven haired mystery woman crossing the street. She continued down a very narrow alley next to the C&O Canal and walked onto Chelsea Street, a charming little area of brightly painted townhouses.

Following her, unlike Red, was very hard. She had eyes in the back of her head. She turned onto a street of brightly painted pink, purple and blue little townhouses, turning again, the colors shifted to green and yellow and after turning a third time, she was gone. I stopped, made no sound. She had just vanished and totally succeeded if her goal was to keep her likeness fresh in my mind. I waited for a while and then walked up to M Street, turned left and made the long walk to the exorcist steps. After clearing my head with their climb, I thought;" what's wrong with me? I've never even seen this woman's face." My obsessing lost steam as a year past with no further contact.

I was again thoroughly ensconced in my routine. Red moved to a house off campus and I lost touch with him. He eventually dropped out of school keeping his secret safe, at least from me. I was taking 21 credits and the workload forced me into spending way too much time in Riggs library. One night, bored out of my mind studying microeconomics, I heard sounds coming from the same general area in the stacks where I had heard them so many months earlier. This time I was not going to wimp out. My heart was racing as I walked up the spiral staircase to the third stack. I stepped off the stack deck to see my "Raven" on the farther most cat walk.

Why am I seeing her now? Her face and her hair were shrouded in her cloak's hood as she motioned for me to sit in the vacant chair next to hers. My legs buckled as she revealed her face. Her beauty left me breathless. Time stopped. Her look propelled me into a feeling of pure joy, not of this world, just by beholding her. Our chairs were hidden from the library's normal traffic patterns and far enough away to allow for a private conversation but no words were spoken. She softened her explosive bright blue eyes. For some reason, my racing heart began to slow. I was becoming more relaxed. My tension dissipated. I was being manipulated into regaining my sensibilities. I was entering some sort of meditative trance. She took hold of both of my hands. Her energy mixed with mine and it settled my body. I began experiencing waves of calmness and levels of peace I had never imagined possible. I remember feeling extremely safe. Little did I know what I would soon experience. Whatever type of meditative state this was allowed my consciousness to calmly slip away from the library and into an ancient setting.

Chapter 3 - Tosh

"I regained my consciousness in ancient Jerusalem, sometime in the early first century. I was incredibly calm in this altered state. My focus was on a man named Samuel Tosh. He was one of Jerusalem's best leather artisans and a cherished member of the Jewish Temple. As Samuel worked on his hides, Roman soldiers combed the overcrowded streets looking for someone. They turned over fruit stands and kiosks in the market exhibiting their obvious frustration suffered at the hands of the Jewish rebels. The smell signified the total breakdown of public sanitation. These conditions were intolerable for the general population.

Samuel's dark coloring provided contrast to his deep set brown eyes. He had a look you would expect from a Semitic heritage. He radiated a very capable hard working confidence. His competitive edge in his business was achieved in obtaining unique hides and other materials from suppliers outside the City. They were not only less expensive but of better quality than those sold by his competition. Samuel was a real mensch, giving most of his time and money to his mother and father. His family and community were at the core of his traditional Jewish life but a new sect was spreading throughout Jerusalem called The True Believers. Their beliefs were considered controversial. Their numbers were growing. His friends were converting. Samuel was determined to find out more about them.

The True Believer movement started after the crucifixion of Jesus of Nazareth. Jesus was taken before the Jewish judicial body, The Sanhedrin. Josephus Caiaphas, the High Priest of the Jewish Temple of Jerusalem was in attendance. The group found Jesus to be a blasphemer and demanded his execution. The Roman Prefect, Pontius Pilate would not put Jesus to death for religious blasphemy but would consent to it if it would stop an uprising. Although the Jews had a titular head in Herod Antipas; Rome controlled and monetarily benefited from its occupation of Judea. If it had to put down an uprising, the result would be the slaughter of hundreds if not thousands of Jews. There would also have to be an example made, a tortured death and a more suitable replacement of the High Priest would be in order. Caiaphas understood this dynamic and as a result, many Jews hated him for his harshness and most never appreciated how he saved their lives in the balance. A side benefit of Caiaphas's harsh leadership style made less work for Pilate who in return allowed Caiaphas more latitude than he would have otherwise been given.

Caiaphas's tenure as High Priest covered the same time span as Pilate's appointment. Caiaphas married into a family of High Priests and his father-in-law Annas was the longest running High Priest in the Jewish

Temple's history. Two of Annas's five sons succeeded Caiaphas as High Priest. Jonathan took over from Caiaphas with Theophilus replacing Jonathan but Theophilus was also a Christian. *Could this be possible? The Jewish High Priest of the Temple of Jerusalem was also a Christian?* Despite the skepticism that many orthodox Jews had about Jesus being the Messiah, the movement received a tremendous boost by the Theophilus conversion. A large Jewish contingent, not to mention the High Priest of the Temple of Jerusalem, had adopted Christianity in the early years. They had very different ideas and concepts from those espoused by Peter, Paul and The Catholic Church.

New converts of the True Believer movement often abandoned their belongings, leaving the City with no intention of ever returning and thus removing themselves as productive members of a tax paying society. Rome was not pleased and began interpreting this behavior as insurrection.

†

My focus shifted to Pontius Pilate, the man. He deeply hated his assignment to the region and the reports back to Rome always included his inhumane and ruthless behavior. He delighted in taunting both the Jews and Palestinians by placing Roman Shields of Emperor Caligula's face on the Temple's altar. Pilate's final undoing came when he slaughtered thousands of Samaritan pilgrims with his cavalry. The complaints caused Vitellius, the Roman Legate to Syria to recall Pilate back to Rome. My vision showed Caligula exiling Pilate to Southern Gaul.

Chapter 4 -
James, the Apostle

The vision refocused on Tosh who had contacted a friend of The True Believers. Samuel wanted to get an invitation to one of their meetings. His friend got back to Samuel instructing him to spend the night in a small village just south of Jerusalem. In the early hours of the next morning, he was taken to James, the Apostle.

James had been part of the movement since the death and resurrection of Jesus. He was sitting warming his hands over a small fire when Samuel arrived. He looked up and asked Samuel why he had wanted to meet. Samuel replied, "To learn more about why my friends are leaving the Jewish faith to embrace The True Believers and the Gospel of the Kingdom."

"Samuel, people join the movement for many reasons but all hope to learn the True Believer's process for attaining personal peace."

Samuel did not understand what James meant by "process." "What is this "process" about? Jesus was a knowledgeable rabbi and teacher. Some say even the Messiah but no one has told me about any "process."

The Jewish population in the City is upset. Many want an insurrection. Can this "process" help us against Rome?"

James provided some background saying, "The reason for secrecy at meetings such as this is because there are only a few of us with the knowledge, which makes it vulnerable to extinction. Powerful people will stop at nothing to prevent us from spreading information about the process. Our methods of communication are poor, our security lax and we are far too vulnerable. That is why you have been brought here in such a manner. We know you have many friends in your leather business. We also know that you have made money and managed to hold on to it. Our cause needs money, leadership and the passion of youth, a rare combination. I foresee you will be considered an adept using the process and will become a very important leader for The True Believers, all resulting in a very different life than the one you presently have. Then James returned to answer Samuel's question. "You will answer for yourself whether it will help our people." Samuel not fazed by James predictions asked, "Tell me more! Why would I want to join this group with its secret? As the words came emotionally out of Samuel's mouth, all those sitting around the last of the burning embers saw the familiar expression come onto James's face.

"Samuel, you're neither the first nor the last to ask these questions. The burden of proof is upon us to give you enough knowledge to make such a decision. The story of Jesus has many facets. The one I will tell you concerns the people in the movement. The years following His death have carried with it much controversy. Cynics think we paid the Roman centurion to take Him down from the cross before death occurred and then nursed him back to health. Others say we paid off the Roman guards to let us sneak the corpse out of Arimathea's tomb so we could claim Jesus had arisen from the dead. The truth will come out over time and you will be the principal scribe documenting it." James went on; "Soon, the followers of Jesus will be persecuted by Rome. They will be tortured and put to death but during their torture, they will be given a chance to live by renouncing Jesus. If they do, the torture will stop and they will be set free. Most will not take the offer. You will be connected to the Court of Herod Agrippa hearing the stories and the screams first hand." Samuel's face went ashen as James told him, "You will learn the answer as to why these people made their particular choices." Samuel's mind was swimming. *Why did James think I would be involved with Agrippa?*

James seemingly changed the subject by asking Samuel to recite a typical day in his life. Samuel did not know how to respond. James clarified his question by asking him to list what tasks he performed at the tannery. Samuel still didn't understand why James was so interested in his day. "Why do you ask me such nonsense?" James sat on a soft pillow, made from animal hides, pointing to it saying; "Is it not true that the first thing you do is salt cure the skin after you remove it from the animal? This step alone could take a month before the skin is ready for soaking, which is also time consuming. Then you have to "scud" the hide by hand carefully removing all the hair and fat."

Samuel could not believe his ears. *How did James know so much about tanning?* "You seem to know a lot about the tanning process but what do you know about me and my business?" James was beginning to like this upstart for his brashness.

"You personally spend most of your day de-liming and dying hides and then you apply your own unique blend of vegetable extracts to the hides." James went on; "You are the only one in all of Jerusalem that finishes with special bee's wax and your customers can only get these unique leather goods from you."

Samuel said; "You could have guessed most of that!" James retorted; "yes, but could I have guessed that you get your bees wax from hives located at the extreme northern end of the Dead Sea or that you talk more with your father than your mother.

James knew he had Samuel's attention. "If you decide to join us, you will learn how I knew all about you without talking to anyone." Samuel was mystified. James finished the meeting by saying, "Do not talk about this place, me or what we have discussed." Before Samuel could respond, he was unceremoniously ushered from the meeting and blindfolded.

On his blindfolded trip back to Jerusalem, Samuel reflected upon the statements James made and how he knew where Samuel got his materials. The competition would stop at nothing to find out that information. *No one knows where I get my waxes, dyes and glazes.* Samuel prided himself on taking long circuitous routes to lose anyone that could be following him when he got his supplies. Conversely, Samuel thought, *someone could have followed me to my parents' house but there is only one window located at the top of a high exterior wall. No one could see in. This truly is a mystery.* Samuel needed to be at the tannery before his workers arrived. He didn't want any speculation even from his closest friends as to where he was or what he was doing.

When the two men removed his blind fold, Samuel found himself at his place of work. If James wanted to impress Samuel, he had succeeded. No sooner had Samuel washed his face and cleaned up when his closest friend, Jonah Levy walked around the stonewall that held up the lean-to.

"Hello Samuel! I went to your house this morning but you were not there. I have news. My uncle has invited me to attend a court feast to honor some of the King's relatives. They have just returned from Rome. He said I could bring you if it would improve my position here at the tannery." Jonah laughed.

This invitation is not a coincidence. How did James know this as well? Samuel remembered his last time at Court but it was not as a guest of Agrippa's. He was a child caught stealing one of Herod Antipas' prize pigeons when he was visiting his aunt in Tiberius. Little did Samuel know that a certain young maiden had spied on him when he was in the Palace's pigeon house. She saw Samuel taking one of the King's plumpest birds to have for his family's dinner. She was so enamored with Samuel's good looks that she followed him outside the gates and back to his aunt's house. Her absence got the attention of the guards, who found her, the pigeon and Samuel. Everyone was summarily escorted back to the Palace.

Antipas loved his pleasures; cooked pigeon was one of them. Samuel was cowed; a long heavy wooden plank buttressed his arms and tied tight to his shoulder blades. The King was about to have the boy killed when the young maiden came out from behind a beautiful tapestry in the great hall. She begged Antipas to hear her, which he allowed.

She told him that Samuel was a boy trying to stop the bird before it flew away rather than a thief trying to take it but he couldn't open the pigeon house's door to get the bird back into its coupe. She said he went with the bird to get his aunt and she followed him. The girl told the King the boy had good intentions. As the King pondered the story, his counsel delivered him a written communication, which so distracted Antipas that he waved the boy out of the chamber.

Samuel couldn't believe his good fortune and ran back to his aunt's house. He never found out who the girl was or why she had helped him. The vapors from the kettle stung Samuel's nose pulling him back from his memories. He agreed to accompany Jonah to Agrippa's event. *This party will give me a chance to see for myself what James said to me.* Samuel had never heard of the "True Believers" being tortured. He wondered if it were true, did they really have an opportunity to go free?

The Palace was surrounded by high stonewalls with three entrances, but for this reception, only the center gate was open. Once inside the walls, the eight wide grand steps served as an elegant invitation into the Palace's main center hall. The ceremonially dressed guards escorted the two young men past the beautifully crafted ornate doors into an arched hallway, which emptied into a torch lit atrium. The atrium had two egresses spilling out onto a flower lined walkway that surrounded a well-manicured garden and pool at its far end.

Samuel needed to excuse himself. Jonah spotted his uncle and waived Samuel on. Samuel walked back toward the main entrance spying a staircase that led to a downstairs corridor. He took the stairs and found nothing but dusty unused holding cells. He saw no guards; no prisoners and Samuel thought, *no truth yet to what James had told me.* Samuel walked back into the garden just as Agrippa and his wife walked onto the balcony above. The outdoor staircase provided a spectacular royal entrance.

Horns blew as the guards announced the King to his guests. As the couple descended down the stairs, the vision shifted to Agrippa and his memory of just a few months earlier when he was on the Roman Senate floor making the case for Claudius to become Emperor.

Chapter 5 - Then along comes Agrippa

My mind fused with Agrippa's. I knew his memories and his perception of his life events. Agrippa's memories took my awareness back to his days in Rome. He had a deep friendship with two Roman Emperors; Gaius; Caligula as he was nicknamed and Claudius. Agrippa mused at how much Gaius hated his nickname, Caligula. The name translated into "little boots" which at best always made him out to be a child. Agrippa saw many sides to his very troubled young friend. Gaius had a mean streak cultivated by Tiberius who murdered both Gaius's father and mother. As a result, Gaius trusted no one and was aloof. Over time, it was apparent to Agrippa that by the age of 19 spending his time on the beautiful Isle of Capri; Gaius had hardened into someone very twisted reveling in sexual perversion and blood sport.

After marrying one of his relatives and spending all of his money, Agrippa was forced to flee Rome from his creditors. He contacted his uncle, Antipas, who gave him a political appointment in Galilee. They fought incessantly.

This situation forced Agrippa to once again flee. This time to Antioch then Alexandria and then finally back to Rome.

Out of desperation, he contacted Gaius for sponsorship but was disappointed to learn that his friend could not help him until Tiberius was no longer Emperor. Determined to help himself and Gaius, Agrippa began orchestrating a coup. Tiberius found out about Agrippa's plans and threw him in jail. He was in prison for seven months before Tiberius died. Once Gaius became Emperor, he paid Agrippa's debts and made him the King of Judea. Agrippa stayed on in Rome. In the early summer of 38 AD, Gaius sent Agrippa on a diplomatic mission to make a determination regarding allegations of brutality and undue harshness inflicted on the Jews by the then Governor of Alexandria, Flaccus. Agrippa found out the Greeks had tricked Flaccus into humiliating the local Jewish population, causing an uprising that ended by Rome soldiers butchering many Jews. Agrippa reported to Gaius that Flaccus was incompetent and unable to control the anti-Semitic behavior in Alexandria. Rome sent a legion to arrest Flaccus who was then tortured and brutally executed.

Agrippa traveled to Judea in 40 A.D. only to have to return to Rome to persuade Gaius to stop the local Roman harassment of his people. Agrippa arrived just in time to find Gaius to be utterly insane and a short time later, the Emperor's own Praetorian Guard killed him. They pledged their support for Claudius to become their new Emperor. Claudius was reluctant and convinced an assassination attempt would be made on his life if he went onto the Senate floor. He asked Agrippa to speak on his behalf. Agrippa agreed and averted Claudius's almost certain death. After becoming Emperor, a grateful Claudius added Samaria to Agrippa's kingdom, restoring the land controlled by him to that once ruled by Herod the Great.

†

Agrippa's memory faded as he refocused his attention back to he and his wife making their way down the staircase to the center of the garden. He thanked his guests for coming and welcomed home his aunt and uncle and their children. Although a Palestinian King, Agrippa was a practicing Jew who needed to maintain a reputation of forging a strong Jewish state in his homeland, while also being known as one of Claudius's closest allies. The guests at the party were coaxing him to tell stories about Gaius, Claudius, and their days together. Agrippa knew he had to be careful. Any conversation involving either Emperor always had a way of getting back to Rome. He did not want to upset any of the perceptions he had worked so hard in creating. One wealthy merchant loudly asked if the rumors about Gaius were true concerning his relationship with his sister.

Agrippa asked in what manner the merchant was referring hoping to shame the man into silence but to no avail. The merchant only got red faced and continued by saying that on one trip to Rome, he heard Gaius and his sister had sexual relations in public. Gaius's incest with his sister was well known and as a result Agrippa wondered if the inference was more of a back handed slap to him as it pertained to his marrying a relative or to the incestuous marriage between Antipas and Agrippa's sister, Herodias or both. Agrippa politely dodged the question but would remember this insult.

† †

Agrippa's mind again wandered back to when Herodias had betrayed him. She married Antipas in an attempt to gain more money and titles of aristocracy for herself. The animosity grew between Agrippa and Antipas as Caligula bestowed more titles and riches on Agrippa. This turn of events crushed Herodias. She felt the title of King belonged to Antipas, her husband and not to her brother. Agrippa recalled when Herodias was committing adultery with Antipas before their marriage. John the Baptist spoke out publicly against this relationship. At that time, Herodias's birthday was coming up and Antipas told her, she could have anything she wished for and he would grant it. She tricked him into delivering "The Baptist's" head to her on a silver tray. This incident forever ruined Antipas' relations within the community and set up what was to follow with Jesus.

Herodias coerced Antipas into going to Rome to persuade Caligula into reinstating him as the rightful King of Judea. Antipas went to Rome where he made false accusations against Agrippa, who was aware of the plan and defended himself well with Gaius. Instead of bestowing titles on Antipas, Gaius banished him to Southern Gaul.

†††

As the scene from the Emperor's chamber ended with the Roman guards escorting Antipas out, my vision slowly dissolved. I returned to Riggs library. My calmness continued for a short time. I kept my eyes closed enjoying the moment. I was extremely comfortable in this twilight experience but these sensations ended all too soon.

Chapter 6 - The Murder

I let the experience wash through me as if I had the most realistic dream one could imagine. I opened my eyes and looked down from the third stack to the tables on the first level of the library, alone. *The vision seemed so real. What just happened? Where did Raven go?*

†††

Ian closed his novel mentally bookmarking dates and people he would later have to identify in his interview. He had 30 minutes before he had to start downtown. He turned on the TV and saw the pretty and cunning assistant DA on the steps of the District court house talking to reporters. She was answering questions about her formal investigation of Paul Bailey and his co-conspirators. As she spoke, blood appeared from the inside of her right nostril and just a bit more from inside her mouth. She instinctively dabbed at it and looked on in amazement before collapsing into the crowd. Ian looked at the TV in shock, realizing he was supposed to meet her in less than an hour. He waited for the news segment to end before grabbing his suit jacket and catching a cab to the D.A.'s office. He knew to anticipate the unexpected thinking she could recover and then subpoena him with attitude. When he arrived, the receptionist told Ian that Ms. Laurie was in the hospital with unknown complications. Ian glanced at the rouge's gallery of no less than 50 pictures hanging in her office posing with every politician in Washington. "I'll wait for a time in case she recovers. I am sorry I didn't catch your name."

"My name is Suzy Fisher." as she extended her hand to Ian.

After waiting long past his appointment time with no word from the hospital, Ian asked Suzy, "Would you like something from the food mart at Union Station? I would be happy to get it." putting on the charm.

"That is so nice of you. I haven't eaten all day and would very much appreciate you doing that for me. Could you please get me a half pint of oriental chicken salad?" Ian said sure, as he walked out before she could give him any money.

Ian had a reason for getting out of Ms. Laurie's office. He had a friend at Georgetown University hospital who could give him some information on her condition.

Ian's original mission in life was to become a doctor. He knew many of the premed students when he was in school, now they were the main movers and shakers in the hospital.

"Could I speak to Doctor Quinn Russell?"

The receptionist responded, "I will page him, who is calling?"

"Please tell him it's Ian."

"Will he know who you are?"

"Oh yes, we go back a long way."

The phone's hold was playing a song by Mike and the Mechanics called "All I need is a miracle." Ian thought. *How appropriate.*

"Hey Ian, I haven't spoken to you in awhile. How are you?"

"I am good. We have a lot of catching up to do but I have an urgent request. Was Debra Laurie brought in to the ER while you were on?"

"No, I was in the doctor's lounge when the guys treating her came in sweating and mad. I don't know that it's out yet but she died on the table."

"No, it's not, I'm looking at a monitor in Union Station and the media doesn't have that yet. They wouldn't keep that a secret for any period of time."

Quinn said, "Please keep it quiet, not that you would say anything but the administration here has been all over us to avoid reporters."

"Sure! Quinn, what did she die of?"

"That's the strange part. According to the ER staff, they couldn't find anything wrong with her. The guys said there was a nasal hemorrhage but that couldn't have killed her. She had no other visible wounds or open sores. They are doing an autopsy to find out more but as of right now, it's a mystery. What's your interest in Debra Laurie?"

"When we get together, I will tell you all about it. The story is too long for the phone. I am in town for a while. I'll call you. Maybe we can go to Houston's for old times."

"That was too many years ago. I can't take the noise. If you want to buy me a drink at Morton's, you got a deal."

"Deal, I'll call you."

Ian hung up the phone and knew instinctively Debra Laurie was murdered. *She was gunning for too many powerful people.* He got Suzy's lunch and ordered a sandwich for himself. By the time he got back to the D.A.'s office, the place was swarming with reporters.

He went through security and found Suzy answering a barrage of questions concerning Ms. Laurie's health, asking why the information wasn't forthcoming on her condition.

The hospital had been successful so far in keeping the death quiet. Ian motioned to Suzy that he was back with her food. She got the reporters out of the receptionist area, came over and thanked Ian.

"I was happy to do it. Have you heard anything more about Ms. Laurie's condition?"

"No, but there are many people in this town who hated her guts and are probably ecstatic she is sick."

"How was she to work with?"

"She was all right I guess. She is known for making political hay out of any case that can advance her career."

Ian thought he dodged a bullet by not meeting with her.

Ian looked at his watch, it was well past courtesy waiting and it would be appropriate for him to leave especially given the circumstances.

"Well, Suzy, it was a pleasure meeting you. I am sure we will meet again. If Ms. Laurie feels better, please have her reschedule."

"Thanks again for lunch. I'll pass the message along."

Ian decided to walk and headed for the Smithsonian. He sat in the lobby of the Air and Space, staring at the planes hanging from the ceiling. Ian's mind drifted to his encounter with Paul Bailey's people months before and knew he had something to do with Laurie's death. Although Ian never met Bailey he had enough experience with his henchmen to know that somehow they got to her. He thought he'd call Quinn in a few days and get the results from the autopsy. After spending a few more minutes in silent contemplation, he went outside and caught a cab back to the hotel. He walked through the lobby atrium, past the front desk, took the elevator to the third floor, and went into his room. Since his last stay, Ian asked for and got a room with a hidden safe. He closed the outer door and went through the mini suite's short hallway into the living room area. The safe was in the floor behind the desk. He opened it and took out his briefcase. He realized his whole world was in that case and the unbelievable importance of each manuscript it contained including the one he was writing. The manuscript delivered at breakfast was different in style from the Grumman manuscript; the body of the document was written in Aramaic, like the Grumman and bound in a similar ancient leather coverlet but its borders were updated in Spanish instead of the French found in the Grumman. The penmanship was exacting which was also similar to the other work.

As Ian puzzled over the manuscript finding its way to him at the hotel, a news bulletin flashed across his TV screen announcing Debra Laurie's death. They reported the cause of death as an apparent heart attack and announced the details of her memorial service. Ian knew he would get a call by some investigator as to why he was on her calendar.

Ian went to Madeleine's down the street for dinner. As he walked back to the hotel onto the cobblestone driveway, he saw an all too familiar black Tacoma parked in front of the main entrance. Ian turned around and walked back past the ice cream store, and entered the art gallery. He walked through it into the hotel's courtyard and used his card key to enter the lobby's side door. He got in the elevator and pressed the button for the third floor. When it opened, he saw men waiting in the chairs directly in front of his room. Ian let the elevator door close naturally and pushed the button for the lower lobby, which opened in the business conference area.

In the second stall of the men's room, he used his cell phone to check his bank's automated teller confirming he still had money in his bank account. He made a reservation under Dr. Quinn Russell and checked into the Georgetown Inn. Lying on the bed, his mind centered on two questions. Who was looking for him and who had sent the new manuscript to the hotel? The next morning he made his way back to his original hotel. No Tacoma and nothing had been touched. His briefcase was still in the safe. He packed and called Carl at the front desk.

"Mr. MacAlester, are you stirring things up again?"

"Yes, Carl! Were you able to find out anything about the package?"

"No, I am still working on it but it looks like whoever it was used a local service and they have not been very forthcoming with information.

"Carl, spend up to a few hundred and I will reimburse you. In the meantime I am going back to New York."

"Very well Sir, if I get any information, I have your numbers. I'll be in touch."

"Thank you, I will see you soon; charge the bill to my card."

"Will do and have a good trip."

Ian spent a few more minutes packing, went out the side courtyard door, and grabbed a cab on 30th Street to Reagan. Going over the 14th Street Bridge, his memories went back to the time of his first vision and how he tried to process the events surrounding it and then what followed.

✝✝✝

I will have to keep my experience very private. No one would ever believe me. I am not sure I believe it, myself. Ian remembered driving to the Hot Shoppe on Wisconsin Ave near Hechinger's. He knew the chances of him running into anyone there would be remote. Taking out his note pad, he sat at the counter, ordered their signature hot fudge cake roll and started writing down questions. He wondered what Raven wanted from him.

Why was there so much about Herod Agrippa and who was Samuel Tosh and why didn't Raven stay to explain what she did to me.

The next night at Apple Pie, Stanley's successor, Ian remembered sitting down with Paulo de la Cruz, the Don Juan of all Georgetown bartenders. Ian never knew what educational program Paulo was on but this man had dated and bedded every good-looking girl in Georgetown and had gotten away with it. Paulo had a habit of greeting his women patrons by shaking their breasts as if they were hands, while saying; "Hello!" Everyone laughed including the women he fondled. Ian would nervously laugh with the certain knowledge that if he did that, he would be imprisoned for rape but Paulo was so smooth, they loved it.

"Hey Paulo, Como esta?"

"Good and you?"

"I have a question for you as the foremost expert in the field.

"Yes, my true calling, women, what can I do for you?"

They laughed as Ian described Raven in detail. "She is breath taking." Ian told him about the hair, the cloak and the night jasmine. Everything he could remember.

Paulo looked at Ian with a blank stare as he searched his mental internal hard drive and after coming up empty he said that if he ever remotely knew a woman like, he would have to marry her. Ian was crest fallen at Paulo's answer.

Surely, Paulo had seen this woman.

More time passed. Ian moved to the new library but couldn't study. It was too crowded so he went back to Riggs and prepared for his last test before the break. Ian wasn't there an hour when he heard the main door open. Raven was standing in its entrance, just looking at him and again, the place was empty. Ian stood at the third stack rail, his eyes lasered to hers.

He put his feet and hands on the top of the railings and flew down the staircase as if it were a spiral fire pole in a station house. His mouth was on FedEx fast. He asked her five questions in two seconds. She didn't say a word but instead led him to the first floor cubby where they could sit. As they walked, Ian suspected something very different about his "Raven." The darkness in the library allowed her aura to be quite visible.

She touched his right hand and Ian again found himself incapable of speaking. She went to grab the other hand but somehow he had the presence of mind to say; "No you don't, the last time you did that, I went off to never never land and when I came back, you were gone. I have been looking for you ever since and I am way beyond obsessed with you. Talk to me!"

Her thoughts went directly into his mind. "Don't be alarmed! You are right in thinking something is different about me. I hope that this method of communication will suffice."

Thinking he had gone off the deep end, she interrupted his mental gyrations; "No, you are not crazy and what you are experiencing is actually happening." Ian realized he didn't have to talk, either. She read his every thought, experience and emotion, all at once. Ian became very embarrassed as he realized she knew everything his mind ever thought, she knew he thought she was the most beautiful creature he had ever seen and the love he had for her. It did not make any sense as to how or why he loved her but he did and it was a love not of this world. There was no lust, jealousy or worry of any type. The experience was nothing like Ian had ever read about, only that it was the most wonderful emotional place he had ever been and certainly never wanted it to leave him.

Tears of joy flooded his eyes as they shared these thoughts. He experienced a new depth of emotion. As her thoughts brought him back, she conveyed a special peace thinking, "Everything is all right, calm, calm!" Ian had so many questions and in his thoughts must have asked her; her name 50 times and each time, she thought back, "it's unimportant." The thoughts of calm and unconditional love resonated in his soul. He never imagined his emotions could be so choreographed as to experience love feelings that resulted in total joy and fulfillment. She waited for him to fully appreciate the moment. Finally, Ian thought to her; *OK, I'm ready, show me.* Ian was no longer sitting in the library.

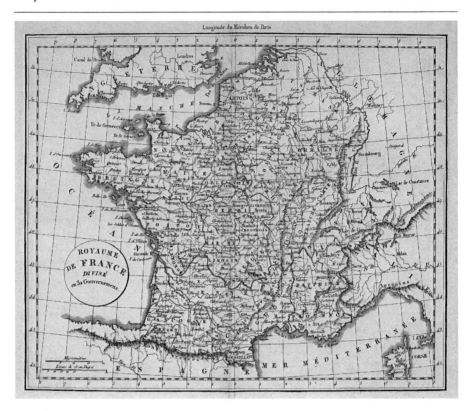

Part 2

Chapter 7 - The Bishop

As Raven's induced mind mist lifted, I paid very close attention to the vision's dynamics. I felt a definite relaxing of my muscles and sinews from every joint. All random thoughts disappeared and a very directed experience began. As in my first vision, I had an awareness of the thoughts, memories and feelings of the people I was led to focus upon.

It was the beginning of the thirteenth century. I watched as a rider, at full gallop, headed toward the English Channel. I felt the man's emotional intensity in delivering a message to the Bishop of North Abby. The rider was Artemus Champaneux; a tall, good-looking man in his early thirties who had been in the employ of the French aristocracy since the age of ten. His father had been a bailiff. His mother died delivering his baby sister. After that, his father's outlook on life gave rise to severe bouts of depression, which often led to drinking himself into unconsciousness. Artemus was taught to keep his mouth shut and his eyes open; a trait that later earned him the gratitude and respect of the power brokers in duchies all over France.

The economy was bad in France and worse in England. At last, Artemus had gotten a legitimate assignment. He was working for a new patron, albeit, one he had never met. His instructions came through his long time friend, Henri Coutard, a well-known go-between, diminutive in stature but large in integrity. Henri owned a tavern in Paris as a front for his work with his aristocratic clients. His instructions to Artemus were simple. "Get this message to the Bishop, make sure he reads it and then get something from him in return."

Artemus had to be careful. There were increasing numbers of unexplained highway "accidents" on the route between Paris and London. Traveling of any sort was extremely dangerous and unwise for anyone but those most desperate. He knew he was carrying a letter of significance; war or something equivalent. Should it get into the wrong hands, his reputation would be lost. He arrived in Calais and waited for the Cog ship to set sail for Dover. Once landed, Artemus purchased a horse and proceeded to an inn located at the southern end of Tunbridge Wells, a small town in southeast England, located between London to the North and Dover to the South.

Plans were made for Artemus to meet the Bishop in the Abby in the next village at night so he had time to kill. Due to his constant traveling, Artemus had frequented this particular inn over the years and was considered familiar to the town's people. His cover was always that of a traveling fragrance merchant and the new mistress of the Inn loved his products. Artemus asked to be included in the evening meal as the

Innkeepers prepared his room. At dinner, he gave the appearance of drinking more than his fair share of wine before retiring. He made his apologies for drinking too much as he expertly stumbled up the stairs to bed and waited until everyone was asleep. He started out for the Abby, arriving in the early hours of the morning but found no one.

The Abby was deserted; something was terribly wrong; there were no signs of life either in the Abby or the adjoining residence. Riding back to the Inn at dawn, Artemus met up with Jamie, the Inn's groom, on the road. He relayed a story that he couldn't sleep and went out for an early ride and was now sufficiently tired to try again. He would go back to the Abby but would have to wait again until nightfall. He checked his torso pouch, his package was safe. Artemus went back to bed and awoke in the late morning. When he entered the Inn's main room, its mistress, Agnes was sitting at a corner table. She asked him to show her his latest fragrances and creams from Paris. She flirted with Artemus taking in his straight ash colored hair, thin build and beautiful white teeth. Artemus caught her amorous looks and hoped the mistress's husband, Glen was close by but he had gone to the market. Agnes smiled asking Artemus,

"What did you bring me today? I was beginning to think you didn't like me." She continued, "I don't think you've told me where you travel to get these wonderful beauty products." Before he could answer, she interrupted; "Tell me about your family?" He smiled and remained silent just long enough for her to say something else. He smiled again, flirted more and never answered any of her questions. Agnes served scones and hot tea to elongate their meeting. "Eat man; you're wasting away to nothing. I think you are getting thinner as I look at you. I would like to see some meat on those bones and when are you going to bring your family around?" Every comment she made was an assumption. She carried on until she verbally exhausted herself, which provided the perfect exit opportunity.

Artemus began to pick out something for her to keep when astonishingly Agnes said she wanted to buy everything. Artemus remarked she must have come into good fortune and was happy for her, trying to get her to open up about herself. Her face grew very serious and said that ever since an aristocrat and his family started staying at the Inn, their fortune had significantly improved. They came every week and stayed for one night, to and from their estate just north of London. Artemus surmised Agnes probably did not know much about them due to her incessant talking but she surprised him, again.

Apparently the lady of manor was a forceful conversationalist and thus Agnes had a hard time getting a word in edgewise so she had to listen to the Lady talk about her husband's awful womanizing. Agnes told Artemus how lucky she thought the Lady was not to have to service her husband, as he was the most homely thing she had ever seen. They laughed. He gave her all of the items and thanked her for her patronage. As he was putting away his samples, Agnes caught his attention when she said something about the Abby.

"There were two murders there not three nights ago where the Bishop and his aid were found dead on the Abby's steps." This could not have been worse news for Artemus. His backup contact was the Bishop's aid. Agnes continued, "According to the Sheriff, no one out of the ordinary was seen that night."

"How were they killed?" Artemus asked.

Agnes said, "That was the worst of it, they had been burned to death. The tortured and charred remains of both men indicated someone had taken great care to make their suffering unimaginable. The Sheriff came by asking if we had seen anything suspicious, as our inn is probably the only rest stop in easy riding distance of Dover and the Abby. The only guests we had were our new patrons and they would not have done such a thing."

As Agnes was talking, Artemus remembered Henri saying the message was time sensitive, *"lives hung in the balance."* His mission was not over even though his contacts had been eliminated. His new employer would want answers as to who killed them and why. Artemus excused himself and went up stairs. As he was packing, he pricked his finger on the bottom part of the bedding. Some of the feathers were coming out of a torn seam. As he licked his finger, his other hand checked out the tear. He felt the needle and pulled a beautiful broach from the fabric. Artemus could hear Agnes on her way up the stairs asking him to stay on a few more days.

He hid the broach in his pocket and finished his packing. Glen had returned from the market and yelled up the stairs, "Where are you going, my friend? We haven't spent anytime talking and now you want to leave us so soon? At least stay and have a glass of wine with me."

Artemus acquiesced and said he would be right down. He went outside and gave Jamie his bags, keeping his pouch securely tied to his chest. When Artemus sat down, he asked Glen what he thought about the murders. "The towns' folk think it's the worst thing that has ever happened to them. They say it is a bad omen and expect to receive God's retribution for letting His bishop die in such a disgusting way."

"Agnes said they were burned to death?"

"Artemus, they were burned with no sign of a struggle. They appeared to be on fire from within their bodies."

"Did the Sheriff say that?"

"He said there were parts of the bodies that exposed raw bone as a result of burning but the outer flesh appeared to be the last affected, not the first as one would expect. The Sheriff said he had never seen anything like it."

The men finished their drinks and Artemus said good-bye to the couple promising to come back soon. Artemus rode toward the Abby. He felt he had to at least survey the area and report back to Henri what had happened. *What if the murderers knew there was a messenger coming to the Bishop? Spies would lay in wait to see who would ride in and then take the message.*

Artemus stopped off the highway, giving his horse a drink of water in a nearby stream. He relaxed under an oak tree and put his hand into his breast pocket searching for the broach. He pulled it out. The design displayed a gold "fleur de lis" on a dark background. The piece was very distinctive and looked to be valuable, very valuable. Artemus had seen something like it many times and hoped he was wrong. He stuck it back into his pocket and resumed his journey.

As Artemus rode into town, he saw the Abby in the distance. The village people were crowded at its entrance listening to someone. Artemus tied up his horse in front of the blacksmith's shop and walked to the Abby, carefully staying to the back of the crowd. The speaker was the Sheriff and his message reassured the town folk nothing apocalyptic was going to happen and they were just being superstitious.

One of the elders asked why this had to happen and "Who could have done such a thing?" The Sheriff said he would report his findings to them when he had more information and then he disbursed everyone, telling them to go home. His gaze shifted to Artemus with inquiring eyes.

Artemus took the look as an opportunity. He went directly up to the Sheriff averring that he was the hired security man from the Church's London office and sent to the village to assist him in any way possible. The Sheriff had reason to believe the story since the only remaining monk from the Abby left days earlier to tell the Church leaders what had happened. The Sheriff said he would appreciate Artemus speaking the following morning. "Please reassure the villagers that everything will be all right and that nothing will happen to them from the Church's perspective." Artemus agreed to do whatever he could. During their conversation, he learned the Sheriff's name was John Tartan and had served in the Third Crusade.

Artemus asked John if he would join him in something to drink which John quickly accepted. John married upon his return from the crusade with a fine military record and was rewarded with an appointment to become Sheriff. Artemus identified with John's situation and a bond quickly formed between them. John validated what Glen and Agnes said earlier about the murders and then added; "In the last day or so, strangers have taken up residence at the local tavern with no discernable business in town."

"The tavern is not suited for overnight guests but there must have been some accommodation reached with the owner." Artemus inquired as to their number and appearance. John said, "Three, I am aware of, one very large man and two smaller men." They had taken over the tavern's upper floor. Artemus asked him if he knew the layout. John provided a description as best he could. After getting the owner to rent him a dark back room; Artemus placed his bags on the floor next to his bed; blew out the room's only candle examining the ceiling. The flooring was uneven and the wooden planks were knot holed which made it easy to see the three men sitting together. He was also able to hear much of their conversation. He got a good look at each of them. One was badly scarred. They were complaining as to how much money they paid the tavern owner for information but were happy their investment paid off in knowing of Artemus' arrival.

The leader, the biggest of the group said, "Draw!" extending pieces of straw. The others took turns picking as the big man spoke, "He who picks the shortest straw must kill the stranger tonight." Artemus put his boots back on and ran to John's house, telling him what he overheard. Artemus suggested they capture these men to find out what they know.

"I wouldn't doubt that they killed the Bishop and then doubled back the next day." John said.

Artemus volunteered to be the bait and went back to the tavern. The smallest of the men came through the bedroom door very quietly with a knife drawn. He plunged it into the clothes Artemus had arranged under the coverlet. Artemus, behind the intruder, put his arm around the man's neck and slowly closed his windpipe.

As soon as the small man passed out, Artemus tied him up. It was hours since his attacker came into the room. *What happened to John?* Without warning, the big man crashed through the door prepared for a fight but found an empty room. Artemus and his captive had moved to the stable's loft. A slipknot in the supply rope dangled the little man upside down about 16 feet over the street. The little man's eyes bulged when he heard that if he moved or made any noise, Artemus would pull the knot free and the man would most surely fall to his death. The big man woke up everyone in the tavern demanding his friend be found.

Artemus silently climbed down from the loft with his hand still holding the rope. He saw John spiked to the ground with a spear driven through his chest in the adjacent corral. *There are more than three men involved here!* Artemus quickly saddled his horse and started out for the Church in London. He was getting closer to his destination when he heard many horses approaching from the rear. Artemus rode into the underbrush and climbed to a place elevated enough to see who was coming up behind him. He saw the big man and his two friends leading three others riding hard toward London. They didn't seem to have the slightest interest in capturing Artemus. *They just tried to kill me yet there is something obviously more important going on.* Artemus would follow them.

Chapter 8 - The Wharf House and The Waif

The band of marauders rode directly to a wharf house located on the Thames River inside London City. Artemus followed staying a safe distance behind them. The perimeter of the wharf house provided very little cover in which to hide. It had a dock to facilitate the loading and transport of goods and also a small muddy beach where a row boat could land. There was a thin strip island that separated the wharf house from the river's main water way giving a slight harbor effect to the ships that tied up at the wharf house dock. The houses to either side of it had service alleys separating each house from one another. Artemus worked his way to see who was inside but by the time he got into position, the conversation had ended and the men were disbanding through the wharf house river door. Cold and hungry Artemus retreated to the small island thicket and waited. After the men left, he broke into the wharf house and sat in the middle of the large first floor single room. He could see the loading floor upstairs with its large oversized doors leading out onto the street. The wharf house was ideally suited as a storage and distribution center for the river trade but was now empty.

Artemus was sure he had become the scapegoat for both the Bishop's and the Sheriff's murder. He decided to wait at the wharf house to see who returned. He fell asleep but was awakened hearing sounds coming from the alley. He scrambled outside onto the muddy beach. Looking through the dockside window, he could see someone come through the street entrance and walk down the interior stairs. The intruder was far too small and thin to be anything but a child or a woman. Perhaps he could get some information from his fellow vagrant but before he could act, the river door opened and Artemus found himself dodging a wooden cleat thrown directly at his head. Artemus managed to jump back into the wharf house and get behind his attacker. He rapped his adversary's head hard against the floor. The form lay motionless in fetal position. Artemus backed off into a corner of the first floor and sat on his haunches waiting for the waif to strike out again. The attack came but found nothing but air.

He applied his sleeper hold. As he was moving the body he felt breasts on the waif. His guest was a woman dressed like a man. He gently positioned her on the floor. Although her face was filthy, he could see that she had beautifully refined features. Her hair was completely shaved but judging from the dark skin helmet around her face if it was allowed to grow, it would be very thick and very dark. She was of medium height, no ass to speak of and her breasts were wrapped. Artemus waited patiently for her to regain consciousness. The little waif woke up in a rage immediately attempting to swing her fists until she realized she was completely bound and gagged. He felt sorry for his new little friend. It was then that Artemus noticed her eyes. They were an almond shaped dark violet. At a glance they looked almost brown but upon closer examination they were something quite different. She made no sound expecting the worst from her captor. Her clothes were filthy and tattered. Rags were tied around her feet in place of shoes. She was furious at herself for being out smarted twice. Artemus gently spoke to her saying he did not intend to hurt her. She finally began to grunt through the gag. Artemus told her, he would remove the gag but warned her that if she did yell, he would knock her out.

After agreeing to this, she immediately screamed and thus spent the night on the floor, gagged. Artemus had been awake for hours purchasing some food and scouting out alternative hiding places before his new little friend woke up. Upon regaining consciousness, she was more livid than ever. Artemus asked her if she liked the way she spent the night and again asked her if she wanted to have her gag removed. She nodded yes and stayed quiet. She was about to yell again until she saw his clenched fists and decided against it. Artemus sensed she was French. *She had to be at least 20*. Artemus whispered to her in English telling her to talk to him no louder than his whisper. She then hurled filthy insults back at him in French. When he responded in formal French, she looked at him in disbelief. She did not say a word but looked away toward the river, tears streaming down her face.

She was on the knife blade dance of feelings, despondency on one side and anger on the other. She reined her emotions in as fast as she had lost them. She stayed quiet and did not move. Artemus kept whispering. She struggled to hear him. She leaned closer to him. Artemus fed her small pieces of dried fish and bread along with giving her small sips of water until she had her fill. She remained silent. *This woman is as tough an urchin as I have ever seen and getting her to cooperate could be difficult.* She whispered to Artemus she had to relieve herself. Artemus was amazed to hear her obvious sophistication as she spoke her words. He loosened her bindings, fully expecting her to run. She surprised him by leaving from the river door and then returned within a few minutes. She went precisely back to the spot where she had spent the previous night and whispered her gratitude for being trusted. Artemus was mystified.

She now began questioning him. He did not answer her but found himself getting quite enchanted. He was impressed as to how well she carried herself. Artemus told her he was there to clear his name of murders he did not commit. He watched her as she listened to his story and realized that despite her youthful appearance, she had heard it all. *Why was she trying to conceal her identity?* Artemus tested the waif by calling her a "mother of swine pigs" in Latin and she spit in his face. She realized he had tricked her yet again and started to laugh. She whispered that no one her own age had ever outsmarted her. She politely inquired if he got the same pleasure by outwitting older people closer to his own age. Finally, she could see a slight hint of dejection in his eyes. He got up from the floor and went to the window.

Artemus looked down the river to where he had left his horse. She asked if she could help him in some way. He shared with her his love of horses and expressed concern for this one's care. She said she could help if he would trust her again. Artemus felt he didn't have much of a choice. If he did not let her go, his horse would starve or be stolen. After agreeing to her suggestion, she left and Artemus found himself mentally running various scenarios in his head.

As the thoughts went through his mind for the thousandth time, she walked into the wharf house from the street entrance with bread, wine and a story of how she got a farmer friend of hers to care of his horse. Artemus was relieved but curious; "How do you know this farmer?"

She ignored his question and responded by asking, "Tell me more about you and I may tell you some small insignificant things about me." Artemus said; "you go first!"

"My real name is unimportant. I go by the name Micah in my role of playing a boy."

"Who would ever believe you to be a boy?" She slowly lifted up her shirt showing her bound breasts and rag padded shoulders. Artemus did not let on he was already aware of her disguise.

She said, "People believe me to be a fourteen year old boy."

"Why are you, with such an obvious aristocratic background, living in this rat infested wharf house?"

Micah replied, "There is an underground war brewing with France, England and others. The Saracens ransomed my father and expected me as payment. The English commandeered the French ship I was on and landed it in Bristol. I fled and found myself here. I have been living by my wits in this house for months." Artemus instinctively knew there was a much bigger story she was not telling. She was beguiling him. He had trouble keeping his eyes off her. He used every trick he knew to distract himself from staring. He remained silent until it was his turn to talk. Artemus spoke. "I was not born into aristocracy but I do have a reputation as someone who can be trusted."

Micah interrupted him; "How do you know so many languages? How do you know how to write? Who taught you how to fight?" He looked into her eyes and at the curious way she held her head while she talked to him. It was as if she was trying to communicate with him on many different levels, all at once. Artemus responded, "My education was a reward for my many accomplishments in working for the Duchies. My patrons felt I could do more for them in the future if I were educated. She nodded with understanding realizing he was also a pawn in their control. Artemus changed the subject. "Micah, tell me about the six men I followed here. They had a meeting with someone that I could not see. That was two days ago and no one has returned. Micah leaned against the wall for support, holding her knees together with both hands clasped around them saying; "I will help you if you get me back to Paris."

"What about your father?"

"After the French ship was pirated, the word went out that all aboard were lost. My father and his captors think I am dead."

"Would you really have gone through with becoming a slave to get your father out of prison?"

"I feel if it is God's will, I am obliged to follow."

"Do you feel our meeting is God's will?" Artemus asked.

"Yes!" and without breaking stride Micah continued by saying she did not know who owns the wharf house just that "He remains always in the background. Even when he is in the house, he manages to stay out of sight. I know he is very powerful. On some occasions, he has been preceded by as many as fifty of his men mingling in the street to get or spread information."

Micah felt comfortable enough with Artemus to begin telling him what this powerful man and his entourage were doing at the wharf house since her arrival.

"These people are using this house to frame a certain group of spiritual believers."

"What are you talking about?"

"The group mimics their spiritual rites with sexual perversion."

"Why do you say, mimics? What do you know of such rites?"

"That's my business!"

Artemus had to remind himself that he should not get too close to her. His chivalrous instincts however, took over and he made a comment about her safety.

Micah screamed. "You do not know anything? I stand more of a chance in here than I do out there. One word with the wrong intonation and I will be raped, garroted and thrown into the Thames with no one being any of the wiser. I hide from these people and watch them in total safety. The other night when you arrived you were so close to me, you could have felt my breath but you didn't and I like it that way." Artemus got a sense of her frustration and anxiety levels. She was shouldering a burden far heavier than what she was letting on. Micah continued, "The patron's black coach has a seal on the side displaying a gold three pointed fleur de lis embossed on a dark background." Artemus pulled out the broach from his pocket and asked her if it was the same.

Micah looked at it with amazement and said; "Yes, that's it. Who does it belong to?"

Now it was Artemus's turn to continue his own line of questioning. "Have you ever followed the coach?"

"No, it is much too dangerous and it is impossible to know how many spies their leader employs. I have been safe staying here and not venturing out other than to steal flowers for my farm girl friend."

"Your farm friend is a girl?"

Micah turned to him laughing clasping her hands behind her head saying, "What better way to avoid having my true identity found out than to flirt with a girl?"

"How long have you known her?"

"A few months."

Artemus listened and said nothing. Micah was extremely well spoken. *So much so that she might play a much larger part in this little mystery. If I had the money, maybe I would pay this well educated young woman to housesit my little "den of inequity."*

He resigned himself to watch her very closely and not tell her more than absolutely necessary. Artemus then asked her when she expected the debauchers to return. "Any day, the first wave should arrive to prepare the house. It's not long after that the black coach arrives."

"Do they know squatters live here?"

"Yes! Some of the advance men have even caught me. I was lucky that when they did, I was so filthy they just wanted to get rid of me."

The advance team showed up a few days later and by then, Artemus and Micah had spread enough dust and dirt to make the wharf house look undisturbed.

Micah's hiding place was a river blind built on the river's thin strip island directly across from the wharf house. The Kings soldiers used it to guard Royal boats navigating the Thames. As they huddled together to keep warm, Micah sensed Artemus's sexual tension growing and wanted it to build. Artemus squirmed so as not to touch her and tried to concentrate on the wharf house. He wanted to catch a glimpse of the person who wanted to kill him. Men arrived from the street entrance. There seemed to be an endless parade of people preparing the wharf house for the next ritualistic ceremony. As the day turned to night, a welcome warm breeze made their watch more bearable. The dark wharf house was transformed with hundreds of candles which beautifully illuminating the newly cleaned and decorated loft.

Micah told Artemus "This is a rehearsal."

"Why do they need a rehearsal?"

"Wait and see!" Micah said.

The advance men began by engaging in a mock ceremonial procession. A man dressed in black robes was the torch bearer. He was followed by the big man who tried to kill Artemus. He was carrying a large grain sac over his head. A third man led a stunning blond woman through the street entrance and down the stairs. She was collared by a ceremonial rope. Her long flowing black robe gave her no shape. Her hair appeared almost white and long below her shoulders. It was pristinely clean and perfectly styled. Micah said this next part of the ceremony offended her and mocked the real spiritual rite with a deception designed to portray "The True Believers" in the worst possible light. Artemus didn't know anything about them but had heard the name. The woman was lifted effortlessly onto the alter after being stripped of her robe by the big man who placed her perfectly proportioned naked body in front of the sac of grain which served as a guide for where an animal would be placed. Artemus craned his neck trying to see more of what was going on inside but was having some difficulty when Micah extended mechanical planks from inside the blind across the water separating the island from the Wharf house's dock. The Kings guard could use these planks extended in the other direction to close off the main river if there was trouble.

Artemus and Micah crawled out giving them a perfect view of the first floor. The big man picked up the sac and placed it down behind the naked woman at the precise moment the lute player hit a certain note. They practiced this move a number of times.

Micah whispered to Artemus the purpose for this spiritual ritualistic rouse was to spread lies in London and elsewhere that this group of True Believers consummated a pact with Satan after the sex act was completed. She continued saying that a fake True Believer priest stabs the animal killing it signaling the start of an open orgy where the entire congregation fornicates. Micah said that the past wharf house spectacles lasted for hours. Artemus knew the motivation for staging all of this was purely political.

"Micah, do you know about this type of ritual?"

"Yes and these people know they are perverting a beautiful ceremony into an abomination to justify their own ends."

"Tell me how you know these things!"

"In time, Artemus, I will tell you in due time."

"How am I to trust you if we don't share our knowledge?"

Micah replied; "Your involvement in things that don't concern you is dangerous for you and therefore also for me. Let us concentrate on their leader and the "why" will become evident."

Artemus didn't like being talked to with such distain but he needed her. He remained quiet and went back to his surveillance of the wharf house. He gave Micah some money and asked her to follow his plan.

Sometime after she left, the street entrance of the wharf house came alive with people coming through its wide passage. The ritual was taking place now and he knew there would be no time to execute his plan. Artemus made his way to the service alley. From there, he walked to the side street where he found two soldiers going into a tavern. Artemus followed them in and sat close enough to begin a conversation.

"What garrison are you with?" Artemus asked.

"We are with the King's personal guard and tonight we have been given time off while our liege is occupied for at least a day in this section of the city."

These "guards" were to make sure everyone in London knew there was some sort of gathering at the wharf house. Artemus asked them questions about anything he could think of to get more information. When they stopped answering him, he worried they had become suspicious. Artemus volunteered to get the next round of drinks and slipped a sleeping potion into his guest's drinks. After everyone finished, Artemus said he had to relieve himself. The two took his lead out the door. The brisk air hit them and they passed out as soon as they rounded the tavern's corner. Artemus then dragged the bodies into the brush and went back into the tavern just in time to overhear the bartender talking with a regular customer saying he was sure he knew every one of the King's guard and those two were not part of it.

Artemus surveyed the wharf house from the street and found the entire area filled with the dregs of humanity. Everyone was drinking heavily and drawing as much attention to the wharf house as possible. Artemus realized *these people are play actors hired to put on this show.* He retreated back to the alley and went around to the muddy beach looking into the wharf house's first floor. The group inside was frenzied. The orgy was at a fever pace. Whatever had taken place before was over and the group was out of control. He watched and waited until all of the revelers finished and had left. The servants cleaned the place and then spread dirt as if nothing had happened. Artemus went back into the wharf house and again sat in the middle of the first floor contemplating all of his questions.

Micah quietly came in the house from the river entrance. Artemus had a knife at her throat not knowing who it was. He was happy to see her. She had a blanket but was not successful in obtaining any more information about who was behind this ritual staging. She listened as Artemus told her the details.

He said he watched as all the people left and the guards rode out of the city. He asked Micah to remain at the wharf house; he would find out who was behind this charade and then come back for her. Micah agreed. He went to the tavern hoping to pick up their trail. As he circled around back to see if his guard guests were still sleeping, he heard someone but it was too late. A blow came from behind and Artemus fell to the ground, unconscious.

Chapter 9 - The Castle Keep

Artemus awoke, yet another day in complete darkness. Freezing still water touched his naked body. Shackles bound his arms and legs tightly to the cell wall, permitting no movement whatsoever. He had been fed and cared for once a day and after being put back on the cell wall, he was deprived of all sensory perception. Fear consumed him. Artemus realized they had his clothes and most assuredly opened up his pouch and read the contents of the message meant for the Bishop's eyes only and they were also in possession of the broach. He had completely failed in his mission. This was devastating to Artemus. His mind turned to Micah. He would probably never see her again, an irony befitting his entire life. He focused in on his own situation. He started ranting at the top of his lungs. He carried on for what seemed like hours with no response. This behavior helped to dissipate the fear. Exhausted, he decided to get some sleep to help prepare for what was certain to be a bad couple of days before they killed him. The first kick woke him up, all the rest reinforced he was still alive. All he could see was the blinding brightness of a very ordinary lantern. The guards dragged him from his dark cell.

His body was pushed outside into the freezing cold and pulled into another building where he was thrown into an iced water open well enclosed by a spiral stone staircase. Artemus knew this clean up was not for his benefit but his inquisitor's. The torture master would not want to endure putrid smells while performing his work. Once cleaned, he was again shackled and blindfolded. He was hit repeatedly in the head, face and groin on the way up the stairs. They put him into a specially built wooden cart that glided on the floor.

He could smell salt air while being wheeled into his torture ready room. The guards manhandled him out of the cart, replacing his iron shackles with leather restraints. These cuffs had metal loops on the outside wrist plates so a prisoner could be attached to chains or lanyards without cutting off circulation, extending consciousness.

After a time, Artemus was taken into a large reception room that had at its center, a huge table. The ceiling was twenty feet high buttressed by rafters extending the entire length of the room with a fireplace at its far end. A "Cu Faoil" Irish wolf hound guarded the door. It was the largest dog Artemus had ever seen. A small thin man entered the room and sat at the table. He motioned for the guards to bring Artemus closer. They dragged him on his knees to a spot about 10 feet from his inquisitor.

"Who are you?" the inquisitor asked.

"I am a messenger sent to deliver a message to the Bishop at North Abbey."

"Liar!" he screamed while he motioned for the guards to hit him.

"Who are you?"

"I told you!"

"Liar!" He motioned this time for the guards to bring the dog closer to Artemus.

The inquisitor spoke forcefully to Artemus. "This dog has been extremely well trained. He will bugger you to death. I will let him have his way with you or we can disembowel you. Unfortunately, I do not have the time for an exquisitely painful torture. I need information and I need it now. If you cooperate with me, I will show you mercy in death. If you do not tell me everything now, I will show you a very different reality. I love my work and reigning terror on you provides me with the greatest personal satisfaction. If you cause delay and take time to tell me what I wish to know, I will be forced to give you my time, something you will not want."

The inquisitor's speech was cut short. He was called out of the room by a messenger giving him some sort of instruction. Artemus could hear they were sending assassins to kill anyone who could be traced back to them. He looked for anything that could free him before the inquisitor returned. He saw a long needle on the table. Something the man was undoubtedly planning to use on him.

Artemus fell on his back and used the momentum of the fall to springboard himself into a standing up position with the result of now having his arms out in front of him. Once on his feet, he bent down and took the needle into his mouth. The laces on his bindings were vulnerable. Artemus folded his hands to create a space between the binding and his wrist. He wedged the needle between the laces and binding and pulled one hand free, undid his feet and other hand. The dog was at the closed door waiting for his master and did not notice Artemus making his escape as he ran through the adjacent room's door.

When the inquisitor returned and noticed his prisoner had escaped, he laughed. He knew there was no escape from this prison. *This is a minor inconvenience.* He yelled for the guards to find Artemus. They entered with swords drawn and ran into the adjacent room. They were shocked to find no one there. The doors were still locked. The inquisitor screaming at the top of his lungs demanded the guards return the prisoner immediately back to his chamber. The guards alerted the entire garrison. No fewer than 30 men were looking for Artemus. As the inquisitor warmed his hands by the fire, his dog turned to check out the sound coming from the adjacent room. As soon as the dog went into the room, Artemus appeared bolting its door from within. He then jumped the inquisitor before he had time to turn around. The needle was at the thin man's throat as Artemus whispered, "Now it is your turn to experience the wonders of pain!" as he put the needle about one eighth of an inch into the man's neck. Blood was flowing and the inquisitor was shaking. Artemus pulled off the man's clothes, bound him in the leather restraints and hoisted him into the air. Artemus began questioning him, "What is this place?"

"A castle." the inquisitor sniveled.

Where is it?

"England!"

Artemus quickly lowered the inquisitor to the floor. He placed the little man's head in the wooden vice panels that were a part of the torture table and started to squeeze. Blood was beginning to come out of the man's ears. Artemus was out of time. The inquisitor defiantly spit at Artemus. After knocking him unconscious, he expertly put the needle into the inquisitor's jugular vein. He quietly expired.

Artemus went through a door that led into a connecting hall. He could hear the guards systematically working their way back to his section of the castle. He surprised two guards, quickly dispatching the first by knocking him to the ground and then, using his open hand, drove it into the guard's nose collapsing it against his skull. He repeated the process on the second guard. He took a back staircase which led to the upper sections of the castle.

Artemus ran up the stairs, through an open room and up another flight of stairs dead ending at an open deep pit with a drawbridge pulled up protecting the other side and barring access to what had to be the master's section of the castle. He jumped the pit's spear-laden floor, white knuckling the top of the raised bridge. Artemus, then, worked on gaining access to the rope and levers of the bridge with a knife he had taken from one of the guards. He found the right combination of pulling the bridge's lever as he held onto its rope.

As it descended slowly, Artemus traversed it to the other side and pulled on the rope to get the bridge back to its upright position. Once it was secure, he walked silently down the formal hallway and stopped at the first room. No one was there. The next two rooms were also empty. He then heard footsteps coming down the hall. He quickly hid behind the door of an empty room. Only after a small child entered the bedroom and closed the door did Artemus continue down the corridor. A room at the end of the hall glowed from candle light.

The sounds of a family were all too apparent bringing back haunting memories of his own wife and child before they were murdered by an unknown assailant. He crept past the care provider's room and headed down the main staircase passing by the empty master suite.

Artemus could hear a great deal of commotion taking place on the first floor as he went down the stairs which faced the massive main entry door. He turned into a guest receiving room just to the right of that door. No sooner did Artemus enter it than the front door flew open. The Captain of the Guard entered leaving his men waiting in the courtyard. The Master at Arms motioned for The Captain to come down a long straight hallway. The door to the office was immediately closed when the Captain entered it but the front door remained open. Artemus hid behind the receiving room's curtains.

A short time later, the meeting ended. The Captain closed the main entry door on his way out and told his lieutenants in Latin to secure the island. This information was more bad news. Artemus now knew he was imprisoned on an island with no means of escape. He went down the hall to the garrison office and looked outside to get his bearings.

The moon was new in the sky. *If the moon was new, then how many days had I spent in that dungeon?* Artemus thought. *Who are these people?*

He entered the now empty office of the Master at Arms and found his sword, pouch, clothes and a drawing of the wharf house. Micah was in the sketch. *What does this mean?* He took his sword and looked into his pouch. All the seals were broken but the message remained inside. He read it and memorized the encrypted note. Artemus took his belongings including the drawing of Micah and the wharf house. He saw a guard in the outside courtyard alone. Artemus subdued him and put on his uniform. Artemus recognized the emblem displaying the heraldry on the guard's tunic. He made it down to the dock where three soldiers guarded a longboat and a small rowboat. He waited until one of the men started his patrol and grunted to see which language was spoken. It was Latin and thus confirmed Artemus's suspicions. Artemus told the soldier closest to the boats he was sent to inform the guards to report immediately to the Master at Arms. All three soldiers started off for the office. He knew he couldn't handle the longboat alone so taking a fresh log from the guards warming fire, set it ablaze and cast off in the rowboat for shore. He could see a swarm of soldiers making their way from the castle to save the boat but it was already beyond salvage.

He diverted the rowboat into a small inlet. More soldiers came out of the local tavern looking at the island. From their vantage point, they could see the fire but could not tell what was causing it. At least ten soldiers got in their boat and started out for the island. The air was cooling down very rapidly. A low-level fog set in making it difficult for the soldiers to navigate. This gave Artemus time to get away. He changed back into his own clothing and blended in with the village crowd. He listened to their chatter and found out he was many miles from London. Artemus needed money and a horse. He went into the stable and rummaged through the goods stored in a livery room off the main stable area for any valuables. He found a few things he could barter. While he was looking through these items, he recalled that the broach was not among his belongings. He found a beautiful grey that would take him back to London. He rode toward the wharf house.

He could not get over his good fortune. The idea he was alive was unbelievable. He needed to find Micah. He couldn't believe he had feelings for her but then reason took over from his heart. *I will do more for Micah by following my only clue.* Artemus changed direction from heading toward London in favor of Tunbridge Wells.

Chapter 10 - Henri

As Artemus got closer to the village, he saw and smelled the devastation created by a massive fire. The villagers had been slaughtered. The odor of their burned flesh sickened him. Curiously, there was no trace of the innkeepers or the groom. He searched the ruble that used to be the Inn but found nothing. He then went into the stable, which was surprisingly untouched. All of the animals were well fed. Someone had left water for them to survive. The only tracks he could find were those left by a wagon or carriage with a notched wheel heading toward Dover. Artemus was hungry, exhausted and badly in need of information. He scavenged what he could from the village and villager's remains. The enormity of these events sank into his mind as he arrived in Dover. He found himself depressed and profoundly saddened. He learned that a boat carrying many people from France capsized in a severe storm and there had not been any channel crossings in many days. *Whoever was in that wagon has not been able to cross the channel. They should still be here somewhere.*

Much of what Artemus retrieved from the dead villagers went to the quartermaster to pay for his boat passage. When Artemus boarded, he positioned himself behind the rudder man on the starboard side of the Cog ship to observe everyone as they embarked. The boat quickly filled up. He did not recognize any of the passengers.

The Cog pitched and rolled across the channel and again Artemus waited for everyone to leave. Out of the corner of his eye, he saw Agnes. Once she was off the ship, she got into a black coach. The same type he saw at the wharf house. Artemus tried to keep up on foot. If nothing else, he would establish its direction. The coach was moving at a very easy pace, and then began to pick up speed. Artemus took a chance. He jumped on the back of the carriage's suspension and held on. The coach stopped in the town of Amiens. As Agnes got out of the carriage, she canvassed the area, looking for anything unusual. Glen appeared in the doorway of a roadhouse and greeted his wife. They went inside. Artemus crawled under the roadhouse window outside where the two took a table inside in its main room.

"Did anyone follow you?" Glen asked.

"I was very careful."

"When are we leaving for Paris?" Agnes asked.

"Tonight, as soon as everyone here is in bed."

"Then what do we do?"

"We must deliver the Bishop's ring to the King."

"What is the significance of the Bishop's ring?" Agnes asked.

Before Artemus could hear the answer, the coachman was rounding the building's corner forcing Artemus to move to another hiding place. He hid in the stable and dozed waiting for the coach to resume its journey.

Later on that night, Agnes, Glen and the driver came into the stable, hitched up the horses, and drove out. As they gained speed, Artemus again took his position on the coach's suspension. As they entered Paris, Artemus hopped off at a small church before the coach went over the bridge to the Palace. Now on his home turf, Artemus quietly entered Lutece, Henri's Inn.

He walked into the large room where most people congregated. Henri's wife, serving as the bar maid, was amazed to see Artemus and motioned for him to go in the back. A short time later, she came to him in tears explaining that the King's guard came for Henri and took him away. "Those bastards kicked him and beat him as they threw a noose around his neck and pulled him behind their horses. The site was awful, Artemus." She continued, "We were told you were dead, that you had been killed by highwaymen and your body taken by a satanic cult working in consort with the King of England."

"Who told you this?"

"By a young boy who was asking about you - just a few days ago."

"Was Henri already in custody?"

"Yes and the King's men were aware you two were friends."

Henri's wife gave Artemus some food and wine as Artemus inquired more into Henri's plight. She told Artemus that Henri was held in the Palace and hoped Artemus would try to free him. Artemus said he could do nothing against the King's guard but thanked her for the food.

His mind was racing. *Henri's wife has always been out for herself. Why was she so curious about what I am going to do next?* Artemus knew that if anything happened to Henri, she and her family would inherit the Inn.

Considering their marriage has been tumultuous at best, it was reasonable to assume that she tipped off the guards. The King probably paid her to tell him about my arrangement with Henri and that I was returning with something of great importance which means she will now tell someone I am back!

Artemus went to the window just in time to see the chambermaid, who must have also been in on Henri's betrayal talking to Jamie, the Tunbridge Wells Inn groom. The girl was about 17 and uniquely attractive. Artemus was sitting at the table when the chambermaid walked in. He had met her before and saw her motioning through the window for Jamie to get the bailiffs while she would do her best to delay any departure. Artemus feigned feeling sick and asked the chambermaid to make up a room that he could use for a time. She rushed to make one ready, thinking Artemus would fetch a tidy reward and she would not have to do anything special to be paid. Jamie returned with a squad of the King's guard. The chambermaid pointed to Artemus' room. The entire unit swooped in to capture him. They found nothing.

The Captain was furious, verbally abusing Jamie and threatening him with wasting everyone's time. Jamie vowed to catch Artemus, himself and get the reward. As soon as the soldiers left, Jamie and the chamber maid fell into each other's arms using the room for themselves. Artemus was hiding under the floorboards. He waited until they finished making love. While the two were still naked and enjoying their afterglow, Artemus rousted Jamie from the bed and had him get dressed. He bound the boy's hands and feet and draped him over the boy's horse. They rode to a remote location outside of the city. Artemus retied Jamie to a tree and started a fire. Jamie looked on "saucer eyed" as Artemus played with the fire heating the long needle he kept from his time in the castle.

Artemus told Jamie, "Don't take this personally. I have a friend in prison probably because of you and I have to get him out. If you make my job easy, I will not harm you, if you make it difficult, I will harm you more than is necessary. Do you understand?"

The needle was a glow and visible from the tree. Jamie started screaming, begging for someone, anyone to help him. When he realized no help was forthcoming, Jamie began telling Artemus everything he knew. The boy's information confirmed that the innkeepers and Jamie were part of a conspiracy conceived by the King of France.

Artemus asked, "Why such an elaborate hoax?"

Jamie admitted that it was all part of the King's plan and that everyone including Artemus helped create a very scandalous event designed to alienate the King of England from the Pope.

Artemus knew more than he let on.

"What happens from here, Jamie? Should I start plucking your eyes out?"

"No, no really I don't know anything else, I would tell you; don't hurt me!"

"Jamie, I am going to give you a chance to avoid disfigurement."

"Yes, yes anything."

"Who are Agnes and Glen?"

"French spies working for the King."

"Who are you?"

"I am their son."

"Who is the street urchin?"

"What street urchin?"

"The one squatting at the wharf house."

"I don't know any street urchin or anything about a wharf house."

"I have to check out your information. You are going to stay with a friend of mine. If you attempt to leave him, I will find you and your family and kill all of you. I will torture the chambermaid and then kill her too. Do you understand?" Artemus brought Jamie to his friend who lived on the Seine. Jamie gave his word he would not attempt to leave. He reaffirmed that everything he told Artemus was the truth. The friend would put Jamie to work until Artemus returned. As Artemus rode back to Paris, he thought about the significance of the Bishop's ring. What was on or in the ring that was so important? He was afraid Henri could already be dead. *Once the King got the information he wanted, Henri would be expendable.* Earlier in the year, one of Artemus' close friends died and left him a small house on the other side of the river in Paris. Artemus's house had been empty since he left for England. After he opened the windows and got some fresh air into the place, Artemus looked longingly at the bed. It was inviting but Artemus could not rest. Instead he walked to the front entrance of the Island Palace, having crossed the bridge, he stopped at the main gate, casing the small cellblock located in the front section.

He stayed clear of the perimeter guards but one of the gate guards spotted him and questioned why he was there. He told the guard; "Ever since those Saracen bastards killed my wife and child, I can't sleep at night." Artemus moved the subject to the guard's necklace, "Hey, isn't that a Saracen good luck piece? Did you take it as a souvenir?" The guard responded affirmatively. After talking for a while about the crusades, the guard eventually asked Artemus if he would like to have a drink after his guard duty was over.

Artemus said; "Maybe I could go over there to wait for you?" motioning to a group of benches at the front gate. The guard nodded his agreement.

As soon as Artemus sat down, he began looking for a way to get into the cellblock.

It was his new friend's turn to walk the perimeter. Artemus waited until he was out of sight before running into the prison building. The cellblock was comprised of twelve cells; all of them filled with as many as 10 people in each.

Artemus found Henri, next to death and badly beaten with multiple burns all over his body. Artemus skillfully picked the lock and opened Henri's cell door but then heard a guard coming to check the prisoners. He went into Henri's cell and blended in with the rest of the inmates. All were in various stages of decrepitude. The guard moved quickly through the area as the smell was horrible. Artemus lifted Henri onto his back, ran out of the cell and through the inner door. He waited until the next guard past and ran into the courtyard with Henri. Artemus put his sleeper hold on Henri as he was beginning to move. *Thank God, Henri is so small!* He could see his new friend walking over to him so Artemus quickly hid Henri under a wagon and sat on the bench as if nothing had happened

"I came to get you, where did you go?" the guard asked.

"I relieved myself over there as he pointed past the cell block."

"That's off limits but I guess it doesn't matter."

The guard continued; "I am off duty soon. Where do you want to go?"

Artemus said, "Let's go to the tavern across the bridge. I will meet you there."

The guard said "Good. If I can get there a bit sooner, I will start without you." The guard went back to his position at the gate and did not notice Artemus tucking the little man into his coat holding him like a pregnant woman holding her stomach. He rounded the Palace's walled corner and broke into a full sprint to get away. Artemus turned into the alley entering his house with Henri moaning. Artemus was satisfied he would recover. *Henri will recognize this place and put together what has happened.* Artemus was going to make his date with the guard. He went inside the tavern, greeted his new guard friend at a table and offered to buy him a drink. The guard accepted.

They drank for hours when the guard said he had to leave. They parted outside at the front door and promised to meet again sometime. Artemus got a bad feeling. *Things were going too well.* Artemus stepped into the shadows to see if anyone was in the tavern or lurking outside to follow him. He waited a short time before seeing two men leave the tavern. They too listened for footsteps but heard only those made by the guard. They met up with a third man standing farther down the street who pointed back to where Artemus was hiding. Artemus ran down to the river and jumped into an unfinished section of a sidewall erected to keep its water from overflowing into the street. He waited there until the three got discouraged and left. The sun was coming up and Artemus was very tired.

As he walked home, he suspected he was set up from the beginning to get Henri out of jail. *Freeing Henri was too easy! The King is still working his charade for some reason.* Artemus entered his house to find Henri still asleep. He prepared an herbal medicine and managed to pour most of it down Henri's throat. After the little man's coughing fit was over, Artemus got some needed rest. When he awoke, Henri had moved and seemed to be recovering. Henri could not believe his eyes, which told him he was in Artemus' house with his "dead" friend taking care of him. The little man started to cry with joy and deeply thanked Artemus for rescuing him. Henri ran at the mouth with information. "We were manipulated, my friend. I have been one of the King's spies for years and thought they would never use me in such a way. I am beside myself with disappointment and feelings of betrayal. They tortured me using horrible instruments, it was awful. I am so angry. I will do anything to get back at them. His Majesty actually came down to the torture chamber and told me what a good job I had done for him in the past and that my mutilation was necessary to complete his charade." Then the King actually said, "No one would have ever guessed that such a hideous mutated diseased dwarf like me had actually been of service to the Crown and that I should take that distinction to my grave" as he walked back up the stairs to his dinner party.

"Calm down, don't work yourself up anymore, it's over."

"This is not over, I will get them, you'll see."

"Did you learn anything while you were in prison? What were they asking you?"

"They wanted to know if you had returned and if so, what you brought back. They also wanted to know if you had anyone with you. They told me you were missing and you had caused them a lot of trouble. I am so happy you outsmarted them. They didn't seem to care about anything I said so I started to lie. I told them anything that would take time to check. I told them that you had enlisted a group of comrades from

Dunkirk to storm the Palace. The lies bought me enough time for you to save me, which is unbelievable."

"They would have boiled you in oil when they found out you were lying."

"I think they were going to do worse than that to me anyway." Henri remarked.

"Did the torture master ask you specifically about the mission?"

"Not specifically! I think the whole interrogation was to make a record which could be shared with someone else. He referred to the English. Does that make sense?"

"Yes! Are you hungry?"

"Yes, when this is over I will pay you back. I cannot begin to tell you how grateful I am. Thank you, Artemus for saving me."

"You would do the same for me, now get some rest."

As Artemus entered the butcher's shop, he saw two unfamiliar men asking for him. He melted into the crowd and walked to the other end of the city, purchased food and came back. They had a good meal and then slept. When they awoke their conversation continued.

"Did you notice anyone new hanging around your Inn before the guards carried you away?"

"Yes, there was a young boy flirting with Anna. I shooed him away on two occasions. Why?" Henri asked.

"Did anybody else come by?"

"Another young lad came in for a meal. He was very thin and had very short dark hair. He asked if many of my customers that stayed at the Inn had business with the Palace." Henri continued, "It was an odd question, I suspected he was spying for someone. The young man wasn't from Paris. He had an accent of some sort. Artemus instinctively knew the young man was Micah. Amazed at this news, Artemus went into deep thought; *this woman exhibits remarkable skill especially, if on her own, she made her way to Paris. If she is working for the King, she would be the perfect spy. I have to be careful.*

After a few days, Henri realized he had best go to his native town of Avignon and disappear until this nightmare was over. In his gratitude, Henri gave Artemus the Inn. He and his family would leave Paris for as long as the King was alive. Artemus told Henri his suspicions about Henri's wife betraying him and that she probably had a pact with the King. Henri responded by saying; "All the more reason to give the Inn away!" as Henri signed over a paper testifying to his gift. Artemus responded, "Thank you! I will get in touch if there is a positive resolution here; otherwise have a good life, my friend."

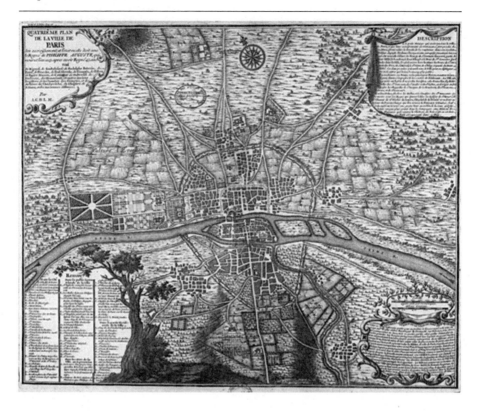

Chapter 11 - Micah in Paris

After seeing Henri off, Artemus went to the Inn to check if any new developments had happened in his absence. He walked into the back kitchen area and found the stableman eating some food.

"Hello, Artemus did you hear about Henri?"

"That he was taken by the King's guard? Yes!"

"No, that he escaped and there is a reward for him. Oh and Artemus, they are looking for you too."

"Did you give them any information?"

"No but Henri's wife talked with the bailiffs for a while. I think she gave them a description of what you look like and approximately where you live."

Artemus asked if he needed anything. The stableman said, "No, we are in good shape, here."

Artemus said he would not be back. He was leaving the City. After making sure he was not followed, Artemus went to his house. He gathered some of his things and waited until nightfall. He, then, secretly moved to a boarding house across the street from Lutece. He paid for his stay in advance and was very nice to the woman proprietor. She showed him to his room on the second floor which overlooked Lutece's stable and grounds. The location also provided easy access to the Palace. Artemus then walked along the river. He could see the Palace where a lavish party was underway. The perimeter guards were in much greater number. Artemus saw the guard he had drinks with in the distance and quickly walked across the road to the Cathedral to avoid detection. He waited there until the guard changed. An area neglected entirely was the formal entrance to the Palace, itself. The challenge was getting past the guards at the front gate.

Artemus went to the bridge and waited for the next guest to arrive. Instead of a coach, he saw a battlewagon carrying supplies pulled by four of the biggest Percheron horses he had ever seen. He jumped under the back wheels grabbing the rear axle and pulled himself under.

The wagon got a cursory look and "a wave through" at the gate. Artemus dropped off before the wagon reached its destination. He ran into some shrubs that surrounded the interior walls. He could see all of the guests and the King. The party was spectacular with jugglers, magicians and a host of the King's croupiers offering his guests a chance to lose their money.

Artemus headed for the lower level of the Palace and found a magician's costume. He put it on and started working the crowd on the periphery, trying to avoid the aristocracy in the center as many would recognize him. He was at the tip of the island where the Seine connected into one river flow when he noticed Agnes in a beautiful gown, speaking to a nobleman. Glen was behind her talking with someone else.

As he was performing a coin trick, he saw Micah in a servant's uniform. She had a look of disbelief in her eyes as she came up behind him. "The wait was too long so I came to find you." She laughed.

"Did you learn more about our friends at the wharf house?"

She said "Some!" A voice from the crowd yelled; "Hey boy bring me more wine!" Micah ran up to the Marquis and responded; "Right away sir!" and left for the kitchen.

Artemus was overwhelmed at seeing her but tempered his enthusiasm. He needed to find Agnes and Glen's quarters. He left the party and found the Palace's guest suites. He climbed the stairs to the third floor and found the couple's suite of five rooms, two bedrooms and three sitting rooms. One of the sitting rooms was turned into a music room. The view was beautiful overlooking the city and down the river. He found a treasure trove beginning with the Bishop's ring and a written account of the elaborate plan to murder the Bishop, the mass killings of the Tunbridge Wells villagers and much more including a part where Artemus would confess to being involved with a Catharess witch. The documents and other evidence showed convincing proof that together; Artemus and the witch had masterminded the plot against King Phillip and were in consort with the English King. In addition, the plan referenced the wharf house and the fifty actors to debauch each other specifically designed to further offend the Pope against the Cathars and alienate him from the English King.

Artemus heard someone coming up the stairs. He hid in the wardrobe closet. Agnes and another lady of the Court were taking a break. They entered the room laughing and making fun of some of the lecherous counts and marquis that were trying to put their hands up and down both women's dresses. They seemed quite amused at their husbands who were having a time of it trying to keep their wives from having sex with the old goats. The women talked as if that notion was beyond the realm of possibility. Artemus instantly knew how very naïve both of these women were and if they stayed much longer at the Palace, they would learn that for themselves. Agnes's friend was about twenty five years old with a very shapely body. Agnes, dressed up, looked surprisingly attractive. The women stepped out of their dresses and lounged in their undergarments on the chaises at the end of their main salon.

A third lady entered the room. Artemus recognized her as the blond haired woman who starred in the wharf house ritual ceremony and orgy. She explained the ladies' role in the night's festivities. "The King, himself wanted me to make sure both of you would be at your best to perform your courtly duties." The blond reassured the women there is no shame in being in the service of their King. A chambermaid came in to attend them and saw the wardrobe door was ajar and came by to close it. Artemus did not know whether she saw him or not but she left without a word. He pushed the door ever so slightly open again to get back into the conversation. The blond woman had left. The women redressed and put white cake powder on their faces in an effort to look as unattractive as possible.

After waiting a while, Artemus came out of the closet. He was positioning his pants to accept his new found bounty when the chambermaid came in inquiring as to whom he was and what he was doing. Artemus told her he was a magician at the party and had come upstairs to set up some tricks, which included putting things in the women's dresses so he laid in wait and did it without their knowledge. He performed a few tricks for the maid and she seemed satisfied.

All of the guests were moving into the banquet room accompanied by their handmaidens to take part in a cornucopia of every imaginable food. They went from one table to another sampling fabulous meats, vegetables and bakery goods. Artemus waited in the ballroom until the last of the guests started to eat before making his escape. He walked casually to the front gate and told a guard he would be back bringing an apparatus for a special trick that the King, himself, had requested. Artemus walked over the bridge and into his boarding house room. He took the cache out of his pants looking at each item. The Bishop's ring had a number of engraved symbols on the outside surface and some very different ones inside it. Artemus knew this ring was a very valuable key to unlocking this mystery. He finished reading the plans for the deception. In addition, there were two journals shrouded in magnificent leather tooled envelopes. Artemus attempted to read them but did not understand the language, only some parts in the margins. He discerned that the journals were very old and referenced back to the time of Jesus. His new priority was to get some sleep and then to get Micah out of the Palace. After sleeping most of the next day, he walked stealthily around "Lutece". Everything was in order. His next stop was the front gate of the Palace. He saw the guard that let him pass the night before saying he was back to retrieve his apparatus. They talked for a while when Artemus asked about the servants. The guard said they lived on the grounds in rooms that are part of the carriage housing. The guard escorted him to the Palace steps where Artemus walked around to the kitchen and saw the chambermaid from the party. She had been crying. Her face was "beaten" red. She did not see him.

He turned into the courtyard when he overheard servants snickering that the King was abusing his new attendant. Artemus assumed it was Micah when he saw her walking up the King's stairs. He yelled into the anteroom staircase.

She heard him and she signaled for them to meet outside.

"I can't believe you are alive." she said.

"I wanted to come back for you but I was being hunted and unfortunately, still am! Did you find out anything more?"

"Yes, I have pieced much of this plot together but we can't talk here."

Micah shoved a piece of paper into his hand saying, "Meet me at this tavern in two days after night fall." She ran back up the stairs before

Artemus could say a word. He would use this time to contact his father to ask about the Bishop's ring and to get his opinion as to what he should do, next. His father lived in a row house in the Rive Gauche section of Paris. He knocked on the old door. No one answered. Artemus entered the small house to find him passed out, drunk. Once Artemus got him up, they sat around a small fireplace in his father's main room. Artemus handed him the ring.

"Father, have you ever seen anything like this before?" Artemus knew his father had knowledge about certain symbols. "Perhaps when you were in the King's service?"

His father looked at the ring carefully trying to focus as he was coming out of his stupor. Artemus told him everything about his Palace adventure giving him as much background as possible. His father said the symbols on the ring show a relationship between the Cathars, the Secret Order of Mary and the Roman Catholic Church. His father was amazed a ring would be crafted to memorialize such a bond and that a Bishop of the Church would own it. He told Artemus that the clergy conducted the communications and interceded in most of the confidential alliances formed by the royal houses in Europe but this ring exposed a serious breach of trust that was reserved exclusively for the Catholic Church. Artemus asked what the symbols meant inside the ring. His father was not familiar with them but suspected a Templar could provide those answers. They changed the subject to things more personal. As they were saying their good-byes, his father warned Artemus to be careful. "Trust no one! This adventure may not end well for you, my son."

Artemus had the recurring thought he might never be able to live peacefully in Paris, again. He went back to his boarding house room but no sooner had he laid down when the door moved. Artemus bolted out of bed with his blade drawn. The proprietor inquired if she could prepare a meal for him. She had not thought of Artemus as being such a proficient fighter or having such a muscular body, both qualities heightened her excitement. Artemus had eaten earlier but asked her to accompany him for a drink and conversation. She agreed. They went downstairs to the main sitting room. He poured two glasses from a new bottle of wine.

Chapter 12 - Languedoc

The boarding house proprietor introduced herself as Catherine Mouton. She told Artemus her husband died in an accident two years earlier. She had no children. Before the conversation shifted to Artemus, Catherine said she had to leave to attend to another boarder. She made him promise they would do it again. Artemus finished the rest of the wine and went upstairs. After making sure Catherine was not lurking about, he started out across the City for his rendezvous with Micah. He was excited to see her.

She was very late and Artemus worried for her safety. "Just be patient!" he told himself but he had been there long enough and was putting on his coat to leave when Micah came running through the door frantically asking him to hide. Artemus had known this particular tavern and its owner for years. He knew about a faux wine cask in the cellar used to hide contraband from the King. Artemus grabbed her hand but she pulled it back. She said the King's men were right behind her. Micah told him she couldn't go with him yet. "There is just too much at stake."

Artemus reluctantly hid alone in the cellar. The two bailiffs came into the tavern.

Micah sat at the bar having a drink. They sat at a table in the corner. When Micah finished, she left her money on the bar and walked back to the Palace. They followed close behind her.

Micah went into the servant's entrance and the two men entered a section of the Palace reserved for the King's bailiffs. Artemus was far behind and waited outside the gates. Micah did not re-emerge. He spent the next three nights at the tavern when he realized Micah would not get off again until the following week. He used this time to visit Jamie, who was still at his friend's house.

Artemus asked Jamie another series of questions but started first with saying, "You are smarter than you look. If you tried to escape, your parents would be dead now. I could have killed your mother with her own comb," he said as he pulled it from his pocket and gave it to the boy.

"How did you get this?" Jamie asked, looking shocked and dismayed.

"I told you; I can kill her at will."

"But how, she is in the Palace guarded by the King, himself?"

"More powerful forces are at work, here and all of them stronger than the one protecting your parents."

"What do you want from me?"

For the first time, Artemus realized he was seeing real fear in the lad's eyes. He had to use that fear to get every ounce of information the boy possessed.

"Where do you come from?"

"Our Family lives in the Languedoc region."

"What connection does your family have in this mess?"

"The King sent for my father supplying twenty of his best men to escort him to Paris. After his meeting, all my father would say was that if everything worked out; we would have wealth beyond measure."

"Why would the King come to your people?"

"I have no idea."

"Tell me again what you know about the wharf house rituals?"

"I told you I don't know anything about them. I was told only what my parents wanted me to know."

Jamie's information did not help. His thoughts turned to Micah. *The "castle keeps" knew about her hence the drawing. She is more than what she has disclosed to me. What is her connection to the Cathars? She looks so young yet she seems to possess true wisdom.*

Artemus told his friend to let the boy go in a few days. The week was over and Artemus waited at a table in the tavern to rendezvous with Micah, if she could get away. He looked out the window and saw her figure coming down the dirt street. She looked more like a man than at any other time he had ever seen her. She wore men's boots that actually fit her and her padding had been adjusted perfectly to reflect a boy's shoulders.

Along with a wide brim hat, her outfit was spot on. She was almost at a trot coming down the street but the bailiffs were just a block back and catching up to her, quickly.

She ran in saying, "We must talk now. I will not be the King's attendant the next time we meet. I must do all I can and that means staying here."

Artemus asked directly, "What can I do for you?

"I need you to get a message to a person named Clovis at Rennes le Chateau in Languedoc. Go to the church there, the priest will tell you where Clovis can be found. Tell him I have sent you. Give him this!" The object was a dark stone with a drawing of a torch and a knife. "I will explain everything when you get back."

Micah continued, "Tell Clovis to prepare, it is happening."

"That's all?"

"Yes! That's all."

"When will I see you again?"

"Meet me on the full moon in the market."

No sooner were the words out of Micah's mouth than the door opened. The same two bailiffs walked into the bar area. Micah was drinking alone. She finished her drink and walked back to the Palace. This time, one of them followed her; the other stayed back thinking someone was coming to meet the King's servant. Artemus had already left from the rear exit before the bailiff's hand ever touched the front door.

After packing his clothes, Artemus went to Catherine's room and knocked. She came to her bedroom door dressed only in a bath blanket. Her shoulders were still wet. She was surprised to see Artemus so early in the morning. He was usually a late riser.

"Where are you going so early this cold morning?"

"I wanted to tell you I was going away for a while but will be back. I will be in Angers until the full moon. I will bring you back a special fragrance, do you have a favorite?" Her body cover was falling slightly while looking into his fragrance case. Artemus could see that she had a beautiful body. Catherine brushed against him picking up a sample to smell when her covering fell entirely to the floor. Her breasts were beautifully formed. Her areolas resembled swirling cyclones. At the tip of each breast was a small hole where the inversion ended replacing a bulbous nipple. Her ass was ample and her legs tapered down to her small ankles and feet. As she turned, she kissed him deeply saying she would be waiting for him when he returned. She retrieved her bath blanket as she told him her favorite fragrance was Lily of the Valley, also closing her bedroom door. He rode off toward Angers very sexually frustrated but doubled back. He was fortunate to hit a mild weather pattern as he headed south. Languedoc had great wealth and spawned legends of even greater treachery. As Artemus was a well known French Chevalier, it was an easy task to plan his trip by alternating horses along the way and returning each horse to their proper stable on his return to Paris. He estimated the trip would take many days each way so there was no time to dawdle. Artemus suspected that

Micah was from the same region however on a personal note; her lack of sentimentality gave him mixed emotions. He hoped she would have at least shown some spark of affection for him during their brief encounters. He questioned whether there would ever be the possibility of a romance. He found this introspection very humorous. For so many years, he only wanted superficial relationships and now after such short sporadic interludes, he was thinking of a long-term commitment. *How are these thoughts even possible?*

He arrived at Rennes le Chateau in the afternoon. The area was sparsely populated but coincidentally the village priest was walking in his direction. He told Artemus that the man he was looking for could be found down the South road. Artemus rode up to the church rectory and asked for Clovis. A monk tending a gathering pond, pointed to a section of the church under repair, "You will find him over there!" He found Clovis working in the center of the cemetery. Artemus was amazed to see the headstones had many of the same symbols found on the Bishop's ring. Clovis suggested they go to the priory as he was finished for the day and Artemus could tell him whatever it was he had come to see him about over a few glasses of wine.

"Who sends you to me?"

"Micah, here is her amulet."

After a few moments spent inspecting the stone, Clovis asked, "What do you have to tell me?"

From his look, Clovis already knew.

"She said for you to prepare, it is happening!"

The rugged man's face displayed deep disappointment.

Artemus had many questions as to what the message meant and how it involved Micah.

Artemus asked; "Could you begin with Micah?"

"What do you want to know?"

"Who is she?"

"She is not what she seems to be, my friend. She is a mystery to all of us who know her. She has remained looking young for a very long period of time."

"What are you saying?"

"She is ageless. She looks the same to me as when I was a young boy and as you can see, I am now old."

Artemus was confounded with this information. Unable to process it further, he changed the subject inquiring as to what the message meant. Clovis began by explaining the Cathars and their beliefs. "The Cathars believe in a specific good and evil, the spirit versus the matter, their doctrine of Jesus Christ revolves around his life and teachings, not his death. Jesus had many mysterious teachings that he shared specifically with Mary Magdalene and Thomas. It is said this knowledge came to Jesus as he practiced meditation. This information was spread primarily by Mary Magdalene and her True Believers after Jesus' death and whose influence spawned what the Cathars have become. If one followed these teachings, one could ascend into the Kingdom of God while still being incarnate. According to these beliefs, Jesus said all of us have the power to do this and transcend into heaven. Part of the process in achieving this spiritual state is to eliminate fear. The best preparation to begin the meditation is to arrive at your spot of calmness with true humility and gratitude and to truly believe in yourself with absolute certainty. The Cathars believe in the spirit as the ultimate in goodness, not anything involving the material. These differences between the Catholic Church and the Cathars are some of the root causes that are leading to this impending war that your Micah is warning us about. Pope Innocent III is afraid the Cathars will expose the true message of Jesus, the Man to the rest of the world and as a result expose the Church's material manipulation of their faithful followers. You understand that if the Cathar beliefs become more widely accepted they could change the concentrated power that the Church currently holds. Artemus, who would the people of the world believe, Mary, the wife and mother of Jesus progeny or Saul of Tarsus, converted Roman torturer and Christian persecutor now known as Paul and the jealous Peter? The Catholic Church has perverted everything into the material with all of their wealth and power. It is for this reason most of all that the Cathars must be exterminated."

Clovis disclosed the story of a number of noblemen financing the First Crusade for the sole purpose of retrieving lost treasure. "They believed the Romans, after sacking Jerusalem in 66 AD, leveled the temple without looting the many floors beneath it especially in the area called the stable. Rumors ranged from bringing back the Ark of the Covenant to something potentially much more valuable." Clovis went on to say, "When

118

the crusade was over, many knights came to make their home here in Languedoc and brought with them some of the missing pieces of Jesus' Legacy. These knights had proof of the existence of the sect they called the True Believers and evidence of how Mary Magdalene was instrumental in helping to start the sect and spread its message in her ministry. The True Believers thought communication with God should be direct and therefore the faithful do not need intermediaries." Clovis continued; "Your Micah was aware of the possibility that there might be a war declared upon the Cathars by Pope Innocent III. She originally wanted to seek Philippe Augustus's help in defending this area. She went to Paris many months ago and learned that Philippe was in league with the Pope so she went to England to see if the English King could help but we have heard precious little from her since except that she had met someone of interest. That someone must be you! She said she would get word to us."

Artemus reluctantly asked; "Does she formally hold a position with the Cathars?"

"No! She is considered a True Believer adept."

Artemus didn't really care about her spiritual beliefs. He wanted to know if she had anyone in her life. "Does she have anyone, romantically?"

"No!" Clovis answered.

"Is she free to marry?"

"Be careful, you do not know whom you are dealing with, Artemus. Your Micah is not who you think she is and I will leave it at that."

What is Clovis not telling me? Artemus tried to get more information out of him but none was forthcoming.

They had many more glasses of wine and talked of the mercenary business. Then Artemus asked; "What is your connection with these people?" Clovis responded; "My connection is with the spiritual beliefs I have shared with you." He switched the topic back to the crusades. They talked well into the night at which time Clovis led him to a room with a bed and offered it to Artemus.

The next morning, Artemus woke up quite hung over realizing he had to be on his way. He found Clovis draped over the table in the main room. Clovis awoke quickly when he heard footsteps but recognizing it was Artemus said, "That was enjoyable last night, I can't remember the last time I talked about the old days with someone that knew them the way I did."

"I liked it too but I must move on, I told Micah I would see her on the full moon which is rapidly approaching. I have some unfinished business I must take care of before I go."

"I am afraid I am going to find myself in this Papal fight whether I like it or not, wish me luck." Clovis responded.

"I will try to do better than that if I am successful, how do I get to Chateau de Bezu?"

Clovis pointed to the neighboring peak, "Go down this mountain trail. You will end up there."

As Artemus traveled along the mountain road he thought; *I could settle down here, if everything went bad in Paris. The location is remote but within a day's ride, there exists a sophistication that rivals any found in Europe.*

He arrived at the Chateau and asked for Bernard II Sermon of Albedun. The servants asked Artemus to wait in a sitting room off the entry hall.

Soon after, Bernard Sermon came into the room.

"You asked for me?"

"My name is Artemus Champaneux, a Chevalier for hire. I have worked for all of the duchies in France. In an effort to regain employment, I took a job over the past few months that took me to England. I met a couple, whose given names are Agnes and Glen. They were posing as innkeepers in the village of Tunbridge Wells. I found out they are from this region and I have come to inquire about them.

"Monsieur, surely you have some reason that led you to me?"

They are involved in a scheme sponsored by the Pope and The King of France. Your name is specifically mentioned as a supporter of the Knights Templar but also a sympathizer to the Cathars. I am here to understand your involvement in this plot and for you to tell me anything about the couple?"

"You know you will be killed for any knowledge in this. Why do you care, it doesn't concern you?"

"This plot involves a woman I am involved with and the information you give me could save her life."

"What do you want exactly?"

"I am in need of food, clothing, money and lodging and during the time it takes you to supply me with my requests; I want you to tell me about this plot."

Bernard Sermon had his own agenda for fulfilling Artemus's requests and sensed Champaneux could be trusted. He had a meal for Artemus brought to their room to fulfill his first request. He, then, asked his second in command to get Artemus some fresh clothing. They walked together into the finance office, where he instructed the knight to give Artemus two bags of coin of the realm, one, good in Languedoc, the other, in Paris. Finally, Bernard instructed a room to be prepared for Artemus.

"Let us go into the great hall, sit by the fire and I will tell you a story."

They walked into the hall where a fire was burning and two chairs were arranged around its hearth. The two men sat down. Sermon began immediately; "My family has been involved with the Knights Templar for decades. We have given substantial sums to the Order over the years.

The reason may surprise you. My family became convinced that the true spiritual instruction from Jesus was not that espoused by Rome but instead from Mary Magdalene whose ministry included spending time here in Languedoc. Her message concerned the spiritual aspects of life's journey, not the accumulation of material wealth. After the first Crusade was over, the knights brought back evidence that the rumors of Jesus and Mary's marriage were true and that there were children, our family supported

122

the idea of receiving tribute from Rome to keep their secret safe. It was a wise economic and political move backing the Knights Templar but on a spiritual basis we all believe that the true message of Jesus was shared by Mary, not Peter or Paul. Over the past number of years, the Cathar adepts have shown many of our local people how to meditate and experience deep levels of peace. One of the reasons Peter's Church gained such prominence was the idea that one could buy their way into God's Kingdom. This could not be more distasteful to the Cathar way of thinking. The locals from this region know they can reach the Kingdom without having to pay to pray. Don't you think it ironic, our support of the Knights Templar gives us a share of the Church of Rome's plate and we in turn help support their arch enemy. Innocent III is a war monger and I expect him to have this entire area annihilated. I am fearful for the Cathars. "

When they resumed at dinner Artemus said; "Thank you for being so candid, can you tell me more about the couple?"

Bernard answered; "They are the only people that the King could trust in this matter. Glen is second cousin to Philippe and Agnes is cousin to Frederick II from the House of Hohenstaufen. Artemus commented; "The problem I have is how they got this ring," showing it to Sermon.

Bernard took the ring and immediately looked at markings engraved in its interior. He asked, "Do you know where this ring came from?"

Artemus responded, "Yes, it came off the Bishop at North Abbey's finger after he was tortured to death by King Philippe's henchmen."

Sermon stated. "The ring's outer markings serve as a recognition instrument allowing communication between the Cathars, The Society of Mary Magdalene and The Church of Rome. It symbolizes the Church's involvement with the very sect that it publicly admonishes and plans to destroy. This would be very embarrassing for Rome should it fall into the wrong hands."

Artemus realized his father was correct in his interpretation of the symbols on the ring and that these markings had a consistent meaning to anyone looking at them. "What do the markings on the inside of the ring mean?"

"Those markings would be very embarrassing to me and my family should this ring find its way either to King Philippe or to Pope Innocent III. They show a relationship between the Cathars and the Knights Templar. The most obvious connection leads to this house. "

Artemus realized that Philip didn't need his elaborate plans of disgracing the King of England with the Pope in part because the Bishop's ring was never shown to the English King and therefore no one would intercede on the Cathars behalf.

The two finished up when Bernard said; "I have delivered everything you wanted. I want you do something for me. I have no time to send anyone to Paris with this important information. I want you to go to Templar House on Place de Grève and give the head bursar this message from Guillaume de Chartres. You do not need to wait or get a response. Could you do that for me?"

Artemus said, "Of course! Please keep the Bishop's ring as a token of my gratitude for helping me. You'll never need worry about your family's safety by it getting into the wrong hands."

"Thank You, Artemus. The Pope or the King must never find out the identities of the people you visited here or that you know anything about the connection between the Cathars and my family."

Artemus had precious little time to get back to Paris, deliver Sermon's message and get to the market at the appointed time. He went to bed and awoke early to discover that the staff had prepared food for his journey and a note for Artemus from Bernard to be read only after he had delivered the message to Templar House.

He rode hard, exchanging each horse with its rightful owner as he made his way back. He reached Paris one day before he was to meet Micah. He went directly to the Knights Templar House and gave over the message to the head bursar. Artemus was now on his way to the boarding house. He arrived to find Catherine cleaning his room. He gave her some money and said he desperately needed sleep. After a passionate kiss, she left. Artemus opened his note from Bernard Sermon.

"Artemus, while you were here I could not tell you that the Cathars will be under attack by the time you read this note. This attack will lead to their complete destruction. They are the Church of Rome's mortal enemy. The Church cannot afford to have the general population believe in the Cathar way of life. Be careful, you and your friends are known sympathizers to Cathar beliefs.

You will be killed. Signed; Bernard Sermon" *The note will help convince Micah not to go back. The Cathars will be dead by the time she reads this. She would only be killing herself by returning.*

Artemus made it to the rendezvous spot in the center of the city. He stood in an ally with an excellent view of the market. He finally saw her coming down the street, carrying a bag on her shoulder. Micah entered the market as he saw Philip's bailiffs round the corner of the block coming up behind her. *She must think that no one is following her or she is the best actor I have ever seen.* Artemus mentally prepared for a fight. She did not come over to him but instead acted like she was looking for something to eat. She ambled through the market and then began walking up the main street that exited the City. As she got further and further from the market, Artemus could see the bailiffs had stopped following her and headed back toward their barracks.

After waiting for them to get out of sight, he started after her. Artemus followed slowly as not to attract attention. Only a stranger, who did not appear to be one of the King's men, took the same road. Artemus let him pass. He thought he had lost Micah when he heard his name being called from a church stable. He slowed but kept his eye on the stranger disappearing over the horizon. Micah had let her hair grow. She was beautiful. Artemus had a hard time concentrating. She looked at him for the first time with warm eyes and smiled.

Chapter 13 - City Prison

Artemus did not feel comfortable trying to kiss her. Things were still distance defined. They never had the time to get romantically close so the fact there was a strong sexual tension only made matters more awkward.

"Tell me what you were able to accomplish?" asked Micah; "Did you make the trip?"

"Yes, I accomplished everything you asked of me and more, but I am afraid I have some bad news. I did not want to hurt you this way but you would never speak to me again if I withheld the fact that the Pope using the King's soldiers is killing the Cathars, as we speak."

"My message to Clovis warned him that things were about to get hard."

With her words, Artemus gave her the message that Bernard Sermon had given him to validate the futility of going back. Artemus reached out to comfort her; she sunk into his chest retreating into her thoughts.

Micah refocused to ask; "How did you know to contact Bernard Sermon?"

"My father gave me his name as a person that could be trusted. I was there to get my own information about Agnes and Glen. You know the only reason I have interest in any of this is because of you. I have fallen in love with you and don't want any harm to come to you. I have never had feelings for a woman like those I have for you and I hope you see that in my eyes and hear it in my voice because it is the truth."

Micah sat for what seemed like an eternity processing what Artemus said and then reconfirming asked; "Is it true, what you just said?"

"It is the absolute truth, straight from my heart. Bernard Sermon asked me to bring a message he had from Guillaume de Chartres to the head bursar at Templar House."

"Artemus, Guillaume de Chartres is the new Grand Master of the Knights Templar and is known to be sympathetic to Sermon. I think you may have provided your new friend with protection and money for his family while all the rest of the nobles sympathetic to the Cathars will be tortured and killed. Unfortunately the note may have betrayed you as the Pope and the King will certainly find out you delivered it and are back in Paris."

Artemus wasn't interested in the politics. Micah sensed what Artemus was thinking. She had to confront this new circumstance. *I have been so dedicated to my mission that I would not allow anyone into my life. I have done everything I can and now I will embrace this man with everything I have.*

Micah reached up to hold Artemus' head as she kissed him. The experience first resonated with the incredible feeling their lips touching produced. The water in their mouths mixed to produce the nectar of the gods. Neither one of them had ever experienced anything like it. Their embrace lasted, completely engulfing both of them. They needed to merge, to create one body. Micah wrapped her now naked legs arounds Artemus and took him into her. They lasted for hours, slow, fast, hard and gentle. Every emotion was displayed. Their first release was the most fantastic either could have ever imagined only to be trumped by the next and the next. Momentarily spent and lying together, both of them realized something else. This was their beginning, never to end. Micah realized Artemus was her missing half. She had a unique timescape knowledge of things and although helping others to experience true love, never did she think it would ever happen to her. She would gradually stimulate Artemus into remembering his eternal existence. Artemus was in bliss. It was the first time he ever felt completely fulfilled in this life. He could not believe his joy and would attempt to keep it for as long as he could but he had to resolve their problems before they could live this unbelievable gift. Lovingly he looked into Micah's eyes trying to keep the moment but also realizing they were running out of time if they were to do anything to help her Cathars.

"What did you learn while in the King's employ?" He asked.

"I tried to get any further information about the war."

"I am so sorry to bring you this news!"

"This is not your fault, if you did not make it to see Clovis, the invasion would have been a complete surprise. At least they might have a chance to escape or fight."

"Do you remember the couple, Agnes and Glen that occupied the guest suite in the front of the Palace?" Artemus asked.

"Yes, I saw them and hear they are now guests of the City prison."

"Tell me everything as we might be able to save some of your Cathars."

Micah began; "They were attending parties and were enjoying life at court but the price of King's favor, as you know, is high. Glen's behavior began to offend the King. He set a trap for the couple. Hidden in a party game was a trick that would expose their non compliance with the King's wishes. When the game's rules required certain outrageous behavior on Agnes's part, she chose to go up to their suite instead of participating. The King was hiding in a secret passageway between the parlor and his own bedchamber and saw the entire scene unfold. Agnes willfully disobeyed the King so he sent both of them to jail. They have been gone for two days. Why are you asking me about them?"

Artemus was familiar with the City prison and knew to make an escape from there was very difficult. He also had to agree that Micah's assessment of Sermon and Knights Templar was correct. The only direct information that may help the Cathars resides with Glen and Agnes. *They were part of the plot in England and hold the proper noble pedigree. Given enough persuasion, they could provide evidence to convenience the English King to help stop the slaughter of the Cathars.* Artemus shared these thoughts with Micah.

"What is our next move?" Micah asked.

"I want to extract the couple; they are our best hope to have something over the King and the Pope and I do not want to be on the run for the rest of my life. If I can get the couple to confirm their role in the charade and the rest of the plot, we can leverage our position with the English King and he may elect to protect what may be left of the Cathars against the Pope if he were to get a payment from the Cathars for his protection."

"I don't understand. What does the Pope know of the charade?"

"The Pope knew he had a leak in his own organization. His Bishop was also "a True Believer" in the Order of Mary and was secretly spying for the Cathars, against Innocent III. He was also secretly spying for the Templars. Philippe did not have hard evidence concerning the Bishop until his people obtained the ring which exposed the Bishop's role as a double agent providing the proof of the Bishops sympathy with the Cathars. Exposing this duplicity would be a huge embarrassment to the Pope. When I retrieved the ring, Philippe no longer had his leverage over The Pope but Agnes and Glen's noble heritage could be substituted for the ring in confirming the Bishop's role with the Cathars, either way eliminating the need for the King to cooperate so completely with his Holiness. The Pope sent his own men to England in an effort to find out what was really going on, independent of Philippe's reports. His people held me captive on a castled island. When his advance men discovered Philippe's wharf house ruse and with the double agent Bishop dead, their leak was plugged. The Pope waited to see what Philippe would do next. The information was to be spun making you out to be a Cathar witch. You would be exposed as the champion of extreme immorality and therefore providing yet another reason for the utter annihilation of the Cathars. When I survived their assassination attempts, it upset their plans. I could confirm you had nothing to do with the debauchery at the wharf house. The Pope and Philippe had to kill me clearing the way for you to be their goat and to justify their murderous intentions.

When I got the ring back from the couple, Philippe adjusted his relationship back with the Pope. The Pope realized he had no time to get a new partner so he continued working with Philippe and the deal went back to its original structure. Together they would kill off the Cathars, eliminating The Church's most serious threat and The King would add territory and wealth to his kingdom."

Micah listened and then said, "I will help you! Your story confirms why the orgies started up again. After the last one, they burned the wharf house to the ground. To your point, they definitely got the word out that there was ritualistic sex being performed, all instigated by the Cathars and have influenced a growing number of people in the region to leave the Church in favor of these sinful practices. Unfortunately, the Church will spin these events as examples to confirm the rampant spread of the devil worshipping practices of these True Believers."

Artemus asked, "Micah, exactly what is your connection to the Cathars? Why did you go to Paris?"

"I tried to stop the war. I thought maybe, just this once I could help change an outcome. I am a True Believer adept, not a Cathar."

"I don't know what that means." Artemus said.

Then he saw something in Micah that conveyed she was no child. She started to explain; "I have dedicated my entire life to practicing and the teaching of the True Believer process for people to get to the Kingdom of God. I won't go into details with you now but know this can turn out very badly for the Cathars. I thought there may be a way to stop the war but with Philippe's involvement in the plot, I had to look to the English King for help. There were clues that led me, just like you, to the wharf house. All along I wanted a French solution because that could provide a local sustainable solution. After I understood what was happening I thought I could get Philippe to betray the Pope by converted him to our beliefs. As his personal servant I had opportunity but he was too far gone into the material world. He hated the sight of me."

"Is there any reason that someone other than The Pope or King would want you out of the way?"

Micah had many secrets and that question perplexed her but no one she could think of came to mind.

Micah responded, "I don't know of anyone."

Recovering, they spent hours more, kissing, fondling, love making and then reluctantly got dressed and headed for the prison. They waited outside gathering information. They discovered the prison had scheduled visiting hours where the prisoners would get money from friends and family to bribe the guards in securing everything from their release to receiving better treatment.

They headed back to the boarding house to develop a plan but Artemus did not want a confrontation between Catherine and Micah. He instructed Micah to wrap her breasts, wear her hat and be the boy she was used to playing. "We don't need any more trouble." Not fully explaining what that meant, they went back to the room. Catherine was at the door in no time and Artemus introduced them. If looks could kill, Micah's stare would have buried Catherine and been a dead giveaway as to Micah's identity but between the light in the room and an awkward line of sight, Catherine could not see Micah's gaze. Artemus said he had to do some business in the morning with Micah and he would see her later. Catherine pouted as she shut the door behind her. Micah was silent and sat in the chair as if to go to sleep. Artemus offered her the bed. "No, Monsieur Lover Boy, you take it."

Artemus knew she was jealous which made him extremely happy. He offered again and was refused so he took the bed first and later felt Micah crawl in bed with him whispering that if he touched her, she would kill him. Artemus chuckled as he moved over. That arrangement didn't last long either. The next morning, they went back to the prison. A visiting group of relatives and friends had congregated to see their loved ones. Micah and Artemus joined them. Much of the prison population was moved into a large caged area. Hundreds of prisoners were herded into the space.

The families of these people were on scaffolding surrounding the huge cage. Communication was made by screaming. Both of them began searching frantically with their eyes, Micah was looking for Agnes and Glen as a couple. Artemus tried to look into each face. Glen was huddled in a corner.

Agnes was nowhere to be found. Artemus began yelling to Glen who eventually heard him and responded into the air. "Who is calling me?" "Hello?" Artemus motioned for Micah to move to the other end of the platform so they had no connection to one another just in case it was a trap. Artemus showed himself to Glen who was very happy to see him. "Where is Agnes?"

"She is somewhere in the prison being molested by the guards." Glen said laughing.

"What can you tell me about all of this?"

"Nothing, they want your head on a platter and I am here to give it to them, you stupid bastard!" as he motioned for the guards to close in on him. Artemus had nowhere to run.

"At least tell me why you are doing this?"

"We are going to share in a treasure beyond your wildest imagination, moron!"

As the guards came onto the platform from all directions, Artemus made sure Micah remembered what Glen looked like, she nodded that she saw him. Artemus had no choice but to surrender. Micah was grief stricken, she knew Artemus didn't stand a chance and would quickly be executed. She turned slowly and left the platform.

Chapter 14 - A Light at the End of a Very Bad Day

Micah had nowhere to go but back to the rooming house. Catherine knocked on the door. Micah answered through the door in her raspiest voice but Catherine asked that she open the door. No cloth disguise could hide Micah's swollen red eyes exposing the fact that the "he" was a "she." Catherine asked her what had happened. Micah had nothing to lose by telling her, thinking possibly Catherine could help. It turned out that Catherine had a friend she had known since childhood who was a guard at the prison. She agreed to find out what she could about Artemus.

Catherine went to the prison to find Andre Bouchard. Andre had been working at the prison for years and worked his way up through the ranks to Captain. He had always flirted with Catherine and was happy to see her.

"What brings you here my darling; I haven't seen you in over two years. How are you doing?"

"I am well, Andre. I've come to ask a favor."

"I knew it couldn't be that you had finally come to your senses and realized how much you want me."

"A man named Artemus was taken into custody. I need to know what they want to do to him. He is staying at my rooming house. I wanted to see if there is anything I can do for him and there is also a little matter of getting paid."

"Stay here!"

Andre walked to registration and asked about the new prisoners. The guard said; "Yes, there were twelve that were taken into custody."

"Give me their cell numbers."

"He wrote down the cell numbers and asked who was in each cell."

Andre looked at the list and did not recognize the name Catherine mentioned. "Is that the complete list?"

"Well, there is a special guest of the King. I was told that no one knew he was here and that he should not under any circumstances, have any visitors.

"Where is he?"

"He is in Cell 14 in the South Tower."

"Thank you, this conversation did not happen."

Artemus was chained to the wall. He had been left there all night without food, water or any attendance whatsoever. André shouted into him; "Hey, you have a friend that is concerned about you! Are you all right?"

"Who are you?"

"I ask the questions!"

"I'm sorry. I have been beaten with no explanation as to why I am here. Please help me if you can monsieur."

"I will see what I can do."

Andre went to the Commandant's office to inquire as to why this prisoner should take up one of the biggest cells in the prison.

"Because my friend, he is special to the King. We have instructions to find out where he has hidden certain items of interest to the King, record everything he says and then kill him. Why, do you have any personal interest in this?"

"I have a friend who he owes money too. Andre laughed as he said, "I guess his debt will go unpaid."

The Commandant's assistant said to Andre, "This one will not last the week. An interrogator is coming in to work on him; he is due in the next few days."

Andre gestured good-bye to his friend and returned to the prison's entrance where Catherine was waiting.

"Your friend is as good as dead. Apparently, he upset the King, who is having a interrogator come to torture him. They do not expect him to last the week. I am sorry, Mon Amie."

"Thank you for your help." Catherine said.

"Anytime but next time, it will cost you." Andre winked as Catherine left the prison.

Catherine went back to the rooming house where she and Micah conferred as to what to do next. They concluded that Micah should go back to the Palace and get her old job back. Micah knew the King would want her close by while he tortured Artemus. The Royal Head of the Household welcomed her back knowing the King's wishes but the King was focused on matters concerning the Pope and the battle raging in the South so he barely noticed who was around him. The couple was now back at the Palace with Glen resolved that life at Court came at a price so he developed a laissez faire attitude about what Agnes did as long as they could freeload off the King until the war was over.

For once, the timing was perfect; no one of significance was in the Palace. The King was at the Cathedral in a meeting and was not expected back for some time. Micah found her way to the couple's suite and waited. Agnes came in first with Glen not far behind. Micah hit Glen in the throat to muffle any noise and then used a kick punch combination that knocked him out. Agnes was in shock, horrified at the prospect of being tortured. Micah said in a low voice. "You have a choice, I will kill your husband and butcher you or you will tell me everything. Do you understand?"

"Yes."

"Start talking."

"We were commissioned by the King and brought here from Languedoc. We were to set the stage for a number of the King's enemies including you and Artemus to be framed for murder and sexual sin. The story would be told all over Europe, especially in France in an attempt to cover up the fact that the King's troops at the direction of the Pope are sacking the Cathars and pillaging all of their wealth, which my husband and I were promised a share. The Pope will get a share and the King will get the rest. Quite unwittingly, we discovered the Bishop was, in secret, a Cathar with his ring exposing his identity. Once the word spread about the Cathars committing sins against God, the King will be vindicated in his avenging role by the neighboring duchies and we would legitimately have our wealth and he will have his new country."

Micah changed the subject.

"Why did you pick that area in England for your hoax?"

"No one would suspect the King of France maneuvering there; instead the English King would be blamed."

"Why did you pick Artemus to be the sacrificial goat?"

"Because Artemus has a flawless reputation and worked at one time or another for every duchy in the land. No one would doubt his word and if he didn't meet you, he would have been tortured and dead long before now."

"You know me?"

"Yes, we know you." Agnes spewing venom from her voice, "The King knows exactly who you are and takes great joy in you being his personal attendant. You will be raped repeatedly and suffer the worst of indignities. We have had you under close observation for some time and want to thank you for bringing Artemus back to us. If he was not so predictable, we never would have caught him and one of our most credible witnesses would not be available to ruin. How do you like bringing such a good man down, you witch?"

"A very interesting story, what do you think I should do with you?"

Agnes lunged at her with a concealed blade but missed her mark. Micah caught Agnes's knife hand, broke her wrist with one hand turn and took the knife, plunging it into Agnes leg. Micah was thinking she could barter the couple for Artemus but Agnes kicked and clawed at Micah and was successful in knocking her off balance.

Glen had recovered and grabbed Micah allowing Agnes to try again with her knife. As Agnes lunged, Micah turned, forcing Glen to take her knife thrust fully in the center of his back. Agnes was so shocked that she hesitated long enough for Micah to place a perfect kick to her throat, collapsing her larynx and closing her windpipe. Agnes died without a sound. Glen was still alive. Micah was unable to control herself. She broke his neck. She had to get out of the Palace and Artemus out of prison. Micah crossed the bridge and entered the boarding house. She learned from Catherine that the King's men had already been to see her. He was offering a reward for Micah's capture dead or alive.

Micah thought, *He had known I would kill Agnes and Glen, saving him the trouble. With a price on my head, who would question anything that had to do with a Cathar conspirator and a witch, it was a perfect set up. I didn't want to see any of this. I wanted to change it.*

It wasn't long before the King's soldiers came back looking for Micah and went through the boarding house, destroying everything in their path. Finding nothing, the troop headed back to the Palace. They would warn the City prison guards of an attempt to break Artemus out. Catherine knew that Andre would not do anything that would jeopardize his position. Micah did not trust Andre anyway and said to Catherine freeing Artemus from jail may be very difficult. Micah had saved the life of Guy De Charter's oldest child on her way to England. He was a Seneschal that worked for a noble house in Orleans. She said she would try to save Artemus without compromising Catherine's position. Micah hoped De Charter's would not betray her. She traveled to see him.

"Hello, my lord, I have come to collect the favor you promised."

"Name it, if it is within my power, I will make it happen."

"I have a friend in the City prison, he is a political prisoner and has secrets that could damage the King but he only wants to live out his life in peace and not be a problem to anyone."

Guy de Charters listened as Micah told him that any help received would be greatly appreciated and would be kept in strictest confidence.

After thinking for a while, he asked her, "Where can I find you, it will take me time to see if I can do anything." Micah gave him the information and thanked him saying, "The King has sent for an interrogator to extract a confession from Artemus. I need to stop him, giving us time."

Guy responded, "I can help you with that information now, your man is leaving the inn down in the village; if you hurry you may be able to catch him before he gets too far. He has worked for me. His victims are never the same, if they live."

Micah rode into the Inn's courtyard and overheard the stable men talking about how Gerald Papillion ate more than any human they had ever seen and that if he had a weakness, food was definitely it. Their conversation gave her an idea. Micah went to the local market and picked up some food and then rode to catch up with this ghoul. She came upon the huge 300-pound man wearing very expensive clothes. He was clean-shaven with a very neat appearance, riding his horse heading for Paris. Micah did not expect him to be so polished especially someone in his profession.

Micah went into her act. "Hello, Monsieur, Are you going to Paris? We could ride together. I am going to the Palace to serve as the Court's second cook. I trained at "Le Tesse de Vin. Ma spécialité est l'agneau de viande en particulier." I apply a special marinade which puts a crisp crust on the skin while keeping the meat very moist and flavorful. It is not surpassed anywhere in the world. Slowing down she said, "I am sorry; I have a bad habit of talking too much."

Gerald replied; "I am going to Paris and consider myself quite an expert in culinary delights. If you like, I would be happy to taste your meal before you serve it to the King. You should know what he likes as I do, before you risk your reputation and possibly your head on a dish that is untested."

"Oh, thank you, sir. Do you know the King?"

"Yes, I am actually on my way to the Palace. We could make the trip together. I know a scenic river side location for you to cook your food and us to eat it."

"That would be wonderful."

After riding a few hours, Gerald found the spot he was thinking of and they stopped to cook the meal. Micah dismounted from her horse taking off its saddle and bridal. Gerald watched as Micah unpacked all the food and gathered the wood to build a slow burning fire. After the fire was well underway, he watched Micah prepare the meat as she cut and tied very thinly sliced fat around the lamb. She then made a make-shift spit slowly roasting her meat. Gerald offered to help with the vegetables but Micah waived him off asking him to make himself comfortable next to the river. He was content and completely facing the opposite direction from Micah as she dissolved a packet of poisons into the vegetables as they cooked. Micah wondered if there was enough poison to do any damage to a man so large. He, literally, inhaled everything.

Gerald belched a number of times, looked over at Micah, and said, "That was quite possibly one of the best meals I have ever had in my life. You are as good at your craft as I am at mine."

"What do you do, Gerald?" Micah asked.

"I am the King's interrogator."

"Is that a tough job?"

"No, only because I don't get personally involved, my responsibility is to extract every bit of information a prisoner possesses. I collect every word and then sort out whether it is relevant. This practice has earned me a very good reputation but those who I interrogate often have crippling outcomes, at best. That was a curious question, why do you ask?"

Micah responded by saying, "You have a difficult job, one that I could never do. I am far too sentimental."

They packed up their belongings, re-saddled the horses and continued their ride to Paris. As they were getting closer to Paris, Micah thought her plan had failed. Gerald exhibited no signs of even getting sick, let alone dying. As they entered the City, he was talking away when he keeled over and fell into the brush. Micah did not slow down and continued into Paris as if she was riding alone. She was relieved but had no idea if the man was dead or would remain sick long enough for her to rescue Artemus in time.

Micah went into Artemus' room at the boarding house. She lay down and was asleep in few minutes. She was awakened by Catherine's screams as a King's man was trying to rape her. Micah rushed to her aid. The man was hitting Catherine and kicking her with his boots. Micah threw her knife finding its mark. Catherine was visibly shaken and convinced that she too would have to spend the rest of her life on the run. The two women spent time at the riverbank after disposing of the body. Micah tried to calm her down. "Catherine, I have made arrangements with the Seneschal I told you about. If things work out, the day might be saved."

Catherine had to make a room ready for a new boarder and asked Micah to check in on her later. As Micah walked around the City, the time went slowly. She was afraid for Artemus. She knew he was being treated very badly and even if he was not being tortured, he may not make it through the week without food or water. She walked back to the boarding house on a side road and entered the barnyard, over hearing voices inside. As she got closer, one of them was Catherine's saying that she had Micah's trust. The man was interested in Micah's resources. He asked Catherine who would come to her aid. Catherine said she had no idea.

"You are wise to cooperate with us, Catherine; we will take everything from you if Artemus gets away. The interrogator has not shown up at the Palace but when he does, we will take him immediately to begin his work, so inform me of any news you get."

"I will, you can be assured of that."

The man left the house and headed toward the bridge. Catherine ringing her hands began to cry. Micah allowed Catherine a moment to regain her composure. She could understand Catherine's motives and it was in her best interest to cooperate with the King.

Micah walked in minutes later. Catherine was more composed but still emotionally upset. Micah was not through the door before Catherine said she was visited by another one of the King's henchmen. "I have them believing I will betray you and Artemus. They talked for a while longer and then Micah went up to her room. A messenger came to the rooming house asking for a young dark haired boy. Catherine showed him into the main room and got Micah.

The messenger handed her a note and left.

It said,

"Artemus will be brought into the general yard this afternoon on his way to a new cell. They found another interrogator who is showing up at the Palace today which means your man is about to have a very rough tomorrow. When Artemus passes through the yard, there will be a commotion in the upper tower distracting the guards but it will not last long enough for there to be any dallying. If you miss this opportunity, he will be lost. I am sorry for this late notice but it is the best I can do. Good luck!" The note was not signed.

Micah told Catherine she had to go to the prison. Catherine was inquisitive.

Micah asked, "What do I tell you? If you know anything, they will get it out of you. If I do not tell you anything, they will torture you for the fun of it and kill you anyway. What do you want to do?" Catherine said, "I am in trouble no matter what I do. I am better off with you two than I am trying to keep this place because they will kill me, too."

Micah convinced Catherine she was wrong. "If you stay behind and have no part in this escape attempt, you will have a better chance of avoiding reprisals, especially if I fail." Micah went into the visitor's section of the prison yard in the early afternoon to participate in the visiting period, alone. A number of prisoners were being moved as the note indicated. The guards assembled to pick up four of them in particular. All were going to the special area of the prison to be tortured. She saw Artemus being pushed through the yard. She stayed behind the gate until he went past. At the precise moment he was passing, a small riot ensued in the North Tower, commanding the immediate attention of the front guards. Micah rounded the gate and was horrified to see how badly Artemus looked. He had been beaten, covered in filth and obviously had not been fed since his capture. He was literally on death's door.

As she got closer to him, she sensed a rear prison guard was looking at her intently. Everything happened in a blur; a squad rounded the corner. The guard that was looking at her so intently lanced Micah in the back. She was impaled but unbelievably able to breathe. She had a serene expression on her face, a look that everything would be all right in death. Artemus tried to fight but was just too weak and after killing the guard to his right, the same prison guard that lanced Micah did the same to Artemus. The escape attempt was over and the prison guard claimed his reward for stopping them as well as having the honor of disposing of the bodies. Artemus and Micah were stripped and paraded through the yard as a deterrent to the rest of the inmate population. A few people were surprised to see Micah was a female. When the King heard the report of their death, he was disappointed. He loved his intrigue with them but he had other evidence he would present and possibly be lucky enough to avoid having to deal with one of his holiness's emissaries for a position in his court. The bodies were wrapped in sack cloth and dumped into a cart that would take them to a spot where they would be unceremoniously thrown into the river.. Two men climbed into the cart and drove through the prison gates. As they crossed the island bridge one of the men jumped back to check the corpses. He opened the cloth shroud and began to dress the wounds on Micah and Artemus. They arrived at a clearing along the Seine and the driver parked the cart under an old tree. He and his partner started their long walk back to Orleans. A number of hours later Micah stirred. Artemus regained consciousness only minutes before. They looked at one another in complete disbelief as to how they could possibly be alive. Before Micah could speak she felt something in her hand. It was a note. She slowly opened it as she felt the throbbing pain in her back. It said; "I gave you my most skilled men who are very good at what they do. You should both recover as I know you can heal your wounds. Thank you for your kindness regarding my daughter and I hope you find it in your heart to accept this gesture as a token of my appreciation." Signed GdC.

Ian began coming out of the vision and knew this story was far from over.

Part 3

Chapter 15 - Life's Little Dramas

╫

Ian's mind returned to Riggs library and to his surprise, Raven was still holding his hands. The meditative vision carried with it deep emotions. He was still reeling from the transmitted pain Artemus and Micah received from the guard's lancing. As Ian recovered, he realized something about Raven. She was somehow connected to his subconscious; a part of it, some type of energy mix. This realization enhanced the telepathic connection between them allowing the sharing of feelings, more than actual words to convey meanings. Ian felt her thinking to him, "Our existence resides outside the concept of time. You are realizing a higher form of communication through increased awareness of your surroundings. This will enable you to feel in every way what we are about, the intent and motivations. What did you get from the story?"

Ian responded; "Was the story, true?"

She asked him to recall the emotions, its pain and the love that went directly into his heart.

Ian was overwhelmed, crying with sadness and betrayal but also the joy of love, all at the same time. He experienced more intensity of emotion.

Raven mentally conveyed to Ian that this sensitivity of awareness when meditating will help achieve better proficiency in experiencing the visions and he will gain unique wisdom. Ian thought to her, "Does everyone have this same ability?" She answered, "Yes, but some people have to work harder than others." She was referring to him as she continued to mentally share her message; "Many incarnates get caught up in worldly emotions. Worry and fear often create illusions. Don't react – wait, become enlightened." Instinctively, Ian's mind flashed to an upcoming exam which activated his anxiety. Raven sensed it and got up to leave. Ian begged her not to go and said he did not care about the test. "Please just stay!" She looked at him with the most understanding loving eyes; "I will return but for now, you must attend to your earthly things. A ribbon will appear showing you a synchronicity of experience particular to your life. It is your Cypher."

Ian didn't want to hear this coming from her now. He was beside himself. As he watched her leave, his heart physically began to hurt. Real pain! Throbbing! His eyes welled up with tears! He had to let the moment pass as he watched his own tear drops hit the chair's arm. As Ian tried to study, he was overcome with the same calm he experienced just before his vision. He could concentrate; retaining all of the study material. He changed his attitude of being abandoned to one resolved in applying all of Raven's instructions, anything that would reconnect her with him. He would pay more attention to all of life's dramas, small and large. When he awoke the next day, he went to his class, took his exam and left for Philadelphia.

As he drove, Ian went over what happened the previous night. *Raven is connected to me. Sharing these experiences with her is as if we are of the same soul split inhabiting other bodies processing various experiences to share and grow.* The drive home took no time. Ian's father and sister greeted him as he walked in the house. All of his friends were home from college this particular Thanksgiving and Tuesday night was the quiet before the partying storm.

Thanksgiving night was one of the best for serious partying. Many of Ian's friends gathered at Bryn Mawr's "Beef and Ale" with the conversation quickly gravitated to an unbelievable story about his friend, Raymond. "What were the odds of two girls from different school districts over twenty miles apart being in the same ladies room in Roy Rogers, strangers with enough time to talk about their boyfriends whose name coincidently happened to be Raymond? The restaurant was 12 miles from one girl's home and 8 miles from the other in opposite directions. The ID bracelets were nondescript and the rings were thin silver bands with different birthstones. How was it that Raymond could be caught dating and sleeping with these two girls at the same time with no apparent connection? The group concluded, "Divine Providence." or perhaps "Divine Justice."

On his last night home, Ian had band practice in Strafford. He had made this trip hundreds of times over the past four years. The band had been together that long and Rusty, the drummer had a separate small house on his family's property that was away from the main house where the band could practice without disturbing anyone. As he drove past the "Paoli Local" train station in Strafford, he saw a car pulled over on the side of the road in a peculiar way. The driver could be in some kind of trouble. Ian stopped, looked inside the car but saw no one. As he got back into his car, he heard a rustle in the bushes where the car was parked. He walked over; "Is anyone there?" No answer! He called out a few more times, still no answer. Then Ian noticed a small child in the bushes who looked frightened. He went closer but stayed far enough away from her not to be threatening. He asked her about her mom and dad. She did not speak. Looking into her face was like looking at Raven in miniature.

No one was anywhere around the car. Ian asked her to get into his car and he drove her to the Berwyn police station. Once there, He called Rusty saying he would be along and to start without him. Rusty informed him that the first bottle of Ron Rico 151 was already gone. They laughed as Ian hung up the phone. Ian answered all of the questions the police asked of him and was on his way 15 minutes later. He drove back the way he had come as he wanted to see if the car was still parked on the side of the road. The car was gone. The band practiced for a few hours but the effects of the Ron Rico were all too evident. At two in the morning, the party broke up and Ian drove home. He normally would not see another car on the entire eight mile ride. When Ian made the turn onto Haverford Road in Rosemont, he spotted a lone car parked at the Conestoga Mill.

The car looked like the same one abandoned in Strafford. Ian drove by trying not to pay much attention to it until it started following him. Ian quickly turned into a driveway to see who was driving the car.

He walked about 20 yards in the direction of Tom's Market but again found the car to be empty. *No one could have gotten out.* Mystified Ian got back in his car and drove the block and half to his house collapsing into bed. He woke up the next morning and said his goodbyes to his father and sister and headed back to G 'town. *What was last night all about? I know Raven is behind this and I am very happy she can't stay away but how is she doing these things and why?*

Weeks passed with no further encounters with Raven. Ian missed her terribly. He was again heading home for Christmas break. Once he got settled, Ian stopped by the Berwyn police station to follow up on what had happened to the child he brought in weeks earlier. The sergeant on duty had no record of the little girl in that night's log. Ian asked him about the other police officers and gave the sergeant their names. The sergeant said he knew them and expected one of them to be coming through the door any minute. Ian waited a few minutes before the officer came into the station house.

He walked over and asked; "Do you remember me?" and the officer replied, "Yes! Yes, I do!"

Ian sat at police officer's desk while he got ready for his shift. He told Ian the strangest story. He said they called the police in the next town up the line in Strafford and asked them to go by the parked car.

159

"They called back and said it was gone. As soon as we hung up the phone, one of the guys went into the lieutenant's office to check on the little girl. She was gone." Ian told him that after dropping off the girl with them, he drove back the same way he had come and the car indeed was gone. Ian said, "A very strange night."

What point is Raven making?

Christmas break was over before it began and Ian was back for the second semester. He picked up his course curriculum at the registrar's office. His first course was American history with Professor Dodd in the Annex which started at 1:40 P.M. so Ian had time to sleep in. The class was interesting but not as interesting as the eyewash created when a certain senior girl came into the class room. She sat in the front row. Ian asked his friend, Paulo about her once he got to Apple Pie for his service bar shift. "Let's play a game, Paulo, name that girl with just three hints and you get an all expense paid trip to Clyde's. Who's that beautiful brunette graduating this year in my American History class?"

"If she's beautiful, I know her."

"Here's four hints; 5'8", 125, Black Irish Hair, Gorgeous face."

"Stop, stop - I know who she is; you are speaking of the most beautiful Joan and I used to date her."

"I knew it, there isn't a woman who remotely fits a description like that you haven't dated."

"She is far too nice for the likes of you and anyway aren't you married yet?" Paulo said to Ian referring to his steady relationship with a co-ed named Leslie.

Ian shook his head in agreement; "Yeah, I know but can't I look?"

"No!" Paulo said laughing.

Ian used the Joan story as a segue into revisiting his Raven quest but Paulo said; "Look if someone like that ever walks in here; she's all mine, Mr. "Married One."" All of Ian's friends teased him that he and Leslie were always together. Ian dropped into the kitchen to get dinner before his shift. He was not in the kitchen two minutes before all hell broke loose in the bar.

Crazy Peter came through the two front doors wearing twin pearl handled .44 caliber six guns strapped to his legs as part of his new cowboy image. Paulo, not missing a beat, asked him to check them behind the bar until he left which Peter, for once, obliged. He had one too many cocktails and started screaming there were way too many "spooks" on M street and he was going to have to do something about it. A few "students" from the Car Barn, the local Interpol training center, confronted Peter about his mouth. That provoked a fight. Ian was an expert in telephone weaponry. He told Peter "it's for you." When he came over to get it, Ian cracked him perfectly on the jaw and Peter was out. Paulo officially started happy hour with a Metro Police car parked literally in the bar's entrance as they removed Peter from the premises.

With the second semester fully underway so resumed Ian's normal routine at Riggs Library. He patrolled the stacks each night before sitting down to study hoping to also find Raven. It wasn't until the middle of February that he heard noises in the upper stacks. His heart raced. He saw her in the corner of the third stack. The chairs were no longer there but Raven stood at the far end of the stack looking at him. He went to her.

The two let their energies mix, nothing needed to be said. Time stood still. They were lost in each other's eyes and all was right with the world. They did not embrace, just beheld one another. Anyone looking at them would know instantly the love energy that was being shared. His experience with Raven was different; no lust, no jealousy, no envy; just pure joy, a sense of belonging and being home. Raven again sensed Ian's soul fear and prepared to leave. No words needed to be spoken. Ian was simply not ready for her. She knew it and, unfortunately, so did he. After reconfirming to Ian how much she adored him, she put on her cloak, looked deeply into his eyes but before leaving conveyed her thoughts; "Remember to find your Cypher." He didn't understand her meaning nor did he care. All he wanted was for her to stay but that was not happening. Ian felt the most profound sense of loss he had ever experienced. She would be gone from him, forever. It was different when his mother died but just as devastating. Again remarkably, the feelings disappeared and an understanding entered his awareness. It was *let's just wait and see.*

Photo by: M. Shades

Chapter 16 - Ian's First Solo

After graduating from Georgetown in December, Ian moved to the New York City suburbs to be closer to Leslie. He landed his first real job in White Plains, NY and then married Leslie, 8 months later. A few years later they moved back to Georgetown and then Spring Valley where they had their first child, Stephanie, a beautiful baby girl. Less than three months after her birth, something awful happened.

"Ian, Come here! Come here! Quickly!" Leslie yelled.

"What's wrong?

"Look at her, look at her arms and legs, look at the way she is arching her back!"

Les continued; "What's wrong with her? I know something is terribly wrong."

Stephanie suffered as many as eighty seizures a day. Fortunately, the couple's friends and doctors connected them to the National Institutes of Health.

The treatment protocol called for them to live on the NIH campus. They spent three months there. Their daughter's condition did not improve and she was not showing any signs of developing. Ian and Leslie took Stephanie to a renowned pediatric neurologist group at Columbia Presbyterian in New York City for a second opinion. After 30 seconds of in-depth diagnosis, the doctor pronounced the little girl, a vegetable. "She should be institutionalized." The doctor advised the couple to think about having another child to replace what they would never have with this baby. Ian said, "This guy doesn't know what he is talking about. I know she'll get better." Ian's comments held little weight with his wife. After she heard the prognosis, Les became totally distraught. It was very long drive back to D.C.

A week passed after the trip and Ian became obsessed with knowing everything he could find out about his baby's condition. Out of complete desperation, he privately looked to God to solve his little girl's problem. Up until this point, Ian feigned religious belief. In some ways he became more like his father every day in that he would only pray if he needed a miracle.

Ian in his prayers for Stephanie offered himself up as the replacement, if one was needed. As part of his effort, he put his hands on her little head asking God to hear him and to heal his daughter. Literally, the next day, the seizures stopped. Ian owned a vacation home in Palm Beach, Florida. Their condominium was the smallest on the island. He thought the family had been though a very difficult ordeal and their tiny place would be perfect to help Stephanie recover. Everything worked out for the little family. Stephanie fully recovered and Ian got a job at a very prestigious firm on Wall Street. Life for Ian and Leslie was very good. They moved to Leslie's home town in New York into a fabulous house where the couple had three more daughters.

After a few years working with some of Wall Street's best firms, Ian went into a private securities practice with a partner. They specialized in private placement investments desperately trying to diversify their clients away from equities in a bad bear market. Ian headed the corporate finance end of the business and his partner worked the brokerage side. During a routine due diligence inspection to take one of their investments public, Ian found a problem. He didn't know the severity of the situation until he halted any further investment into the company in question. The incoming operating cash was not sufficient to pay outgoing debt. Even though Ian was deceived by his partner, Ian blamed himself for not paying close enough attention to the company's operations. He was sued by people he had never met and fought regulatory authorities over the company's remaining assets. The day Ian went to Philadelphia to give a regulatory agency deposition, his wife surprised him by asking for a separation. His attorney compounded the injury by actually telling him to plead the fifth. "Off the record tell them anything they want to know." This was the worst nightmare Ian could ever imagine. He followed the attorney's advice but hating every minute of it. Ian's world was crashing down all around him.

After the inquisition was over, Ian returned to New York. On the train ride, Ian began meditating. He just wanted to recuperate after a very grueling day but instead found that he was in a vision of his own, his first solo. Ian's eyes were closed. He was breathing deeply and felt what could only be described as angels wings wrap around him. He had a feeling of extreme well being, fully aware of the train, the sounds it made, his seat and the fact he was heading toward New York but then the scene changed. His mind went from angel's wings to a room full of people. Jesus made his way through a small crowd to hug Ian. *Why am I here and why would He ever hug the likes of me?* There was no voice or message just a knowledge that he had been visited by someone who Ian least expected to ever see. Suddenly, Ian found himself back in angel's wings still riding the train. He was again very calm and serene. He would have preferred to stay with the angel indefinitely but the train arrived at Penn Station. The meditative trace lingered even after Ian opened his eyes while still sitting in his seat. As he got up to exit the train, Ian noticed that every person leaving was more beautiful than the next, not attractive or handsome but really beautiful. He was fully awake and experiencing beauty beyond anything that would be considered normal. Ian's left-brain began working overtime, telling him *This is New York, pal, you know that the people here are not ALL beautiful, you've gone crazy; snap out of it.* Ian's fear took over just as it had in Riggs Library the last time he saw Raven. Ian trying to snap out of it as he was walking into the concourse thought; *this world requires a certain paradigm. This bliss is too unreal. It is too far outside the box. I cannot exist in this world with an outlook on life like this. Everything is too nice, too beautiful.* Ian lost the vision's glow as the cab made the right onto 42nd Street to drop him off at Grand Central to go home to a home he no longer had. He rationalized the experience thinking he had hypnotized himself, just a right brained reaction to a horrific day but then he remembered the other visions and realized that he had actually caused one without Raven's help.

Chapter 17 - Taos

It was time for Ian to ride in the barrel of life. His once charmed existence turned into a perpetual personal hurricane. Every day, it seemed like he got another registered letter from some lawyer demanding money. Everything Ian had worked so hard in obtaining was lost. His wife sued him in a bitter divorce. Federal Regulatory Agencies regularly convened grand juries that subpoenaed Ian to testify. He couldn't imagine anything worse.

Ian's new life as a joint custody dad was properly reflected in his first Christmas. His holiday decorations consisted of a string of lights strung on his living room ficus tree. The actual divorce papers were served to Ian on the evening of the 23rd during his "Christmas Eve" dinner with his children. From that moment Ian referred to Leslie as "The Queen of Darkness." After dropping his children back to the marriage house on the 24th to spend Christmas with their mother, he flew to New Mexico with his sister on the 25th to get away for a while by attending a five day spiritual seminar. Ian's sister felt it was the farthest thing from his current life she could think of so she booked it.

Christmas night at the hotel in Taos was straight out of an old Western. The fire in the huge hearth danced to a three-piece, fancy dressed cowboy band playing on stage. The locals wore their western hats, turquoise stick pins and cowgirl fancy dresses. The goose feather snow was outrageously beautiful as it fell over the mountains. After a brief introduction by the guru, the day started at 4 A.M. for a meditation and back at 10 A.M. for the first group class.

The core theme of the experience was to eliminate fear by overcoming extraordinary obstacles. After the first day's exercises, Ian's group of eight began a ritual of a cocktailed debriefing at the bar covering lessons learned. Finally the day had come where the locals from the surrounding area came to watch the lunatics' fire walk. Waiting bare footed on the iced covered parking lot was far more painful than walking on the "cold moss" of the burning embers.

Ian met the guru at the bar afterwards and told him about his unexplained visions and meditations. He gave the guru the short version of his Raven experiences and asked for guidance regarding his soul fear.

The guru seemed fascinated by Ian's description of "soul fear" and asked what he meant by it. Ian responded by saying it seemed to emanate from his core essence, somewhere beyond the "fight or flight" response. Ian continued, "This fear transcends the physical world." Ian shared how it frustrated his meditation practice. He explained that his meditation progresses to a point where he sees a white light but when it appears suddenly, his fear takes over and the focus is lost.

The guru responded, "You have fire walked, rappelled down cliffs hundreds of feet high above the river, and had six pythons put all over your body but nothing we do here will stop the fear you describe. Intense prayer and mystical calm is the only way past it. I wish I could help you more but you must find your own path" An encouraging aspect of the conversation confirmed that experiences like those Ian described were not unique and certain people were far more receptive than others in experiencing them.

Chapter 18 - Alphabet City

The trip to New Mexico re-enforced the notion to look deeper into Ian's experiences. He didn't want to address Raven's parting thoughts to him, "find your Cypher" but he had to do something. Ian's world was upside down and these most recent events forced his hand. He was sure none of these experiences was coincidence. He needed to piece them together. He knew a ribbon would emerge. Professionally, his clients lost money and everything Ian tried to do to prevent that, failed. Personally, he was divorced and alone. The great reputation he wanted so badly was utterly shattered. He would salvage whatever he could for his clients and maybe something for his children but even if he was successful, he knew it would never overcome the losses suffered by everyone at the time. He promised himself to find out the connection between his spiritual experiences and those he had experienced in the physical world. Ian didn't want to get too deep too quickly so he began his research by looking into Micah's amulet. Ian thought this reference was innocuous enough, but it turned out to be even older than Samuel Tosh's story. The symbols on

Micah's amulet were those of the ancient goddess, Hecate. Legend had it she presided over the crossroads of life. Ian knew he was at such a cross road and Ian's guess was so did Raven. *My second vision was more than a connection to the True Believers; it was an invitation to analyze the ribbon found in one's life path. Clovis was speaking to me, not just Artemus regarding Micah. Why?* Ian realized his soul fear was aggravated by something. He needed to find out what. He thought a spiritual teacher could help him get past this hurdle. Ian's sister had a friend, Elizabeth, educated as a lawyer but hated it so she became an editor of an astrology magazine. She knew Ian well and felt she could help. After a few months of looking, she called him. "I think I have found a man who may fit your needs. He lives in New York in an area called Alphabet City off of Avenue B around 12th Street."

Ian gave Mark a call to set up an appointment. They agreed to meet on a Tuesday at 11 AM at Mark's apartment. Ian arrived promptly and took in the neat and tidy surroundings. Mark was an environmentalist and a carpenter among other things and was utterly shocked at Ian's punctuality. He was a few years older than Ian and in very good shape. His long wavy grey hair was tied back showing off his strong Jewish heritage. As they sat down in the kitchen, he told Ian that he had done Ian's astrology chart and it fit the profile of a substance abuser. Mark took Ian's hands, poked, prodded, and then proceeded to tell Ian what no one could have known. He intuited certain knowledge of details in Ian's life that even Ian's closest friends were unaware. After the "reading" had finished, Mark said he was hungry and invited Ian to have lunch. They went to the Avenue A Café for a late breakfast. Ian was pushing for Mark's outside observation on Raven's Cypher instructions. They talked about Ian's recurring life themes. Mark was curious as to Ian's material obsessions.

"Ian, your soul fear may be directly related to your childhood?"

"Tell me more."

"When you were offered different options outside the materialistic box by Raven, you weren't interested. You were outside your comfort zone. You told me your father would never understand you heading down a spiritual path. Perhaps it was really you that did not want to understand that direction. It frightened you."

"I agree. I didn't want to see it then. What about the experiences I have had? Could the soul have its own agenda that influence life outcomes, regardless of the ego's conscious desires? My life couldn't be farther from what I consciously planned." Mark pondered the question. He didn't answer Ian that day.

As time passed, Mark earned the distinction as one of the best palm readers in the world. He was a regular on many TV talk shows. Ian continued in his entrepreneurial career and worked through his layers of soul fear by meditation, prayer and reading books. Everything he had worked for in the material world was gone and everything Ian thought would never work in his life had helped to save it. He remembered Raven's last look in another, more haunting way. *She knew I would have to overcome the illusions created by material desires and face my soul fears, head on. She also knew that out of all the work I needed to do, the most important tool to dissolve fear and*

develop spiritual depth was meditation; stop my talking in prayer and instead listen in
meditation.

Each morning Ian would quiet his mind and worked on eliminating
his prideful arrogant self, concentrating on humility and gratitude. In the
beginning it was all contrived. Ian was angry over the course of events
but knew anger would not solve anything. He had to fake it before he
could make it. After years of disciplined practice, praying for 10 minutes
and meditating for 20, one to three times a day; Ian's mind's eye began to
regularly see a minuscule light; usually white, sometimes, yellow gold. Each
time he looked at it directly, the light disappeared. Sometimes the light
would appear suddenly. Every time this happened, it startled him exposing
his fear. Ian tried everything to get past this problem. He diligently kept
thinking; *"Look at it only out of the corner of the mind's eye."* Nothing worked.
Ian needed to change something in his spiritual practice.

Chapter 19 - Tyson's Recipe

After another morning of failing to retain the light aspect, Ian got an idea. He called Lindsey Campbell, a friend and member of Ian's weekend golf foursome. Lindsey's day job was the sports editor and part time science writer for The Times. Ian moved the subject from tee times to neural pathways. Although they spent countless hours together, Ian never divulged anything to his friends about his meditation practices. He knew there was still a significant negative stigma attached with practicing meditation. Everyone still remembered the Beatles doing massive quantities of weed while proclaiming the virtues of Transcendental Meditation and Maharishi Mahesh Yogi. So after getting a ton of verbal crap dumped on Ian's head, Lindsey felt sorry enough to offer up the cell number of an expert that maybe could help Ian.

"Professor, my name is Ian MacAlester. I would like to present a proposition to you?"

The man on the other end of the phone was not amused at Ian's directness or how Ian got his telephone number.

"Who are you and who gave you my number?" asked John Tyson, a world-renowned neuropsychologist.

"I am someone who might be able to help you. I got your name from some friends at the New York Times."

"What exactly do you want?" Tyson barked.

"I am blessed or cursed with a strange ability to experience absolute calm. As a result, I have had extraordinary experiences. I am contacting you to inquire if you would entertain the prospect of developing a way to measure my brain activity during my meditative sessions. I am quite sure I can provide you with some unique brain waves. Does this interest you?"

"My only availability to discuss this further is tomorrow morning. Come by my office at 6 AM." Click. Ian did not know where Tyson's office was let alone how get to Los Angeles so early in the morning. He caught an early evening flight and found a relatively inexpensive place to stay in Century City. He was at Tyson's office at 5:45 AM. Ian entered the second floor hallway to find an overweight short squatty white coated Tyson moving boxes out of his office. Without any introduction Tyson snapped, "Pick up this end." Ian found himself moving three quarters of Tyson's instruments into his car. Tyson got into the driver's seat and was about to leave when Ian asked; "Don't you know who I am?"

"No and I don't particularly care." as he started to close the car door.

Ian grabbed the door and the keys from the ignition and said; "I flew here from New York last night and I am going to have a word with you whether you like it or not."

"You are the lunatic that called me yesterday?"

"Yes, I am that lunatic."

"Talk!"

Ian sat on the curb and went into his explanation. After about five minutes, Tyson said; "Enough, I understand what you want. As it happens, I have received a grant to measure brain activity in various stages of stimulation such as you describe. I am looking for subjects. I will notify you when I'm set up at Berkeley. I must tell you, MacAlester, I am not expecting anything to come of this."

"Thank you for your time, professor."

Tyson slammed the car door and looked into the rear view mirror with disgust as he drove away. Ian watched the out of control white curly haired Tyson making the turn out of the campus parking lot and knew this mad professor was interested.

He flew back to New York and spent the next two weeks consulting for one of his clients when the phone rang.

"Hello?"

"MacAlester, its Tyson. Can you come out here in the next ten days?"

"Name it."

"How about next Wednesday."

"I'll be there. What time?"

"9 A.M."

"Done." Ian heard the all too familiar click on the other end of the line.

Ian was excited about the possibility of graphically depicting what happened just before his soul fear took over. Perhaps Tyson could help him through it.

†††

The day came and Ian was in Tyson's lab. "Put your head back and hold still. I want to get these electrodes on properly." As Ian started to talk, Tyson instructed his assistant to test the instrumentation. "MacAlester, I don't want to hear anything out of your mouth unless I ask you a specific question or give you a command. Do you understand?"

Ian shook his head yes.

"Good, now that you are hooked up, we will use your base line MRI scan as our starting point and compare it to your brain activity when you are in meditation."

Ian started. He could not get comfortable. After about 10 minutes Tyson asked, "What are you doing? The instruments are recording no change. I see you fidgeting. Are you really who you say you are?"

"Yes, but I am nervous."

With that, Tyson came over and pinched Ian in the tender area under his right bicep. Ian got so mad; he punched Tyson hard in the arm knocking him into a stainless steel stand.

"Isn't that what you have wanted to do ever since you called me?"

"Yes!"

"Do you feel better?"

Ian did feel better and was better able to focus.

Ian went into his normal calming practice by relaxing each body part and muscle group working up from his feet to his head starting with his toes. Once he completed this procedure, he mentally re-emphasized relaxing his shoulders, neck, jaw and face; Ian then started his visualization technique. He guided his meditation into picturing a beautiful staircase in a tropical paradise where each step he took down resulted in a deepening of peace and calm.

"Fantastic, fantastic, keep it up!" yelled Tyson.

Ian did not hear anything and slowly brought himself out of his trance to the ecstatic jubilation of a frenzied Tyson.

"I did it! I did it!" Tyson screamed as Ian watched Tyson strut up and down the hall.

"What did you do?" Ian asked.

"I measured your brain activity during the meditation using my unique algorithms. As Tyson calmed down, Ian could see that he was going deep into thought. The once jubilant Professor was morphing back to the terrible tempered mad scientist.

"What's your problem?" Ian asked.

"Now that I have documented results, we have to duplicate them."

"Ok, I will go back into a meditative trace and you will have them reproduced."

"Do it!"

Ian sat on the lab floor as the staff hooked him up again and Ian repeated the procedure. The results were the same. The pen graph mirrored the previous images.

"MacAlester, how do I help you improve your meditations and eliminate your soul fear as you call it? And how do I prove an alternate conscious experience instead of defending allegations of a malfunctioning electroencephalic neurofeedback device? I have no clue what to modify for the next experiment."

"You measured my brain activity. I can document my techniques using guided meditation and selfless consciousness to listen." Tyson was non-plused with this explanation.

"Spend the next few days out here. I'll come up with something." Tyson said as he was walking into his cubicle in the basement of one of Berkley's labs. Ian shook his head in agreement. He drove to San Francisco and checked into the Fairmont. Ian, then, caught the cable car to Fisherman's Wharf, bought an order of mini bay shrimp and after exploring the City a bit found his way into a curiosity shop in Chinatown. The place was old and desperately in need of a new coat of paint. An ancient Chinese man was sitting behind the counter. Ian picked up a book whose cover displayed the same curious symbols he encountered in his vision about the Cathars. A $10 price was on the back cover. The old man asked Ian to return it when he was finished and he would give Ian his money back."

"No wonder this place looked so bad, it was a lending library." Ian laughingly thought.

Ian left the shop and went back to his hotel. Entering his room, he saw the light flashing on the hotel phone. He retrieved the message from Tyson instructing him to be at the lab at 10 AM the next morning.

Ian crossed the street facing the Mark Hopkins, and negotiated the steep hill just to the right of the Mark's driveway. At the bottom of the first block was a restaurant Ian had eaten in years earlier. The hostess sat him at a small table by the window and he opened up his new book.

The story began with a young man on a spiritual quest. He was taken in by a monastery in India with each of the monks having their own personal message for the main character but if all their advice were distilled it would translate into simply treating others as you would treat yourself. The main character's first lesson focused on prayer. In order for prayer to be more effective, the young monk had to learn to eliminate desire, carnality, and hubris. The oldest most experienced monk advised the novice on the importance of also adding intense feelings which imprints the prayer thus providing the best results.

Ian came back to the hotel after dinner. His message light on the hotel phone was dark. Ian then climbed into bed and started back reading.

The young monk was sent out from the monastery to gain experience. He journeyed into the mountains near Kashmir. As he walked by a tree next to the road, a very old man beckoned him to come closer. The young monk stood directly over the old man and was surprised at the heat coming from either the tree or the old man.

"What manner of trick is this, old man?" the young monk asked.

"The heat comes from my meditation." the old man replied.

"What type of meditation could cast off such heat?"

"The meditation acts as a catalyst. The process forms a harmony between those energies found in my body and those of the tree."

"Old man, how do you know such things?"

"I have been meditating in this spot for years. Many people have remarked, as you have, about the considerable heat emanating from either the tree or me. In my meditation, I become one with the tree so I now know to respond that the heat comes from both of us."

The young monk had to learn about meditation as part of his journey toward enlightenment so he asked the old man if he would teach him how to meditate and explain why in the old man's mind, meditation was important. The old man agreed and asked the young monk to help him stand up. As the young monk helped him up, the old man proceeded to beat the monk with his walking stick.

"Why do you beat me with this stick after I have helped you?" the young monk screamed.

"To show you that fairness is in the eye of the beholder and that the mind experiences disruption by such things as injustice. Now, my young friend, I want you to sit under this tree and meditate the best you can with no instruction."

The young monk still upset and lacking the understanding of the lesson, sat at the base of the tree furious, thinking he had picked the wrong mentor. As he sat there, the young monk realized the tree seemed to be providing him with a calming influence and indeed helped him in regaining his composure. The old man returned after a while to the monk who said; "Old man, it is not you that provides the calm, it is the tree." The old man asked the young monk to get him dinner as a payment for the successful completion of his first lesson. The young monk reacted. "How did you teach me anything, it was I who noticed the power of the tree?"

The old man responded. "It was I who put you under the tree, mad and upset so you could feel its power."

The young monk thought for a moment and conceded.

The old man continued. "The disturbing emotions gave you the opportunity to be comforted by the tree, going from agitation to peace. When you acclimated to the tree's energy, the disruption actually helped amplify its calming effects."

The next day, the two men came upon a river. The old man danced across it and patiently waited on the other side for his new apprentice. The young monk set out, seeing the first rock just under the surface of the water and lost his footing. Emerging drenched from the water, he noticed the slippery moss growing on the rock.

"How did you get across the river so easily, old man? I am young and agile, you are old and frail yet you skipped across the rocks as if they formed a wide road."

"Listen to yourself and you have your answer!" The old man said walking away from the river.

The monk got out of the water, replayed old man's words in his mind. He saw the pattern in the water and jumped from one rock to the other, and ran after the old man saying, "Look at me old man, I did it. I did it."

The old man stopped. "How does this connect with meditation?"

The young monk was stumped.

The old man did not reply but continued walking toward the small village that lay ahead. Once in its center, the old man sat down next to the community well and the young monk watched in amazement as many young people of the village came up to him, bringing food and water, and sat down in a circle around him.

"Old man what are these people doing and why do they treat you in this manner?" the young monk asked. The old man did not respond again to the monk but addressed the small crowd that had gathered.

"Thank you for your generosity and caring. Today I am going to tell you about "the old man and the young apprentice" and proceeded to tell them the story of the past few days. When the old man finished, the people applauded and went back to what they were doing."

The old man motioned for the young monk to come closer. "Young man, what do you know about fellowship and how does that apply to meditation?" Even though he didn't know that answer either, the young monk thought perhaps he had chosen the right mentor after all. He would pay closer attention.

"Old man, I concede there may be a relationship but I don't know what it is."

"Good, you are learning; you became aware of the pattern the rocks formed in the river and you are now aware of the pattern of behavior exhibited by the community in the village. Any increase in your awareness helps you in achieving better meditations."

†††

Ian fell asleep. The next morning, he walked into the lab and followed the cloud of smoke created by Tyson's Lucky Strike while connecting electrodes to a large machine.

"Come over here MacAlester, you can make yourself useful. Hold these wires."

"Dr. Tyson, why are you hooking up so many leads to this machine?"

"Connectivity."

"What do you mean connectivity?"

"I believe we can view your brain activity, your sympathetic energy system and their combined influence on your heart."

"What will that prove?"

"That brain activity generated by guided meditation combines with the sympathetic nervous system to form its own independent energy, perhaps one capable of creating an altered state of consciousness."

"So?"

"Your mind somehow gets inside this combination of energies. This interchange of energy vibrates at a higher level enabling you to experience a form of Trans-dimensional travel and leaves your corporal body, a dream state."

"Is that your explanation of how I achieve my visions?"

"Let's see, shall we?" He said fading into the control room to test the equipment. Tyson returned and began to prepare Ian.

"How many leads are you putting on me?"

"Just a few more!" as Tyson reveled in putting connecting tape all over Ian's hairy chest."

"Think of this as a waxing for your next conquest." Tyson said.

The rest of Tyson's staff arrived. They were amazed to find Ian all hooked up and ready to go. Tyson immediately began shouting orders to each of the four technicians as they walked in the door expressing his unhappiness with having to prepare MacAlester, himself.

"All right MacAlester, do your thing."

Ian began to meditate. He relaxed his body parts sequentially then concentrated on his organs. He even tried to relax his blood vessels as he pictured them to have extreme flexibility and clear of any obstructions. Ian then focused on his own internally guided instructions.

The machines began recording altered brain wave patterns. Ian's breathing decreased and became noticeably deeper. His breath originated from the belly not his chest. This method of breathing resulted in a higher oxygenation of cells. The machines in the control room were also registering all of Ian's vital signs and a few other metrics that Tyson kept to himself. Ian was in a standard meditation, nothing extraordinary and certainly, nothing that compared to some of his unique experiences.

The meditation lasted for approximately 20 minutes and when Ian came out of it, he could see on everyone's face that the results were lackluster. Ian searched his mind for a fix and then his new little book provided an inspiration. Ian shared with Tyson there could be another way to achieve the results. Ian felt that if he could provide an emotional afterburner once he was in his relaxed state, the results might be better.

"You are already hooked up. It would be a shame not to give it another try." Tyson said thinking of a way to get Ian emotionally charged.

Ian voiced his concern about an adrenaline surge and thought that another type of intense emotion may provide better results.

Tyson had an idea.

"Ian, come over and sit down."

"What do you have in mind?"

"You have a unique gift in meditation; I am going to apply an electro-stimulus to your frontal lobe." Tyson attached more electrodes to Ian's head. The idea was to stimulate Ian's brain just at the spot where he saw that elusive "spec of light."

"MacAlester, go back into the quiet room and prepare to meditate."

Ian again went into his meditative state. As he reached the level of brain activity to where the graph indicated Ian should be experiencing "the spec of light," Tyson activated the electrode. He had never seen results like this in his career.

Tyson said to one of his technicians; "Jones, get the paddles ready, MacAlester's heart has almost stopped."

Tyson, in the control room, watched the gages in utter amazement screaming; "Are you seeing this? Are you seeing this?" knowing that Ian could not hear anything.

The recorder was an old pen and tracer unit but it provided the evidence that Tyson had always known was there if he could ever find the right subject.

The entire meditation room filled with a bright light with no point of origin.

Tyson was beside himself in awe. In the meantime, Ian found he could enter the light but knew he had to mentally get back to the lab because this time something was not right. His experience said something was very wrong.

"NO! NO! STOP! GO BACK! I am not finished. NO!" Tyson screamed.

"We have perfected the recipe; haven't we, Doc?" as Ian came out of his trace.

"What you mean "we?""

Ian could take it. After all, he was the only one in Tyson's entire group that could reproduce these results.

"Let's do it again MacAlester."

"NO!" I have achieved what I came here to do."

"Tell me what you experienced, tell me right NOW!"

"Hey Doc, pound sand!" Ian left the lab and headed up to his parked car.

"You ingrate, you worm, you insect!" Tyson shrieked chasing Ian up the stairs.

Ian did not turn around as he spoke; "Maybe that will teach you a few manners and some humility."

"Call me, Ian, we can work this out, I know we can, please?"

"Let me think about it, I'll call you."

Part 4

Chapter 20 - The Mysterious Force

Looking down, flying over the Golden Gate Bridge, Ian recalled what happened in Tyson's lab. *There was something very wrong in reaching the Kingdom that way.* Ian couldn't believe he had found a spiritual afterburner to open up the light tunnel but the "feeling" was all wrong. Ian instinctively knew that by forcing the spirit, the experience was bastardized just as it was referenced in the New Testament. He did not explain any of this to Tyson but left a voice mail saying that he was going back to New York and would call him in a few days. Sitting in his seat, Ian took out the small Gospel of Thomas and his notes. *Certain of the Nag Hammadi scrolls do provide the recipe to meditate into the Kingdom. I have just got to figure it out!*

The Gospel's opening verses give instruction on getting proper interpretation, seek out true wisdom and look within for the Kingdom. Ian cross-referenced the Gospel of Mary, "the son of man is within you." The Gospels of Thomas, John and the Truth were primers for this meditation.

All of them point to looking within, not to guide your meditation outwardly but inward. Ian put down his books and began going through his meditation prep steps to get some sleep. As the plane cruised at 33,000 feet, Ian felt the familiar sensations. His meditation was hitting its normal state of quiet. Ian visualized putting his consciousness into his heart rather than his mind. This effort started the speck of light in the corner of his mind's eye. Ian's mind calmly thinking, *do not look directly at it, just stay the course.* As the thoughts were clearing the way for his next set of self guidance, Ian experienced a breakthrough. He found himself in the beautiful Kingdom square with his beloved Raven sitting on the retaining wall of the fountain. She smiled at him extending her hand. He felt her touch. She focused on Ian's emotional afterburner entry into the light. Raven amplified her thoughts into Ian's vision reflecting her sincere concern. "This is not the way to the Kingdom. Do not attempt anything like that again, do you understand?"

The words struck him like mental thunderbolts. The effect numbed his vision. He felt the warning deep into his soul. The word "mission" echoed in his brain. Ian never thought he was on a mission but Raven interjected; "You are on a mission, we all are and you chose yours. You must expose this suppressed information." Ian began feeling like a scolded schoolchild and thought; *Yes, I am so sorry I did not know....* Before Ian could think anymore, Raven calmed him with waves of love. Ian found himself back in the plane hearing the flight attendant announcing their preparation for landing.

╫

Ian returned to his life in New York. Not long after Raven's rebuke, in a routine meditation, Ian found himself back in Jerusalem picking up where his first Raven induced vision left off. He was focusing on Hiram Abiud, Temple Officiate and Counsel to King Herod Agrippa. Walking past the alabaster walls of the Palace, Abiud felt the pressure from the Pharisees to stop the defection of good Jews joining these splinter groups like the Jesus movement. Agrippa met him at the King's Chamber door screaming; "I want to know everything about their beliefs and why our people convert to this way of life?" Abiud had another problem. The core of the "True Believer" movement did not renounce Jewish tradition. Quite to the contrary, they embraced all of Judaism but accepted Jesus as the Messiah and his teachings as the Word of God. Abiud's spies infiltrated their secret meetings. He learned of a "Kingdom" that was available for anyone to embrace.

This teaching provided even the most pathetic individual a way to attain spiritual enlightenment. Abiud was superstitious in thinking this movement was being propelled by a mysterious force of some kind. He heard about the rift between Peter, on one hand and Thomas and Mary Magdalene on the other. The rumor was that Peter accused Jesus of imparting important information about God and the Kingdom only to Mary, Thomas and James that he did not share with the others. Abiud spied on all at court and identified Levy, one of the King's advisors as having a nephew about the same age as most of the recent defectors.

Abiud demanded Levy's nephew and any of his close friends be brought to the Palace immediately. Samuel Tosh was among those summoned to appear before Abiud. He was convinced it had something to do with his meeting James. He and Jonah went to the Palace. The throne room was intimidating. The two guests awaited the Counselor's arrival from touring the Roman barracks.

"Thank you for coming Jonah" Abiud said as he walked into his huge office. "I have known your uncle for many years. He is a very well respected member of the King's court. I would like to discuss a matter of some delicacy regarding this Jesus business. I am aware that your friend here has met James, the Apostle. I am told Samuel, you were somewhat enamored with this man but have not been back to see him. This is good from my prospective because it shows you have not betrayed your roots yet you were curious. I want both of you to work for me. Samuel, I want you to infiltrate the sect where James preaches. Tell me what he says including all of his mystical secrets. Jonah, I want you to keep seeing that girl you have been sneaking around with and gain her confidence so she will introduce you into the group that follows Mary. I know that we understand each other when I say that the King does not tolerate failure and likes to get quick results. I expect both of you to give me a full report within three weeks time. I will pay you well if you succeed or with a blade, if you don't." Abiud waived his hand signaling their meeting was over as the guards escorted the two men out of the Palace.

As soon as Samuel and Jonah got to a place where they could speak, Jonah turned to Samuel and said, "Abiud's spies are everywhere. He even sets them on my uncle, a prominent man. We obviously have been watched for some time. Samuel, I didn't know you went to see James. What was he like? Why didn't you tell me?"

Samuel responded, "I thought it was too dangerous for any of us to see the group again and I didn't want my parents to find out. By the way, I didn't know you were seeing a girl." as Samuel smiled for the first time since their meeting. Jonah did not immediately answer.

"Well?" Samuel asked.

"Yes, I have been seeing someone and I love her. I would like to have a little more money saved before I ask her to marry me. I may get a dowry from her father who is very wealthy. What am I going to do about this problem?"

Samuel responded by saying, "It is a simple problem to solve. I am going to my leather suppliers and wait for "The True Believers" to come, get the information Abiud wants, and relay it. That will be the end of it."

Jonah said; "I have a much more difficult problem. If I betray my beloved's friend, Mary; I am kissing good-bye my relationship and any trust she will ever have for me."

They talked for a while longer and parted with an understanding that they would come up with a plan for Jonah that would not ruin his relationship. Samuel finished his duties at the leather works and was on his way to his parent's house when two men shepherded him into an alley and then down the street to an empty house.

James was waiting.

"How do you like being a member of Agrippa's court, Samuel?"

"How did you know that?"

"What does Abiud want you to do, betray me?"

"Yes, he wants to know all of your mystical teachings and I only have three weeks to do it."

James thought for a moment and then outlined his plan. "You will not come to any of our regular meetings. You will not meet any new prospective members. Instead you will meet with me alone and then go back to your business and parents. This will work for Abiud and will not betray any of our followers." James went on. "Abiud will get infuriated when his spies can't give him further details on the group and you will later be asked to betray all of us which I am counting on."

"And when Abiud wants me to do more?"

"Leave that to me." James said.

Samuel left the house looking for any sign of Abiud's spies but saw nothing. He went to his parent's home and they ate together. His mother saw his troubled look. He told them he was working very hard and under some strain to get certain hides tanned and sold. He did not want his parents to worry. He would not lie to them directly but instead omit telling them everything. When he awoke the next morning, he packed for his scheduled trip to get his tanning supplies on the north shore of the

Dead Sea. Along the road, Samuel saw a man dressed in muslin robes who stopped him.

It was James in disguise. "Let's spend some time now on the teaching." James spent a few hours with Samuel teaching him the principals of the "Light" technique.

After the lesson was over, Samuel continued on his way. He arrived at the oasis where his trading suppliers had pitched camp. The next day he was met by another one of James followers who was a True Believer adept to teach Samuel a lesson in "the light and the calm." This lesson put Samuel on a training track to be ahead of the time period Abiud outlined.

Samuel went into the tents to finish his business and enjoy a wonderful dinner. Afterwards, when everyone had gone to bed, Samuel looked for Abiud's spies. He found them in the near-by dunes overlooking the camp. *Abiud has people everywhere.* Samuel thought. The next day, the adept returned, dressed as a wealthy merchant throwing money around for everyone to see. After making a spectacle of purchasing some of Samuel's hides, they retired into the tent. As soon as they were inside, the follower taught Samuel a technique to help with his "tracing the light".

Samuel was amazed at how complex the exercise was but he worked hard and was able to do it. He was successful in sustaining the white light continuance.

The rest of his attempts were spent asleep validating his failure. The initiate also relayed other information to Samuel. "The same energy needed to transcend the mental gulf in the "light acquisition" exercise is spent if a person is sexually active." The initiate continued, "The rule of thumb is to remain sexually inactive for at least nine days, harnessing light before that time usually produces poor results." Samuel headed back to Jerusalem. No sooner did he arrive than one of the Palace guards came to the tannery and physically took Samuel to Abiud.

"Samuel, you have been to your suppliers and have been visited by one of the Christians."

Samuel nodded his head affirmatively.

"Have they started training you?"

Samuel again nodded yes.

"Tell me what the teaching is about."

"I have learned what they call "The light and the calm" and a number of other techniques that provide deeper levels of peace."

"Tell me how to do it."

Samuel started to show Abiud the exercise but Abiud stopped him saying he did not have time and would wait until Samuel completed all of his lessons before Abiud would start learning any of it.

"Samuel, it has been one week since our first meeting. You have done well, keep it up. I will see you again in two weeks, don't disappoint me."

Samuel walked out of the Palace thinking he had dodged the first of Abiud's menacing threats. As he walked, he could not help think that Abiud must have so many people on the Palace payroll that literally nothing goes on without him knowing about it. He would not underestimate Abiud or do anything that could jeopardize his family.

In the meantime, Jonah continued to see his ladylove but had not yet confided in her and was falling behind Abiud's time schedule. When he did talk to her, she was repulsed at his duplicity. She said she never wanted to see Jonah again. He did not know what to do. He went searching for Samuel at his parent's home. As he entered, Samuel and his parents greeted him and gave him a meal. After thanking his hosts, Jonah took Samuel outside. "Samuel, I am in trouble, she left me when I told her what Abiud asked me to do and now I have no way to comply with his request. My failure will ruin my uncle and the rest of the family."

Samuel replied; "Jonah, let me see what I can do to get you a direct audience with Mary. She, in all likelihood, will accept you and work with you to fulfill Abiud's wishes." Jonah felt somewhat relieved.

Samuel's plan was that when James or one of the initiates contacted him to further his own education; he would ask James to help Jonah.

"Hello Samuel!" James said from the shadows of the tannery the next night.

"Hello, James; I have another favor to ask of you?"

"I will help your friend meet Mary. I have received her permission to have Jonah meet her in two days' time at the valley of Hinnom."

"How did you know?"

"You will soon be able to answer that question for yourself."

Samuel said; "You have been two steps ahead of me and now Abiud since all of this started."

"Both of us will soon be faced with some very interesting life tests, Samuel." James responded.

Samuel did not like the ominous way that sounded. James continued, "Samuel, you need to perfect the calmness technique." The next night, they sat in Samuel's little workspace and worked through another exercise when the most unbelievable thing happened. The fear that Samuel always had in seeing the spec of light in his meditation, disappeared. He had peace of mind. Samuel had a vision of the Kingdom. He saw beautiful flowers everywhere. His vision was more vivid than any physical experience he had using his empirical senses. He actually smelled the fragrance of the flowers in his vision. As Samuel walked through his vision, he saw people in the streets. He knew some of them. "Hello, Samuel!" one of his father's friends said. "We are surprised to see you here but glad for you." Samuel was also surprised to see them as he would not have picked those people he met.

He walked further and saw a fabulous square where people were congregating. He found himself pushing his way through the people to see who was speaking. The speaker exhibited the most powerful physical presence Samuel had ever seen but every time he tried to look into the man's face, Samuel found the Sun to be in his eyes no matter which way he positioned himself. He could hear the man's tone of voice but not his words.

†††

Samuel's vision faded and he found himself back in his workshop staring at James, speechless. His thoughts jumbled but managed to hear James say, "You have just experienced the Kingdom, Samuel."

"What an experience, the most wonderful place I have ever known; I never wanted to leave. How do I get back?"

"You have much work to do here. You must give Mary's invitation to Jonah and relay your experience to Abiud and finally be prepared to share it with King Agrippa, himself."

"Why do you want me to give this information to our enemies?"

"Do you think they will be our enemies for long once they experience the Kingdom?"

Samuel acknowledged James' point and went to find Jonah to tell him about his arranged meeting with Mary. Jonah thanked him profusely for his help and in two days time went to the rendezvous location where he found Mary kneeling by a fire.

"Hello, Jonah, I am Mary Magdalene."

"I am honored to speak with you; I know you are aware of my plight. I have been asked by Hiram Abiud to find out about your followers and tell him everything."

"You will tell him everything he wants to know."

"What would you have me do?"

"Our meeting will be reported to Abiud." Mary gave Jonah all the information Abiud asked him for and then said, "You will tell him you have done what he has asked of you. You will also tell him his spies are incompetent which has compromised your ability to further execute his request." Mary ended their meeting but before she left, Mary turned to Jonah with compassion, "I hope your lady friend recovers."

In the morning, Samuel rounded the corner to the tannery just in time to see Jonah taken away to the Palace. The guards were much rougher with Jonah than they had been with Samuel but as Samuel looked on, he thought the information Jonah had would keep him out of any trouble. Jonah could not understand his bad treatment. He was feeling concerned that something had gone terribly wrong. Abiud came into the hall calling Jonah a bungling idiot and that Jonah had compromised the plan because he disclosed information about his mission. Abiud took Jonah to a group of cells in the Antonia Fortress.

In one of them, he saw his beloved, badly beaten. She was bleeding from her head. This infuriated Jonah but he stayed silent. Apparently, the spy who was following Jonah had not yet reported in to Abiud. This possibility sent shivers up his spine as he remembered Mary's words. Abiud said; "you are a waste and we will deal with you, later."

Jonah responded. "I have met with Mary and soon I will be a member of her inner sanctum of followers. If your informant was competent and had properly reported to you on time, you would know all of this. I met with Mary for hours last night and will do so again. I respectfully ask that you return this woman back to her family with no more harm coming to her."

"Tell me everything you have learned from that whore." Abiud demanded as he motioned for the girl to be released. Jonah could see she was already dead. His heart sank. After Jonah debriefed Abiud as to his meeting with Mary, he asked who beat his fiancé. Abiud gave him the jailor's name and told him he could settle things as he saw fit. As Abiud walked toward the King's Palace, Jonah turned to go back inside the Fortress. He overheard the jailor boasting that his fiancé had firm breasts and he would have raped her himself but just as he was about to mount her, the King's counselor entered the cell and violated her, first. Jonah evaporated into the walls. He waited outside until the jailor's duty was over. The night was dark and as the jailor turned onto a side street, Jonah took him from behind and slit his throat. He dragged the man's body to the Palace gates, attaching a note around the jailer's head addressed to Abiud, "You're next!"

I had hoped for this. Abiud thought as he read the note. He told his guards to round up Jonah's family, rape the women in front of the men, and then kill all of them. A Palace squad surrounded Jonah's uncle's walled house. They called for them to come out or face the King's wrath. No movement came from inside the compound. The soldiers stormed the house. To their surprise, they found nothing. The families and their belongings were gone. Only a gate was open leading to the garden. As the troops went through it, a trap box opened releasing 10 rabid squirrels who managed to bite a number of the soldiers. Panicked, the guards killed both the squirrels and the infected soldiers. After hearing the report, Abiud was visibly upset and told the guards to go to the tannery and destroy it. Samuel and Jonah hid as the tannery was being demolished. They hoped to hear something about Abiud's next move but heard nothing. Jonah asked, "Now what do we do?"

Samuel said, "My parents are bewildered but they were willing to leave the City. They are afraid to start life all over again."

Jonah said, "We didn't have any choice. Even though we did as Abiud asked, we still have ended up in a bad situation."

"The only thing we can do now is warn our new friends and meet up with our families. We will get money from the sale of these last hides and be able to start again. I am going to find James. You find Mary and we will meet in Gaza."

Jonah said; "Let's make a pact, Samuel. If one of us is caught, the other will take care of the captive's family and not attempt a rescue. We cannot afford both of us dead for our families' sake. Agreed?"

"Agreed!"

They split up. Samuel went back to a spot in the City where he knew he could get word to James. The streets were crawling with soldiers; everyone was looking for Samuel and Jonah. Abiud put a hefty price on their heads. Samuel waited until he saw one of the adepts making his way through the market and approached him. The adept told Samuel where he could find James in a one-room enclosure that was part of the City wall.

"James, I moved my family to safety outside the City." Samuel continued; "Please get away from here as I fear for your life."

"You are a true friend, Samuel but I must provide an example for the people."

"James, how do I get back to the Kingdom?"

"I will send someone to you. They will teach you how to find it, again."

James told Samuel to go to his family as they are not yet out of danger. They hugged and Samuel left. He had packed hides, equipment and supplies onto two mules and rode for about three hours before making camp in a valley for the night. Samuel was about to start a fire when he heard riders coming through the pass and hid in the bushes. They were Abiud's soldiers. They rode past him and bedded down a few hundred yards farther down the trail.

The squad was on their way at daybreak, moving toward the sea, seeming to know exactly where the families had gone. Samuel followed. Gaza was an independent state and not under Roman rule. Samuel knew they would not enter the city as soldiers. When they stopped to change their clothes, Samuel would go directly to the families.

He went to Jonah's family first and told them about the soldiers. Jonah's family had eight men in it; six in Gaza. They were Jonah's uncle, four brothers and his father, all were in good physical shape. Then Samuel went to Jonah's dead beloved's family and warned them. Finally, he went to his parents. They were the oldest and very frail. He moved them to another section of the settlement, closer to the sea.

He told them to stay away from the marketplace. Samuel then contacted some of his business associates to guard his parents while he returned to fight with Jonah's family. The soldiers attack came in the middle of the night. Jonah's brothers were good fighters and proved to be more than a good match for Abiud's killers. Jonah's father and uncle walked behind the men while they were fighting the family and quickly killed all but the youngest soldier. After Samuel tied him up, the soldier gladly volunteered all of his information beginning with the fact that Abiud had captured Jonah.

"He will be kept alive until Samuel comes for him. My Lord Abiud said to make sure you know Jonah's stay will be as unpleasant as possible. He is being held in the Fortress. We are not to return without the heads of all of the family members as proof they have been killed." Jonah's family was beside themselves. They knew this man was telling the truth otherwise, there was no way Abiud would have known where the family had gone in the first place.

Samuel immediately went back to the City. Abiud's spies spotted him and public notices were posted commanding Samuel to come to the Palace. Samuel complied.

The guards pushed and beat Samuel before allowing him access to the inner sanctum of the Councilor's offices, a small repayment for outsmarting Abiud. Afterward, Abiud came into his huge office complex and ordered Samuel to kneel on the hard stone floor as they talked.

He was abrupt but the tone of the conversation was markedly nicer than Samuel expected. Apparently, Agrippa had told Abiud to produce Samuel. The King wanted to know everything about the mysterious force, which was so much a part of the True Believer movement. Abiud told Samuel, "If the King is displeased in any way, you will be killed directly after the meeting. Jonah's death will quickly follow." Samuel was confident he could entice Agrippa with the knowledge about "the Kingdom" as he had been foretold by James.

The next day, Samuel was bathed and properly attired for his meeting with Agrippa. He was led through the reception hall to the great chamber. A number of people were paying homage to the King and asking Agrippa for favors. Now, it was Samuel's turn for an audience. Agrippa dismissed his court and began the interrogation. "I understand you have experienced James' mysticism; is this correct?"

"Yes, you're Majesty."

"Who are you?"

"My name is Samuel Tosh!"

"Describe what happened to you?" "Who did you meet?" "What did they teach you?" "Hurry up, answer quickly!"

After being scared out of his mind, Samuel regained his composure, and started his story about James and his wonderful ability to see into the future. Samuel explained that the teaching enables a person to experience heaven in a dreamlike state. He riddled the story with mystery. Agrippa pondered Samuel's account and then said, "Tosh, we will make a place for you here in the Palace. I am well versed in all types of magic. You will prepare me for my meeting with James. He can lead me into the Kingdom." After finishing his meeting with the King, Samuel was escorted into Abiud's office suite.

Abiud had Jonah brought into the office from the Fortress and made Samuel promise that as long as the instruction was going on with the King, he would not flee the City. Samuel also had to let Abiud know what was being taught to the King, if he so desired. Jonah was so weak he could barely crawl let alone walk. Once out of the Palace, Jonah vowed to kill Abiud. "Samuel, it is awful in there. The prisoners experience continual molestation in their cells. The soldiers do unspeakable things to both men and women. These poor people die and then are tossed into shallow graves. The Romans defile everything we believe in. Agrippa has to end these atrocities. Abiud has his own agenda and seems to enjoy fostering this inhumane treatment."

Samuel responded, "Please don't have vengeance on your mind now. Heal and recover as fast as you can. I will take time with the King, as much as I can, before he threatens to cut off my head. You must be able to fight or run."

"I will be ready."

Samuel started teaching Agrippa, spending considerable time getting the King focused on the "Light and Calm" techniques. The King's knowledge of mysticism made his understanding of these concepts easier. The King's patience also surprised Samuel.

As time went on, Agrippa got quite good at the techniques, which impressed Samuel but also was a reminder that the lessons were rapidly approaching a point where Samuel could no longer contribute and James would have to intervene to take Agrippa to the next level. Samuel informed Jonah of Agrippa's progress at dinner one night saying that during the day's lesson, Agrippa managed, all by himself, to get to a level where he thought he could see the Kingdom.

"The King knows he has used my talents to their fullest and he will ask me tomorrow to see James. I can try to stall by saying that I want to drill him on the calm technique but I will have to get James for the next level of instruction."

Jonah responded; "I have recuperated well enough to fight and have met someone who is caring for me."

"Jonah, how do you do it? I had a business and money but could never find anyone. It seems all you have to do is walk down the street and women find you. As payment for saving you, you will find me a woman to marry?"

"It is certainly the least I can do."

Samuel pushed Jonah hard in the chest testing his progress. Jonah pushed back and was indeed ready. The next day, Samuel went to the Palace and started with the calm technique when Agrippa yelled to the guards to bring in one of Abiud's spies. The spy looked familiar to Samuel. He was one of the people Samuel saw when he was in the dreamlike state of the Kingdom.

"Tosh, do you really think I would blindly believe your fantastic story. This man has been in my service since the time when I lived in Rome. He told me he saw you in the Kingdom and that everything you have told me is true. Lucky for you; bring me James!"

"Yes, Sire!"

Samuel left the Palace and met Jonah in the Temple.

"I need to get in touch with James immediately. We are out of time. I met one of the spies that work directly for the King. He lives next to where your parents used to live. That's how they could so easily observe us."

"That would also explain how they caught my beloved." Jonah said. "I will make that spy pay with his life after I torture him for the way they raped and killed her."

"Jonah, keep your voice down."

No sooner did the words come out of Samuel's mouth than one of James's initiates approached. "You are to come with me."

They walked through the City's main gates and out to a nearby orchard. James, talking with a small group, excused himself when he saw Samuel.

"Is it time?" James knowingly asked.

"How did you know so many months ago that I would be teaching the King?"

"You have only experienced the Kingdom as an observer. Time folds in upon itself there and as such, I was able to know what role you would play with Agrippa."

"Then you must know I have been sent to get you to finish the modest education I started with Agrippa."

"Yes, I know. I will come with you to the Palace, now. He will not be expecting you to return so quickly. That will be to our advantage."

James and Samuel walked through the City into the Palace. They were instructed to go into the great hall. Agrippa cancelled the audiences he had scheduled for the rest of the morning. The King instructed his secretary to work around his meeting with the Procurator who was coming to the Palace from Rome.

Agrippa spoke first. "I see you are back with James. I loath to meet you James as this cult of yours has caused me considerable problems. I am trying to avoid action against your people but if the disregard for Roman rule in general, and my authority in particular, persists there will be no choice but to punish them. I am sure you and your group will not like the outcome that would ensue. On a more positive note, your apprentice here has instructed me on the Light and Calm technique of which I have grown quite proficient. The practice enables me to sleep and is good preparation for your instruction. I desire to be shown the Kingdom by you. I am ready to experience it now."

James instructed the King to prepare himself and then he would do the rest.

Agrippa went into a mild trance. James assisted the King in gaining access to the Kingdom.

The experience was the most wonderful Agrippa ever felt. When James brought the King back to the throne room, Agrippa was furious. He wanted to go back immediately to the Kingdom but his secretary reminded him of the meeting with the Roman Procurator. Agrippa backed off and became so docile it shocked Samuel. The King was actually polite and used his fabulous charm to ingratiate himself to James. He was so courteous that Samuel forgot all of Agrippa's tyrannical traits and quickly fantasized about the possibility that the King could become a True Believer. Agrippa instructed James to come back tomorrow. As the two walked outside the Palace, James became very serious.

"What's wrong, James?" Samuel asked.

"You and your friend must go to Gaza, tonight."

"Why James, I want to be there when you take the King back to the Kingdom. I want to be known as someone who was with you when you turned King Herod Agrippa into a True Believer."

"The problems will start tomorrow and only intensify. Please gather Jonah and leave. The King asked me to come back tomorrow, which I will do. He did not ask you and I will point that out to him for his court to hear in the morning. In that way, you did not violate a direct command. Samuel, go in peace."

"But I want so much to be with you and become a member of the Kingdom; I have so many more questions?"

"Please go, all of your questions will be answered."

Samuel went to Jonah and told him everything. Jonah was happy to hear he could visit his family but saddened by leaving his new friend in the City.

"She could also be tortured and raped by Abiud and his men." Jonah said.

The two men agreed to meet outside the City's gates. Jonah arrived at the gate with two beautiful women. One looked to be about 17, the other, 22. They were sisters and part of the family that helped Jonah recover. Jonah introduced them as Rachel and Ruth. Jonah said their father had instructed him to make sure they arrived in Gaza safely and unharmed. The women rode on the donkeys, the men walked in front of them. Jonah said he hoped his taste in women was sufficient for Samuel to consider Ruth as a potential marriage candidate. Jonah laughed saying, "I am working on satisfying my obligation to you, Samuel." He told Samuel that the woman's family was one of the best in all of Judea and was sure Samuel's parents would approve. The men knew that as soon as things settled down, their families would resume arranging marriages.

James arrived at the Palace in the late morning giving Samuel and Jonah more of a head start should Agrippa decide to send his troops after them.

Agrippa was waiting in the throne room for James.

"I know Tosh and his friend have left the City."

"Sire, you specifically asked for me, today, not Samuel. I told him I would take care of your education from now on thinking that he had shown you all he knew. Which in my opinion, he did. I, please, beg your forgiveness."

Agrippa knew James was protecting Tosh but couldn't risk any alienation of James at least until he had mastered the technique of entering the Kingdom. They talked for a while longer and then got to work getting Agrippa back to the Kingdom. Agrippa loved the experience and made time for James on a daily basis. This went on for months. Passover was upon them and Agrippa was getting bored. He suspected there was more to the Kingdom than James was showing him.

He experienced a bifurcation in his vision where he could see himself inside the Kingdom but his thinking mind remained outside, separate and apart. The separation from the people inside Kingdom made the experience increasingly more frustrating. "James, I am experiencing being in two places at the same time. I see myself inside the Kingdom with other people yet I cannot understand or comprehend what is being said and I cannot seem to get the attention of any of the heavenly creatures that I have encountered."

"You have come to the point in your education that requires you to make some adjustments in your life style in order to experience the next level of the Kingdom."

"What adjustments?"

"To begin with, if you want to attain the next level inside the Kingdom, you have to abstain from any sexual activity for a period of not less than nine days."

Agrippa was not happy with that but asked James to go on.

"You also have to eliminate as much of your own personal desires as possible."

"What?"

"The act of desire in material things grounds you in this realm. The more you desire to dominate things and people, the less likely you will be able to rise to a higher level in the Kingdom."

"Is there anything else?" hoping the answer would be no.

"Yes, you have to embrace the concept of unconditional love."

Agrippa was beside himself. He recognized James had intentionally not mentioned any of these conditions to give those retched Christians time to escape and allow his new addiction to gain a stronger hold over him.

The King said, "The traits you want me to forfeit are ones I have coveted for a lifetime. I am the King of this land. No mystic will ever tell me to be otherwise. Guards! Guards! Take this man away. When you have a better solution for me to interact within the Kingdom, I will let you go, until then I will keep you as my guest in the Fortress."

The court and many of the Jews in Jerusalem thought James had some mystical hold over Agrippa and openly cheered when James was imprisoned. James was completely resigned to his situation and willingly went into his cell. Agrippa continued his duties as King and began to get away from his routine of visiting "the Kingdom" until one day when no one was in the throne room; the King performed the ritual himself.

He had abstained from sex for 11 days, offered up a sacrifice to God for Him to help rule Agrippa's realm and went so far as to pray that he be given the ability to love unconditionally. Agrippa made the journey to the Kingdom on his own. Agrippa was spiritually imprinted with the mysterious force. Upon his return from the Kingdom, Agrippa was consumed with the foreboding knowledge that the Jesus movement would be very detrimental to him and all Jews. Agrippa summoned his entire court to appear before him. He declared that they and all future Jewish generations be involved in an unbreakable alliance, against the "Believing Jews" or "True Believers."

Agrippa said; "Despite every attempt in showing our people that this Jesus was a charlatan, his followers grow in number and in strength. Therefore, we must stand together to defend our religion and way of life."

Passover was approaching and in a frenzied display of emotion and arrogance, he beheaded James. After that, Agrippa was unable to recreate his experience. He lost his ability to visit the Kingdom.

Agrippa became more obsessive than ever to master "the mysterious force." The absence of going to the Kingdom took its toll on Agrippa. The King could not get "The Light" aspect of the practice back. He finally had Mary Magdalene summoned to his court. He did this during the festival of the Emperor in the city of Caesarea. The night before the festival, Mary Magdalene was brought to Agrippa. He told her he must return to the Kingdom. Mary said to him that because he abused his power by killing James, all the work he had done was lost but he could work himself back and God would forgive him.

He was enraged at the idea of starting over again and that God could command him to do anything. Mary begrudgingly granted him his wish to go to the Kingdom. Agrippa called in his tailors and had a royal suit of clothes made with silver and golden threads. He experienced the Kingdom under forced circumstances. He went into the light. Agrippa later appeared to the crowd at the festival in the morning sunlight. His voice sounded godly and not of this world. After his speech, Agrippa settled back into the earthly plane where he, immediately, became grief stricken.

He died five days later. His son, Agrippa II only 17, was so scared of the mysterious force, he quickly arranged for Mary, Philip, Martha and Lazarus to have safe passage to Southern Gaul.

Chapter 21 - The Mission

When word of Mary's journey reached Gaza, many of her followers made pilgrimages to Gaul in support. Samuel and Jonah accompanied the sisters, who had become very involved with the True Believers. They had dedicated their lives to spreading the gospel of the Kingdom. The two men had hoped to marry these women but it was not to be. Samuel became the scribe to Mary Magdalene. His job was to write down her wisdom and bind it for the ages.

Mary was the most knowledgeable of all the Apostles in these mysteries. The levels or "mansions" in the Kingdom allowed for many degrees of attainment. When she left Judea, only a few adepts were capable of achieving inter-activity between the Kingdom and their incarnate bodies. What James had prophesied to Samuel came true as he and many of the most knowledgeable believers were martyred. Extinction had indeed become the gospel of the Kingdom's worst enemy.

By the time Mary started teaching in Gaul, there were many "churches" preaching different aspects of the Word of Jesus but Mary concentrated on teaching the True Believer process to the masses. The higher level adepts provided more intense training to those capable of traversing the carnal plane of existence. Lazarus and Philip worked with the intermediate students. Anyone seeking power on Earth would stop at nothing to destroy this knowledge. Mary also traveled extensively throughout Europe and the Mesopotamia region. Her mission was to enlighten as many people as possible using the path taken by the True Believers.

Mary had Samuel organize and divide the mysteries and meditative steps into a full discourse on the spiritual preparedness needed to experience the Kingdom. Samuel separated what he termed The Meditation Manuscripts into five books. Each manuscript contained different aspects and points of view using meditative practices that outlined both positive and negative outcomes. She also had him show correspondences that referred to elements of the Old Testament. Jesus' mystical teachings connected to all aspects of Jewish tradition.

At Mary's direction, Samuel picked families that were best suited to protect the information until a time when it all could be reassembled for the betterment of human kind. The vision moved hundreds of years into the future with its culmination focusing on the Universal or Catholic notion of emphasizing the resurrection as its primary focus. There was no role for women. This teaching proclaimed a follower needed to have the scriptures interpreted and the only people qualified for such duties were priests.

Ian's vision dissipated. He then realized he was connected to this story, not just as an observer but something more.

.

.

Part 5

Chapter 22 - Sasha

Ian continued his introspection; examining every pattern and practice to determine where he had made mistakes. In an effort to get a fresh perspective, he went back to Georgetown where his adult life began. He also thought the trip would provide a distraction from his loneliness in New York. He had just seen his four daughters for the weekend so it would be days before he would see them again.

Ian hadn't been on campus in over 15 years. He walked into Healy, climbed the three flights of stairs to Riggs Library and found the doors, locked. Looking through the glass, the library looked more beautiful than ever. He went to the administration office where he was given the keys to the library for a closer look. The stacks were in perfect order except for one book that had fallen on the floor. It was a yearbook open to a picture of Ian in his car, dog-eared with one sentence written, "You have made it through yet another level" signed with a beautifully scripted "R."

Ian was beside himself. *If I get another chance with Raven, I will not screw it up.* He placed the book back on the shelf, turned off the lights and returned the key. *The magic is still there.* On the way back to his hotel, the

message in the yearbook consumed him. *What was so special about the library*

for Raven? He had to find out more.

Ian finished a great dinner at the 1789 restaurant and attempted to

walk it off by going back on campus. He first walked around the quad and

went into the chapel where his first born daughter was baptized. Sitting

in the last pew, he remembered a dream about Raven being in Rock Creek

Park cemetery located at the upper end of Georgetown. He instinctively

headed toward that spot. The day had been warm but the night was dark

and cold. Ian wore a long blue polo coat, collar up and a white silk scarf

tied around his neck. He walked around the cemetery for about 30 minutes

wondering why he had thought of such a crazy idea when he saw someone

he hadn't seen in years.

Ian yelled "Rosco, is that you?" Rosco turned around, looking the

same as Ian remembered years earlier. Ian considered him a good friend

when he was living in Georgetown during his last residency.

"It has been a long time." Ian said

"It sure has, fool, you don't call or come down here ever and now

I see you walking around a cemetery in the middle of the night." As he

laughed "By the way, I haven't figured out whether to thank you or hit you

for fixing me up with my wife but enough about me, how long are you in

town."

"I am here for the next ten days."

"Good, I'll meet you at 7 for dinner tomorrow night at the East India. I'll call "Bammer.""

"Great, I'll see you there."

Ian thought. *We had such great lunches at the Press Club with Sleepy pouring the cocktails and us causing so much trouble with our obnoxious questions to every resource speaker. I have been very bad at keeping in touch with these guys. I deserve all the crap I am going to get from them at dinner.* Ian could see Rosco looking for an explanation as to why he was walking around the cemetery. Ian turned. "I'll explain everything tomorrow night." Ian headed slowly down 31st Street and waited for Rosco to enter his town house before doubling back to walk through the cemetery one last time. He found no one and worse, felt no presence. He was hopeful that maybe after all this time he could get faster results but nothing had changed. *Tomorrow I will go to the Library of Congress to do some research. Maybe something was written about Raven in the D.C. archives.*

Ian worked most of the next day in the LOC occupying the same area where he used to study so many years earlier. He spent the day researching anything that resembled Raven's true name and the Kingdom as it pertained to Jesus and Mary before packing up his notebook and going back to the hotel. He was looking forward to seeing Rosco and Bammer. He dressed for dinner and walked across the street, down the alley and entered the basement of the Guard's restaurant which housed the East India Club. His friends had not yet arrived so he went to the end of the bar where he could see everyone as they came through the door. Ian had not been there five minutes when an old classmate of his came in and sat next to him.

Ian glanced over and said, "Hi Jim, How are you?"

"As I live and breathe, I haven't seen you here in many years, how are you?"

Ian responded, "I'm fine. Do you still get into conspiracy theories?"

"You remember those days; I got a few awards for the JFK thing."

"I remember you would come into Stanley's, get liquored and start talking about debunking the grassy knoll long before it ever became fashionable."

"You protected me! I remember one night when I couldn't walk."

"That was a long time ago. The juniper does crazy things to people."

"I switched to vodka and have been much better off since."

"I bet!"

"What brings you back?"

"I am doing some research on a hobby of mine and it's funny that I would run into you because you may be able to help me."

"What? Do you need any help? Can you pay me?" Jim tried to offer an explanation for his directness by saying other people got rewarded for discrediting the JFK conspiracy theories. "I made a few bucks but never had a pay day."

Ian thought about it. Jim was one of the best "bird dogs" he had ever known.

"Yes, Jim, I do need help and I can pay you something. How much do you need?"

They came to an agreement. Jim was anti-social in college and had gotten worse with age. He sat on the same bar stool every night for years. He never seemed interested in a relationship, had no friends, and barely acknowledged the bartender whom he had known for over 20 years. Ian asked him for breakfast to set up the parameters of the assignment.

Jim said, "Is seven all right?"

Ian said, "Sure!" As the words were spoken, Ian's friends arrived.

Everyone knew each other. The banter started immediately.

"Look who jumped out from under the rocks and with his boulder buddy, "Sneaky Jim." How are you, Jim? Long time, no see" Jim said hello to both of them and left. Ian and Jim shook hands and confirmed breakfast.

Rosco started in. "Bammer, can you believe I caught this guy walking around the cemetery last night, no explanations, no apologies for not calling, nothing, I think the least he can do is buy us dinner."

After they both agreed to bankrupt Ian by ordering Crystal to warm their pallet, they proceeded to the Chateau Lafite Rothschild accompanying the most expensive meals they could find, finally ending with $150.00 per glass port. Ian could have taken both of them to Paris for what dinner was going to cost. The check was presented to Ian. When he opened it up, it came to $3.87. "How did you guys grab this?" as they all were known to be consummate check grabbers. Ian continued, "Neither one of you left my side all night."

"He even forgets who he's with." Rosco said laughingly.

Ian was told that he had to earn his meal by telling them his story. They wanted to know why he was back in town. Ian told bits and pieces and said, "I may have discovered something regarding The Grail Story."

"Oh, come on, you've always been crazy but this?" Bammer commented.

Rosco interrupted, "What about the Grail and what do you think you've found?"

"Eternal Life from Jesus' chalice or Jesus Bloodline in the womb are the rumors du jour but I think there something else!"

"What?" Bammer said

"The continuation of the Jesus bloodline was supposed to be the big secret where the Knights Templar supposedly got rich off blackmailing the Vatican by getting a percentage of the plate for their silence. The Templars said they had proof that Jesus married Mary Magdalene and that they had children together perhaps the reference to their bloodline as the Holy Grail.

Although there might be some truth to the stories, my Grail story was always known to the Catholic Church who has worked very hard to eradicate any trace of it. Peter and Paul knew all about its existence. King Herod Agrippa actually used it and King Philippe Augustus and Pope

Innocent III waged the Fourth Crusade to ethnically cleanse any remnant of it. Philippe got money and the southern provinces of France and the Pope got the license to begin their 800 year extermination campaign." ·

Rosco said, "You are actually getting me sucked into this."

Ian was laughing out loud now telling them he was practicing his "hook" to sell the book as he told them, "You have to buy the book for the rest of the story."

"We want to know now."

"That's why I am down here. I need to research the rest."

"Is that why you were talking to "Jimmy, the worm?""

"Rosco, why are you so hostile towards him? Did he do something to you?"

"Jim has a shady reputation. Whatever you do, watch yourself."

"He will take your ideas and use them for himself. The Pulitzer he got was ripped off from his partner. The thing ended up in a bad lawsuit with his partner getting nothing. Just be careful!"

Ian acknowledged the warning. He would be careful.

The three finished up their evening and as Ian walked back to the hotel. His walking gait reflected the big meal and numerous cocktails in a way that when Ian stood at the curb to cross the street, it could be interpreted as wanting to hail a cab. A taxi driving by stopped with the driver asking Ian if he needed a ride. Ian looked in the back seat. Two absolutely stunning nuns were looking at him to make up his mind. *I bet these two aren't going to The Visitation School. What the hell?* He got in and said,

"Take me to Old Anglers Inn." The driver said he would "drop off the nuns first and then we will head out to Old Anglers."

Ian put his head down as if to sleep. The nuns were talking in the back about their day. They agreed that once they got settled, they would have to report to their superior. Ian anxiously waited to see whether the nuns would be dropped off at 34th and P but no, the driver continued up to Reservoir Road and made a left. Now Ian was intrigued. The cab took the right hand fork on Foxhall and drove no more than two minutes before making another right into a beautifully landscaped estate high enough to have a view of downtown Washington and the Washington Monument. Ian had never known any Catholic residences to be in this section of town. The two paid their share of the fare and the taxi began to turn around. Ian looked at the driver and said, "Please do it very slowly." They both laughed.

Ian told the driver he had reconsidered and wanted to go back to Georgetown. The driver responded, "Sure that's better for me anyway." Ian asked him if he had ever driven to the estate before. The driver said once and then confirmed Ian's suspicion. "You know, the last fare I took here was also a young beautiful nun, I mean really pretty, Mister. What do you think about that?"

The driver said he had driven a cab for 30 years and recalled that the estate had long been vacant until a wealthy businessman bought it and gave it to the Church.

"The story was in all the papers, about 10 years ago." The driver continued, "Then everything died down and no one has talked of it since."

"That's an interesting story; do you remember who the businessman was?"

"No, Mister."

They had arrived at The Guards. Ian paid the driver a handsome tip, walked across the street and went up to bed. The alarm rang at 6:45 AM. Ian got boarding school ready - 1-minute shower, 1-minute shave, and 3-minutes for the coat and tie. Ian entered the breakfast area, which was the formal dinner dining room. Jim was already there drinking a glass of fresh orange juice. Ian asked the waiter for the same. He brought a small pitcher sensing he had another victim of the Irish Flu.

"How did you sleep?" Jim asked.

"I had a good night."

Ian got down to business, "I don't have the money for a blank check investigation, so we have to cap the effort by me paying you "a number of days certain" so no one is disappointed. I want you to find out the following things!" as Ian handed him a list of twenty-five items all connected to what they had just talked about. "You have three months on my feedbag, that's all I can afford. I want you to get me as much information as fast as possible on each topic. If you finish earlier, I'll still pay you for the three months. Do we have a deal?"

Jim looked at the list and smiled. He obviously knew some of the information or where to get it on the list. Jim had some questions on a few of the items. Ian had information on all but two of them. Ian thought finding the answers on the rest would point them in the direction of the two unknowns.

Ian told him about the previous evening's sighting of the nuns, which was exactly where he wanted Jim to start his research. Ian then refreshed Jim about his experiences at Georgetown during his three plus years leaving out particular information concerning Raven and his visions. He focused Jim on the "warrior" priests and the strange relationship Ian suspected the Georgetown Jesuits had with the Vatican. He told Jim he had no evidence, just feelings. Ian knew Jim had Jesuit friends. They finished breakfast and Ian passed five $100 bills across the table. Jim was very appreciative. Saying good-bye Jim would not let go of Ian's hand. Ian finally had to say, "Jim, Jim, you're welcome! Thanks for your help."

"You won't regret it. I'll remember this!"

Ian remembered how short Jim's memory could be and that he could get stabbed in the back if it was worth Jim's while to do so. *At least I can see this one coming unlike so many others.* Ian went back upstairs, retrieved his notebook computer and left for the Library of Congress. Ian needed to know more about other aspects of the mystery, especially those pertaining to the Kingdom Gospel. Everything Ian looked into led him to Gaul, modern day France. The more he read the more Mary Magdalene's name kept appearing.

Many in France thought Mary had three children, two boys, and a girl and that a union with Jesus, the rabbi was well within messianic law. All of these theories seemed to contain elements that could be true and would make an alternate Jesus story all the more plausible. He had to go to Southern France. Ian became momentarily despondent. *How can I ever hope to find out answers to these questions? Jesus living a sexually active life was out of the question for the Catholic Church. Mary was the wrong sex to be a part of the Church's hierarchy. Peter and Paul discredited Mary in particular and women in general. Agrippa and Abiud knew of the mysterious force and had taken steps to eradicate it. Do the Gnostic gospels tell of this force?* Ian's research suggested Agrippa died of it. His son set Mary up in the Heriodian estate in Lyon for a time. Ian thought the only thing that would spark such behavior was pure abject fear.

Ian jotted down his many questions:

Where did Herod Antipas live in Gaul? He was the King that killed John, the Baptist and let Pilate crucify Jesus. Pilate, too, was exiled to Gaul. Did he commit suicide or live out his life in the area? Indeed, many of the people very important to all of the Jesus stories were eventually banished to Gaul. Everything Ian was looking into suggested that if there was an alternate Christian scenario, it would be found in France and he had run into a dead end in Washington.

The day was ending and Ian booked his trip to Nice. He only had a few days to go there and come back in order to be with his daughters. As he walked into his room, he could see his message light blinking. He called the concierge who confirmed that he had three messages and they would be right up. A minute later, an envelope was shoved under the door, *"Old School" hotel service.*

The first message was from Jim, who already had some information on the man who bought the place for the nuns and his background. He wanted Ian to call him back. The second was from Ian's sister who just wanted to see how he was doing and the third was from a woman, Sasha Burnes who was referred to him by Bammer saying he thought she might be of some help. Ian called Sasha back first, catching her as she was leaving work for the night.

She said she would be out of town for the next three days but offered to meet him for a drink. She told Ian she worked off K on 18th street. Ian suggested Duke Siberts. She said OK. They met 30 minutes later.

Ian was impressed. She looked like an attractive librarian, her frosted hair pulled back in a bun, glasses and very loose clothing. Her fashion sense down played her appearance. They talked for over an hour about her background and her passion, Freemasonry. She said that the location of the Freemason headquarters in Washington had geographic and mystical implications. Ian, then, asked her "What is your interest in this area of study and how did it even come up with Bammer?"

She said she had helped supply research to him from time to time. Her current day job with a builders association gave her time to freelance. She said that during a charity fundraiser, she and others including Bammer got talking conspiracy theories and wondered about a possible connection between the Freemasons and the Catholic Church.

Sasha continued by telling Ian that they all wondered whether there could be a secret agreement between the two organizations calling for an unofficial cease-fire between them for maximizing their independent effectiveness. Sasha was hooking him and Ian suggested they have dinner to continue their discussion. She liked that idea. They went to a place in Georgetown called "Le Steak." Monique greeted them at the door. Ian said hello, complimented her on her place, and ordered one medium and one medium rare. Sasha shared a legend about Agrippa and Abiud having a strong belief in the mysterious force. They might have conceived of a unified approach in combating or controlling it, which eventually could have evolved into some of the precepts found in Freemasonry. Ian didn't let on that he knew anything about Agrippa and Abiud.

Sasha told Ian the movement spread to the South of France and from there over the rest of the world, moving west. "There are no coincidences in life." She said. "This meeting is not one of them either." As they talked further, Ian noticed Sasha's hair falling down ever so slightly. The bun was losing its tightness. She excused herself and walked through the little hallway off the main dining room where there was a pay phone and two small bathrooms. Ian went up to Monique at the bar and talked about her places in Ft. Lauderdale and New York. Sasha rejoined them at the bar. Her hair was down, the glasses gone, and a belt appeared around a very thin waist that accentuated quite a voluptuous body. She was stunning. They talked for a few more minutes when Ian invited her to his hotel for a nightcap and promised to put her in a cab after just one. They went into the bar but Sasha asked him if she could see his room. She said she had never seen a room there and wanted to know what it looked like. Ian said sure thinking he might steal a kiss.

No sooner had he closed the door than "the librarian" put a lip lock on him that was one of the best he had in recent memory. They spent the next few hours exploring each other and then she said she had to go. Ian really liked this woman. She was smart, good looking and they were interested in many of the same things. They kissed good night as Ian put her into the cab. He paid the driver and went to bed. He was happy and care free when he hit the breakfast room, the next morning. As he sat down to read the Post, Jim came in. Ian thought. *He must be stalking the dining room waiting for another freebie.*

Ian indulged him and thought, *what the hell maybe he has something.* Jim couldn't stop talking. Ian slowed Jim down. "Wait, stop, hold on!" Jim calmed down long enough to tell Ian that he had come across some amazing information about the nuns and the man who used to own the place.

"I found out that this Mr. Paul Bailey is a very rich media mogul. His specialty is print but in recent years, he has started acquiring a number of TV stations and has also invested in the cable business. He is a staunch supporter of a number of community service groups including some church organizations but known in his inner circle of friends as an agnostic if not an outright atheist. The man has lived in France for 20 years and hardly ever comes to the United States. About 12 years ago, he made an unexpected trip to Washington. He bought the estate on Foxhall Rd. During the same trip according to the press reports, he gave it to the Order of Notre Dame. It's a mystery as to why Bailey would do such a thing. The Order of Notre Dame has been difficult to research." Jim continued.

"I thought this nunnery was a part of the Catholic Church so I called the Archdiocese in D.C. to get the telephone number. They told me the only number they had was for a "The Sisters of the Order of Notre Dame" in Cleveland. I talked to the Mother Superior who transferred me to the finance department. The Administrator there had no idea what I was talking about and assured me that if they had something of that value in real estate, he would know. He had more questions for me than I did for him. Finally, he said he would check it out and call me when he got more information. If it is a religious Order, it's not Catholic." As Jim was eating his eggs, Ian asked him if he could look into something else for him.

"Sure, sure what else can I do? I'll work day and night!"

"I want you to see what you can find out about my warrior priests."

"I will get right on it."

"Jim, I have to leave town for a few days. I know I told you that I would be here for a while but my plans have changed. I will call you when I finalize my plans. I also want to thank you for following up. I am sorry I didn't return your call last night."

"That's Ok, I'm used to it."

"Still, please keep after me if I don't respond. I have a lot on my plate and sometimes I let stuff get through the cracks."

They talked a bit about what Jim had been up to for the last 15 years but after hearing an hour of "Me, me, I, I; life has been harsh and I have been such a victim." Ian couldn't take it anymore. "I have to get going!" They split up. Jim said he would call Ian as soon as he got anything concrete. In the elevator, Ian realized he had opened himself up for Jim's constant bugging but perhaps some good would come from it.

After an uneventful day at the library, Ian went to Nathan's. *I never thought I'd be back here single. The place hadn't changed in its women to men ratio.* His mind went to Sasha. *She was great.* Ian had no idea if the relationship would grow into anything but he thought he would play out that hand. He should call her if only to leave a message saying what a nice time he had and that they should do it again.

Ian got up and walked down the street to get her card. He wanted to give the right impression and he didn't want to wait until it was very late even though he knew she was traveling. Ian got in the elevator and got off at the third floor. He could see his room from the elevator and the door was ajar. He walked very quietly up to it and listened, nothing. He pushed on the door. Someone had ransacked it. His stuff was everywhere. The good news was that his notes, wallet, notebook and everything else of value were with him. After fixing the place up, Ian realized that he could have left the door open. He called Sasha's home number and got voice mail. He left his message and asked her to call him sometime. He obsessively triple checked the door and went back to Nathan's. The place was jumping. Everyone was having a good time and Ian recognized some of the customers but couldn't remember their names so he remained quietly on his stool. A short time later, some administrative staff that worked on Capital Hill very smartly dressed came in and sat down beside him at the bar.

They were talking amongst themselves and it looked like they didn't want to be disturbed. At least three guys tried to pick them up, each being denied an audiance with the last being verbally assaulted. Ian laughed as he finished his bar meal. He didn't feel quite so alone sitting there rather than eating in a booth. One of the girls got up to leave and said to her friend in a loud voice that she was going but maybe this gentleman over here pointing to Ian, could buy her a drink. "Are you talking to me?" Ian said in his best De Niro, "Sure, why don't I buy both of you a drink."

The one with her coat on said no she had to go home to her kids and husband. Ian said he understood. She left. Her friend was cute. They talked for a while but no "sparks" so they split up about an hour later. Ian walked over to a place called the Pall Mall. The name changed many times but it was the same bar, inside. The bar's reputation was known to be the only place on M street that the locals didn't frequent and was the type of place that businessmen could pick up women or have "drunk fests" without calling attention to themselves. Ian walked in and saw a guy he knew from his old Georgetown days. "Hey, Sabado, how are you doing?" He turned and said "Son of a bitch, you're still alive? The last time I saw you, you were getting me fired for improving my retirement fund."

Ian said. "That was one very slick move."

Ian flashed back to when Randolph, the bar's owner, asked Ian to find out who was stealing money and how it was being done. If Ian found out, he got free drinks and meals for the rest of the semester. Sabado would wait until happy hour was over and then bring in his own duplicate cash register creating the exact dupes used in all of the rest of the machines. The employees suspected nothing and the only questions occurred when doing the inventory. Ian made sure Sabado wasn't pouring his drink when he asked what the bartender had been doing for the last 15 years.

He thanked Ian for talking the owner out of prosecuting him for grand larceny. "No problem, I thought anyone with your "bolas" deserved to get mercy." Little did Sabado know that Randolph made much more money having his father bank roll the bar than he ever did from its actual operation. After the drink, Ian walked further up the street to "Winston's." Ian's ex brother-in-law used to work there and it held some very funny memories. Once Les went in there with Ian for a drink and her sister's boyfriend was working that night. He fixed her a stinger in a mug and every time she took a sip of her drink, Harry would top it off when she wasn't looking. She walked up 33rd at 2 AM singing in the middle of the street. The best part of the story was when Ian woke up for work the next day, she lay on her back, saying, "Don't talk, don't open the shade and please leave very quietly." Ian laughed all the way to Connecticut Ave. When he returned that night, she was in the same position. Harry was forever on her shit list. Walking to the hotel, Ian thought maybe some roses would be in order for his new friend, Sasha. As Ian walked into the atrium section of the hotel, he started to reconsider thinking that she may not want a relationship and he didn't want to scare her off. By the time Ian stepped into the elevator, he had talked himself out of doing anything. Ian walked into his room and everything was as he left it. "Someone in the hotel or a kid must have been fooling around. Ian checked the closet, his computer and notes were all untouched. He got ready for bed, turned off the light and his mind started up. *Where was Sasha going anyway and why didn't I ask her any questions? Why was a girl like that still available? Bammer knows, I'll find out!* Ian's mind was already working on new scenarios, maybe moving back to D.C. but no chance, remembering his children in Fairchester, he fell asleep. The next morning Ian went to Madeline's for breakfast. After ordering, he went to a table with his wooden block displaying his order number. He picked up a paper at the newsstand. On the front page was a picture of Mr. Paul Bailey who had just made a purchase of a Rembrandt for just over $50,000,000. The painting looked a bit bigger than a post card.

The picture of him was taken in Paris at the auction with the caption saying he was coming to the JFK Center of the Performing Arts to attend a charity function held for the benefit of homeless children. The article went on to say Mr. Bailey had a sincere interest in this particular charity as his parents abandoned him early in life. He had to live in foster homes growing up. One of Madeline's service staff came with his food. Ian didn't get the fork into his eggs before he heard Jim's voice behind him saying, "I am sorry for bothering you every morning but I found out much more about the nuns and Mr. Bailey." Ian gave him the paper and said, "Read this while I eat, we'll talk afterwards." After Ian finished his omelet, Jim started by saying; "In talking with one of my sources who sells Chinese knock offs, Bailey's name came up. My friend said Paul is into young girls and nuns. I asked my Mr. Chow how he knew this. He told me that before he got into knock-offs, he fulfilled the sexual needs of wealthy businessmen when they came into town but it got too much for him. Chow said that there was something very strange regarding the clergy living at the Foxhall estate but he didn't elaborate."

"Did Chow supply Bailey directly or was it through someone else?"

"Bailey's credit card paid for Chow's services. Chow never talked directly to him nor did he say the girls ever talked about him. Chow said that Mr. Bailey was a very bad man and was one of the toughest guys he had ever dealt with even if it was indirectly." Ian asked Jim to find out more.

Jim said he would and shifted the conversation; "Let's go to your warrior priests. There is an interesting connection between Bailey and The Knights of Rhodes. These particular knights have been in the service to many different Pontiffs over hundreds of years and said to have evolved out of the Knights of Malta but there is also speculation that this order has been used as a front for many privateers. Bailey claims to support this order in Washington, D.C. They have access to the Foxhall estate."

"Is there any connection to the Jesuits?"

"Not that I could find but I have only just started. I will find out more about these priests and their connections here in Washington especially since they don't seem affiliated with the University."

"My question is why are they here as much as who they are." Ian said.

Jim continued. "I will be checking on any rumors concerning a rift between the Jesuits at the University and the Vatican and will keep you informed as to what I find out. I have an appointment with an old friend and will get back to you."

Ian was initially concerned as to Jim's commitment when he hired him but no more. *The trick will be keeping the project's true meaning from him until I finish my work.* Ian went back to the hotel and found a better flight leaving at 8 o'clock to DeGaulle connecting to Marseilles for a ridiculously cheap price. After packing his bag, Ian left a message for Jim that he would be gone for about four days and would be back Monday night.

Ian figured that he would have enough time to check out a few things and come back to DC before heading on to New York. Ian flew out of Kennedy that night after grabbing his passport, repacking at home and calling his girls.

Chapter 23 - Southern France

After landing in Marseilles, Ian drove to Montpellier. It was equidistant to all of the places he needed to visit. His first stop was Rennes le Chateau. Many of the Grail theories mention this location. Its name is always used in connection with mystery and was thought to be the hiding place of artifacts proving a special relationship between Mary and Jesus. Ian walked the grounds and then tagged along with an English tour group. Their guide was knowledgeable but conveyed only the most basic of information. He wandered through the ruins in the cemetery where rumor had it that there were two gravesites of significant importance. It was the same cemetery Clovis was working in when Artemus found him.

Ian came upon a snow white haired thin older woman sitting on some broken stones. She was dressed in an elegant jacket and skirt looking at Ian as if she expected him. Ian asked if there was anything he could do for her in his worst French. She replied saying she wanted to go home. He asked her where that was and she said it was about ten kilometers down the road. Ian told her he would be happy to take her. She extended her arm.

Ian helped her into his rental car. Along the way, she admitted she could speak so-so English. Ian said her so-so English was probably a lot better than his French. They talked about why Ian was in France and she asked him if he thought he had a different interpretation of the Grail. He told her that he did but was uncertain as to ever chasing down so many of the leads he had developed. Ian expressed his frustration with even finding any references to his theories let alone actually finding anything in the short time he had before going back to the States. They pulled up to her house. The old woman asked him in. Ian admired its ancient construction. She said her family had been in the area for all most two thousand years and this family home had gone through many of its generations.

She told him about the German occupation and that her family lost their home a number of times but always managed to get it back. She was the last of her line and after her death; there would be no one to take it over. They talked for a while longer when she said, "I think I can help you with your research."

Ian was startled at the suggestion and asked her, "How?"

She said she had information about Mary Magdalene but if Ian was interested in material treasure, he would be very disappointed. Ian said, "The treasure I seek is about the truth not wealth although I could always use some money."

The old woman seemed to have already made a judgment about Ian even before beginning her story. She told him her ancestors came to the region from Gaza. She was a direct descendant of a Samuel Tosh, a respected Jew who was part of a pilgrimage to follow Mary Magdalene. She said her ancestor came with a woman named Ruth, who he loved deeply but was unable to marry her. She was committed to preaching the Gospel of the Kingdom. "Have you ever heard of that?" she asked Ian.

Ian was stammering for her name as he said, "Yes, Mrs.?"

"My name is Ruth Grumman." she said. Yes, its German but that is another story for another time, young man." Ian told her; he was very much aware of the Gospel of the Kingdom and thought it held a key to finding out the real meaning of the Grail.

She sat back in her chair and continued by saying that her family was entrusted with a book that Samuel Tosh had written. "Each generation's job was to make sure the message remained fresh in that day's current language. If the book's leather coverlet or its pages were worn, it was that generation's obligation to repair it. We had to make sure the spiritual recipes were preserved. No one in the family could tell the story, not publicly, until mankind had gotten to a point where the family would not be persecuted for sharing the book's contents." She went on to say the story is fantastic but now she was certain, even though no one would believe it, the time had finally come to where at least the storyteller would not get killed by telling it.

"I want you to know that I feel privileged you would confide in me, Mrs. Grumman." Ian told her everything, his visions, their stories and bewilderment as to his involvement. She listened and then smiled.

"You must be a distant relative somehow. This would explain our immediate and unexplainable close connection in such a short time. I will tell you the rest of what I know. She spent the next two hours explaining how Samuel Tosh came into the region and how he suffered heart-ache for his Ruth. "He did get some consolation in hearing her once say that she really did love him and not to take it personally but she was committed to Mary's message and could not be responsive to his advances. When Samuel turned 33, he decided to take a wife and married a woman from Judea. Her family was of noble birth serving out their lives as Roman exiles. The woman was from the Herod line." Ian thought it must be the same girl who liked Samuel in Antipas's Palace.

Ruth said, "Samuel thought it all very ironic that he ended up with someone of Agrippa's blood. Their first child was a girl. Ruth told Ian that the book reported this child to be one of the most beautiful creatures God ever put on the earth. Samuel adored her. He had five children and all of them were beautiful but his first-born was his favorite."

Ian interrupted, "I had met someone who showed me a vision of Samuel Tosh. Could that have been your ancestor?" Mrs. Grumman continued as if she did not hear him. Ian was polite, listened and made no further interruptions.

"Little Sara, Samuel's first born, went everywhere with her father." Ruth told Ian, "Samuel's first section of the book consisted of interviews with all of the major influences in the region that had any connection with Jesus and John the Baptist. This led him to taking trips to Lyons and Provence.

Samuel interviewed Pilate's family. According to Samuel, they thought Jesus was a threat to the Roman occupation. Pilate's family said his handling of Jesus gave him limited popularity with the people and problems occurred when the body was no longer in Aremethia's tomb. Pilate apparently told the Roman Guard that "If anyone disturbs or tries to take the body of this rabbi, all of you will be tortured and killed." Pilate's family told the story that when the Captain of the guard reported the body's disappearance, a calming effect seemed to come over Pilate. He accepted that either some of Jesus' followers took the body or someone paid off the Centurion to let Jesus down off the cross while he was still alive. Either way, it did not seem to matter to him! Normally, Pilate would have followed through on his threat and killed and tortured all of the soldiers to make an example of them. Instead, he did nothing.

Samuel wrote about Antipas who was very bitter over losing his kingdom to Agrippa. He said he never should have helped his nephew in the first place also blaming his misfortune on John, the Baptist and Herodias. He could not believe that John, the Baptist told him before his execution that Antipas would suffer severe indignities. Antipas was shocked that the movement had grown so large. He recalled how common place it was for "Messiahs" to come to Jerusalem and claim to be the chosen one. Despite the high number of messianic crucifixions, it was Jesus that was remembered and sanctified. After interviewing Antipas, Samuel would spend the rest of his life serving Mary Magdalene. He experienced the same type of calming effect when he was with her as he felt when practicing his Kingdom meditation. She discussed every aspect of the meditation with Samuel who wrote in extreme detail from the most basic preliminary steps to achieving the state of what Mary called "Light and the Calm."

The teaching allowed the true adepts to have one foot on the Earth and the other in heaven." Ruth Grumman continued. "Samuel became a true adept. He could be on the earth but not of it. In fact, if any adept ever became "of the world," he or she would revert back to their normal corporal existence." Mrs. Grumman stopped and inquired if Ian understood all of this information.

Ian said yes but was surprised the practice could be so easily reversed. Ian was curious if the practitioners of the Kingdom Gospel could attain the riches of this world. Mrs. Grumman answered him. "You have tapped into one of the deep secrets of the Grail. The only thing that stops this power from being abused according to my ancestor, Samuel Tosh is that "being of this world" negates the vibration needed to be part of the Kingdom. The two cannot work simultaneously except if the practitioner never allows the desires of this world to enter his or her consciousness. This doesn't mean that the knowledge contained in the manuscript is only used for accessing the Kingdom. This information can be perverted with catastrophic consequences. When you digest the manuscript's contents you will understand."

Mrs. Grumman offered to let Ian read Samuel's manuscript. Her only stipulation was that he could not divulge any of the information until she died. Ian promised her he would do as she asked but couldn't help himself. "How old are you anyway?"

"How old do you think I am?" She asked. Ian could not even begin to tell. She had a look of about sixty. "You look about sixty." She laughed. "Don't worry! If you are a person I can trust, I will go on soon enough." Ian's paranoia started to get the best of him. *How was it that I met this woman so conveniently? How did she size me up so fast to entrust a secret of this magnitude?* They talked for a little while longer. Any other questions Ian had, she referred him to the book. Finally, Ian asked, "Are there any other books or copies other than the original?"

She said, "There are four other manuscripts; each deal with a different aspect of the True Believer process. They can be very dangerous in the wrong hands. The most general information is provided in the one you have. If you work with it diligently, you will have something that humankind can surely use. All right, young man I am old and tired. You may read this book and return it to me, tomorrow. I will then determine what I will do with it after you tell me your thoughts. If I like what you have to say, I will allow you to keep it, as long as you keep your promise." Ian thanked her profusely and went back to his hotel.

He had enough food at Mrs. Grumman's to sustain him for the night. The manuscript was easily 500 pages, written in Aramaic with French sidebars. Much of it, Ian did not understand. He fell asleep around

7 AM. When he awoke in the late morning, he drove back to the old woman's house. He turned onto her gravel road but when he arrived, there was nothing there but rubble where the house stood "just yesterday." Ian could not believe this was happening. He must have made a wrong turn. He drove around for an hour looking for the right road. He went into the little town and asked if anyone knew this woman. Everyone said "No!" Ian looked at the manuscript on the passenger's seat and knew he hadn't dreamt it. Finally, he went to the police station. No one there knew her but the desk officer did say he knew of someone. He suggested Ian find an elderly man who spends most of his day in the city park. The policeman gave Ian directions to the park and told him where he would find the man. Ian found him and introduced himself. The man was highly suspicious and very standoffish until Ian mentioned Mrs. Grumman by name.

He looked at Ian and asked; "Did you say you saw Mrs. Ruth Grumman yesterday?

Ian said, "Yes but I can't find her home."

"Can you drive me to where you say her house was? By the way, my name is Otto Grumman. I am Ruth Grumman's brother-in-law."

Ian said "Sure. It is a pleasure to meet you." They got in the car and ten minutes later, both men were on the street Ian remembered.

"I swear I was in her home yesterday. Where there is a pile of stones and mortar stood a house." The old man gazed out the car window saying, "She finally did it. Ruth said she would do it and I thought she was crazy."

Otto told Ian that during the war, the Nazis were all over this area searching for religious artifacts. "The High Command was convinced there was a secret in the region, valuable beyond comprehension." The old man described how he and his brother, Oscar came to the region as officers in the SS and stayed on after the war. They both married local women. Oscar married Ruth. He told Ian that Ruth Grumman was a direct descendant of a prominent Jewish family dating back to the time of Jesus.

He began his story by saying, "One day many years ago, Ruth and Oscar went for a walk in the same park you found me." Ian nodded his comprehension as the old man continued. "She told Oscar that her time on Earth was finished. Oscar tried to console her but she would not hear of it and continued saying she was going to "the Kingdom" and would not return until she had been instructed to do so. All of us, who knew her, thought she was crazy but it wasn't long after her declaration that Ruth disappeared." Mr. Grumman continued. "I am an old man. I would love to think there is something beyond life on Earth."

After Oscar and my wife died and all my children moved away, I started losing faith. Something happened when I met you, today. I was overwhelmed with a sense of calm that I have not felt for decades. Now I know you are the reason she came back. Describe for me what you did after you parked the car here with Ruth in the passenger seat."

"I opened up the door for Mrs. Grumman and helped her into the thatched roofed house." Ian continued, "The thing that really got me…"

Mr. Grumman interrupted saying, "Stop, stop, let me tell you! You walked directly into the sitting room. A red chair was next to a long divan and hand carved figurines were everywhere. The home itself was spotless. How am I doing?"

Ian looked in amazement and said, "How did you know?"

"My brother loved that home and the way I just described it was the actual way it was over 50 years ago. You walked into a higher vibration, one that transcends time. Ruth always said it was possible. She said that a True Believer adept had the power to bring others with them. You cannot imagine how excited I am to hear all of this. Did she ask you about any of us?"

Ian had to say, "No but she did entice me to come back here and she must have known that I would check her out. She also must have known that somehow I would find you."

"Ruth was considerably older than Oscar. We thought she was well into her fifties when they married."

"When did they get married?"

"In August of 46."

"When did she vanish?"

"April of 1966."

"Am I correct in saying that her age yesterday would be well over 100?" Ian asked.

"Oh yes, why?"

"She didn't look much older than 60, yesterday."

Ian was curious about Mr. Grumman and knew there was much more to this man than what he was letting on. Ian asked, "Tell me about your life."

"I was in advertising until a few years ago. I could never save any money. My pension didn't cover my life style so I continued to work and eventually became involved with the local TV station." Mr. Grumman abruptly finished and asked, "Could you take me to my home now?"

They drove up to a very long driveway. Mr. Grumman asked to be dropped off at its entrance. Ian said good-bye and thanked him for the information. Ian was careful not to tell Mr. Grumman anything about the manuscript and looked under his coat in the back seat to make sure it was still there, which it was. He had to get to Lyons and was running out of time but his curiosity got the better of him. As he made the turn to go back to the hotel, he parked and walked up the driveway toward the main house. One shrub was prettier than the next, all expertly sculptured and together made up one of the most exquisite topiaries he had ever seen. The smell of boxwood was everywhere. The driveway must have been a thousand feet long ending in a cobble-stoned courtyard surrounded by a house no less impressive than any of the finest French country estates.

Why was Mr. Grumman concealing his wealth?

Ian finally got to Lyons and found the small hotel where he had reserved a room. His bathroom was down the hall supporting four other bedrooms. The sanitation in the place left a lot to be desired but it was late and he did not have much of a choice. Ian took the manuscript everywhere. He memorized as much of the French sidebars as he could. *What part does my Raven play in this story?* He knew even if he deciphered the Aramaic in the manuscript, there would be interpretation errors. Many words have alternate meanings with various connotations reflecting subtle variants depending on certain points in history. He would not be able to work on them until he got to a place where each word could be researched. Ian looked at his watch. The time was 8 o'clock at night, early afternoon in D.C. He called Jim leaving a short voice mail telling him he would try to get back in the next few days. The owner of his hotel suggested a restaurant just up the road that served "the best lamb dinner in France. You can walk, Monsieur."

Ian walked into Le Petite Marmite's very formal entryway. He was seated immediately. By the time his entrée had arrived, the place was filling up for the main seating. He noticed a customer demographic very different from what he expected; an understated elegance that rivaled any wealth Ian had ever seen. The watch du jour was not Rolex but Patik Philippe. The men's dress shirts had thin double backed collars making the shirt more elegant and insured a perfect fit. The women wore vibrantly colored silks from the Lake Como region and their shoes were custom lasted making their feet look small and perfectly formed. The most noticeable feature however was their youthful appearance. All of the restaurant's patrons had a glow. Ian couldn't help but wonder if some of the True Believers managed to escape the inquisition and taught their meditation exercises to the people in this region.

Ian left around midnight and called his daughters from his hotel.

He had translated enough of the manuscript to know he had

something extraordinary. The level of esoteric knowledge needed to

understand its true meaning was complex. Ian thought it odd that his own

unique personal experience was figuring into decyphering the manuscript.

The masses would not believe the concepts offered within its pages.

Ian had one objective left on this trip, to see if any Roman or

Herod ancestry had survived in the region. He contacted a man whose

name was given to him by Sasha Burnes the night they met. She told Ian

this man was of Herodian descent and may have information that might

be helpful. Ian drove for hours. The roads were so poor the axles felt

like they were coming through the floor boards. Ian reached the address

and knocked on the door. No answer. He knocked again. No answer. Ian

knocked one more time, this time he heard someone stirring and pounded

on the door. The man finally arrived at the door. Ian introduced himself as

a friend of Sasha Burnes.

The man told Ian he would need a few drinks at the local bar to

loosen his tongue. Ian said, "Sure!" It was 10 AM. *For this story, why not?*

After exchanging pleasantries, the man confirmed he was a descendant

of Herod Antipas. Specifically, Ian wanted to know if Antipas had any

interaction with Mary Magdalene during his exile in France. The man didn't

know the answer to the question but replied; "Did you know Abiud ended

up here after Agrippa died? Abiud had to know if Mary or Lazarus had

put a curse on Agrippa or himself. He was obsessed with the mysterious force. There are legends that suggest Agrippa and Abiud, after being indoctrinated with James and Mary's ideas, helped found the Freemasons, did you know that?"

"So what if that was true?" Ian thought.

Not really gaining any new information, Ian got up to leave when the man lamented he was once very much in love with Sasha. When she wouldn't have him, he turned to the bottle. Ian sat back down to listen. The man said Sasha was a project and that if Ian had any romantic thoughts about her, a word to the wise was to stay away. Ian asked, "Why?" The man said she has the idea she would lose her identity if she got too close to any man. When he started repeating himself, Ian made his excuses and left.

On the drive back to his little hotel, Ian decided to spend the night in Cannes. He would catch the next plane back to Washington in the morning. Once there, Ian went into his room and tried again to get in touch with Jim. Still no answer; he left another message but was vague as to when he would be back but promised to be in touch.

Ian arrived in Cannes and went to the Carlton Hotel. The bellman took his car and bag and told Ian they would check him in but his room was not yet ready. The hotel had a seaside beach patio overlooking the Mediterranean decorated with colorful shade umbrellas. Ian asked for a grapefruit cocktail, a combination of freshly squeezed red grapefruit juice, vodka and a splash of cointreau. The topless women sunbathers added the perfect garnish to an already perfect setting. After finishing his drink, Ian walked across the promenade and checked in. His room overlooked the concourse and the beach. He changed and went for a walk.

The streets were small and very quaint. Many of the local artists sold their watercolors in the street around the hotel's entrance. Ian bought postage stamp watercolors, one for each of his girls, and walked farther into the antique shop section of the city. The furniture was some of the finest he had ever seen. In looking through one of the windows, he saw expertly crafted Louis XVI period pieces. After going inside, Ian asked a few questions about the furniture. The dealer was very knowledgeable.

Ian said he was learning about two periods in France, 50 AD, and the time around 1200. The dealer looked at Ian and said, "You must be a student of Mary Magdalene. Ian responded "precisely!" The dealer introduced himself as Jacque Le Fleur and quickly told Ian what he knew about Mary and her followers. Ian was amazed at the information the man possessed. Jacque said he was closing the shop and offered to buy Ian a drink. They went to a little bistro a few blocks away from Ian's hotel. Everyone in the place knew Jacque.

He introduced Ian as a good American as opposed to the ugly type and told them that they should treat him well. Ian thanked him for the good reference as Ian hoped to get back one day for a real vacation. They sat at a corner table away from the crowd. Jacque told Ian that when he was young; there were rumors that a priest had found a great treasure at Rennes le Chateau around the turn of the century. He said his family knew Béranger Saunière, a strange but very shrewd man. The priest apparently found a number of artifacts, gems and most important of all, a cache of documents concerning the fourth crusade and more specifically about Pope Innocent III's obsession with the elimination of the Cathars.

According to Jacque, the priest had succeeded in convincing certain people in the Vatican that he had found evidence so damaging that the Church should pay him "hush" money to keep it hidden. Jacque said that although there was not a lot of money paid for his silence, the Priest managed to live quite nicely for a time. When Saunière asked for more, the Church refused. By that time the Church was successful in retrieving whatever it was the priest was using for his extortion. Apparently, when Saunière was denied the money, he started selling church favors and kept the money for himself. The Church removed Saunière from the priesthood only to later mysteriously reinstate him. There was no explanation given but the speculation was that the Church did not want any disparaging remarks to be made by this man so they would allow him to make a modest living in return for his allegiance.

Le Fleur said that the priest left all of his worldly possessions to his housekeeper, who vowed she would reveal everything on her deathbed. She died before revealing anything. He told Ian that when he was a little boy; his parents would take him into the mountains of the Languedoc region for vacation.

Jacque pulled out a rock from his pants pocket that shimmered as if it had its own light source. He said it was an example of special rocks found in that area and told Ian about local legends regarding their formation resulting from rituals performed by Mary and her followers. The story was these rites changed the rocks into what the locals called "Kingdom" rock. Ian looked at the rock and it did exhibit a strange small glow. He asked Jacque if it was perhaps radioactive. He said, "No, I had it tested many years ago. The rock is indigenous to the region but some, not all have unexplained properties." He then took Ian's hand and said, "Watch this!" He rubbed the rock all over Ian's hand. The glow transferred to Ian's hand and then went back into the rock. Ian was fascinated. Jacque said that during his holidays, he would explore the area and follow many of the trails that were long since abandoned by the many hikers that came to the area. He turned to Ian and said; "It was some of the most boring times I have ever spent except for one day.

"After years of hiking, I found a cavern in the mountains well off the tourist routes. I went inside and returned with some stones. That cave is where I found this stone and others like it."

"Is it still there?" Ian asked.

"Yes but now it is heavily patrolled by the Pope's Swiss Guard."

"How can they keep this a secret without someone knowing?

"The property is owned by the Church, dating back to 1200 AD. Jacque leaned toward Ian and quietly said, "I have a form of very aggressive cancer and have been told I have very little time left. I have not met anyone until now that shares any interest in this aspect of history which currently is nothing more than a fairy tale. Someone with a passion for fully researching these spiritual tidbits needs to tell the real story about

Mary Magdalene and all the people connected with it. You must promise to follow through with exposing this intrigue."

Jacque gave Ian the location to the cave and said, "The last piece of information I have was obtained from the housekeeper, my great grandmother's sister. She said that the most important place in the church was the old kitchen in the Saunière's Church's rectory. I was never able to get back up there and could never tell anyone about it. Now, you know everything I know. You must see if you can find out what happened there. I am living on borrowed time and don't expect to see another season but if you find out anything, please contact me as I would love to know something before I die."

Ian assured him that he would do everything possible to achieve what Jacque asked of him. They exchanged numbers and shook hands. These revelations were getting more unbelievable by the hour. "There are no coincidences" was reeling in Ian's head. Ian walked back to his hotel, got room service, and went to bed. The next morning, he flew to Paris and from there to Dulles.

Chapter 24 - A Farm called Rome

Ian arrived in the early afternoon and went directly to his favorite Georgetown hotel. He was still reeling from all that happened in France. After checking in, he walked the few blocks to Jim's place. The front door was slightly opened so Ian called in to Jim as he entered the tiny townhouse. The place had really been tossed. Blood spatter was on the floor. *What happened here?* Ian made a wild guess and called Georgetown University Hospital. He got Quinn on the phone who told him that Jim had been there for a couple of days and checked out just that morning. Ian surmised that Jim never came back to his house after the disturbance and whoever messed it up didn't come back either but when Ian walked out onto Jim's street, he saw two men sitting in a black SUV, a surveillance team of some sort just looking at him.

Unfortunately, Jim has plenty of enemies. Any number of things could have happened to him that have nothing to do with me.

Ian went back to the hotel and called information for Tony's number, an old friend and neighbor of Jim's. He got it and then called.

"Hey Tony, it is Ian MacAlester. How are you?"

"I recognize that voice. OK, I guess, how are you?"

"I'm good but having a bit of trouble tracking down Jim, do you know where he is?"

"No, but the cops were here the other day looking for him."

"The cops?"

"Yeah, apparently he was working on something that offended somebody to the point that some guys visited old Jim and beat him up but that was all the information I could get out of them."

"What did they want from you?" Ian asked.

"They wanted background information."

"Did my name come up?"

"No, should it have?"

"I was talking to Jim about working for me." Ian told Tony.

"The cops were very interested in his University days and his contacts there."

Tony and Ian talked for a while. He hung up and then Ian thought to call Jim's sister who lived in Alexandria. Jim answered the phone, "You really do have my number, don't you?"

"Yes! What happened?"

"Where do I begin? The short version is that I have not been home since you left. I came home to find it trashed and then two guys came in and started punching me. They asked me all sorts of questions as to what I was doing and who I worked for. I must have passed out because

I woke up in the hospital. After being discharged, I came straight to my sister's place. The problem is I don't know what I found that could have somebody so upset or who called 911 to take me to the hospital."

Ian said, "Maybe together, we can figure it out. Let's meet at that coffee shop on King Street or do you want me to pick you up?"

"No, I'll meet you there. I'm OK."

They sat in a booth. Jim ordered breakfast for dinner while Ian just had coffee. He was excited to tell Ian about his discoveries and the possible connections to the University. Ian asked him how he could track down any information while being in the hospital. Jim told him the nurses were very helpful. He said he had more female contact there then he had in the past five years. "All in all, a few punches had been well worth it." Ian asked what Jim did after they met the morning Ian left town. Jim told him that he followed the nuns all day around the City and then followed them back to the Foxhall estate. He looked in the windows and saw some very interesting things.

"The women are housed in billets on the grounds and are intensely trained in many different skills. I held my camera up to the windows and took some pictures but they are still being developed. The common denominator for all of the nuns is their beauty. They are just gorgeous."

"So you think it's all a cover? Maybe that's the reason somebody beat you up? Someone must have seen you."

"If that is the connection, you're right. It is obvious that somebody doesn't want me talking about what I found."

Ian said, "You know the cops are involved!"

"No I didn't. How do you know?"

"Because I talked to Tony to find out what happened to you and he said the cops had been talking to your neighbors asking about you."

"I stopped telling Tony anything a long time ago. He stiffed me on a few deals and we haven't had the same relationship since. I suppose he left that part out, didn't he?"

"Yes, but why didn't the cops come to see you at the hospital?"

Then, Ian started thinking aloud. "Maybe they weren't cops."

"You may be on to something. I'm staying here for a while."

"Can they find you here?"

"I don't think so and I can still follow up on some things but I will have to be more careful."

"Don't get hurt over this, we can find another way."

"No, I am really close to something big here. I can feel it! I need this for my career and self esteem." Jim said passionately.

"Take care of yourself, call me when you have anything, better yet, call me even if you don't, I want to know you're OK." Ian said.

Jim finished his food and Ian went back to Georgetown. Jim gave Ian the ticket to pick up the film. "Maybe the pictures will show us something?"

Ian parked the rental car in the hotel's circle and asked the valets if they would leave it out, he would be back in a few minutes. After making more phone calls, Ian drove to the Spring Valley drug store where Jim took the film to be developed.

Ian presented the ticket and the clerk gave him a very thick packet of prints. The pictures showed "the nuns" with their habits off. Each woman had beautiful hair and a face to match. The next series of shots showed "the nuns" learning martial arts followed by the women being taught some sort of computer skills. These pictures confirmed what Jim had said. Ian looked through them again. One of the pictures showed an older man in a hall doorway. He looked familiar. Ian remembered where he had seen that man; he was the White House's Chief of Staff. Ian called Jim. They met again in Alexandria. When Jim looked at the shots, he didn't remember seeing anyone but now understood why there could be a problem. He told Ian that he was setting up a meeting with some people that could tell him more about the women and their training center. Ian went back to his hotel and tried to piece together all of the last week's events.

What about Sasha? Ian called her. Sasha's assistant answered and said she was out of the office at a meeting. Ian left a message. Ian decided to lay down on the bed. He closed his eyes and started to meditate trying to regain "The Light and Calm." The daily exercises rarely yielded vision results but the practice improved his awareness. The bed was so comfortable. Ian was resigned to falling asleep. When he started meditating, he relaxed everything in his body. Ian visualized looking straight ahead into the gray scale of his eye lids and saw the light out of the corner of his mind's eye. Normally again, at this point, Ian would lose the light and a rush of fear would occur resulting in yet another failed attempt. He would start over again but not this time. Ian was in the light.

He repeated to himself "stay calm, get more relaxed." Ian, then, transcended. He found himself in the Kingdom's square. Raven, sitting on the fountain's retaining wall, thought to him.

"Hello! I felt certain you would have to incarnate again to reach the Kingdom by yourself. I am glad to see I was wrong. You must have worked very hard."

"I have worked very hard for many years not just to get back to the Kingdom but to see you. A day hasn't gone by that I haven't thought about you."

Playfully Raven thinks, "You exaggerate. Remember, I can check your thoughts."

"Ok, maybe every other day." Ian laughingly thought.

She was more beautiful to him than ever. She radiated! As she tuned into Ian, her muscles tensed and relaxed around her mouth, nose and eyes ever so slightly to create an ever-changing facial sculpture which gave Ian a kaleidoscope of her beauty. This vision was something Ian would cherish for the rest of his existence.

"You do know that I have made up a name for you since we have never been formally introduced?"

"Yes, I know you call me Raven which pleases me. My real name is Sara."

Ian didn't know why but thought "Tosh."

She looked comforted in him knowing her name.

"I have just returned from France and was told about a Sara Tosh and given the manuscript kept by your descendant, Ruth Grumman. I know you are attracted to me romantically. Your energy must be thousands of years old. I couldn't bring myself to imagine that possibility but I knew it. I have so many questions. Where do I begin?"

Raven put on a very serious expression. "I have also waited for you a very long time but you have work to complete and relationship karma to correct. You must work the exercises found in the manuscript. The visions showed you the history; you must use them to piece together the truth."

"I understand." Ian said as his vision dissipated.

Everything was very complicated. Ian thought that finally his Raven was back in his life.

Just as Ian fell asleep. The phone rang. It was Jim. He said they had to meet right now. He sounded scared. Ian said, "I will see you in 45 minutes on King Street."

Jim was in the same booth and he looked awful.

"What's wrong with you? Are you OK?" Ian asked.

Jim motioned to a car parked across and down the street. "Those guys have been staking out my car. It's only a matter of time until they get me." Ian thought about it and decided to get Jim out of there. Once they were in his rental car Ian started driving toward his hotel. "Where else can you go?"

Jim said he had friends in Easton and others in Annapolis. Ian asked, "When was the last time you spoke to either of them?" Jim said, "The guys in Easton, just last week but the people in Annapolis, it has been years." Ian gave him three hundred dollars and told him not to call, just show up in Annapolis. "Stay there for a few days. Now tell me what you found out!"

"The nuns are connected to the estate but not to the Catholic Church. The military priests are also somehow connected to the estate. Certain people, both here and abroad, sense weakness in the Church's ability to maintain control over its parishioners. They want to accelerate its possible collapse by publicizing more sexual perversions by its priests and expose a cover up led by the Pope, letting the media do most of the work. The Vatican is doing everything it can to institute damage control but the Church can do nothing but react and deal with the onslaught of even more lawsuits."

Ian switched the subject. He told Jim that if they were successful in piecing together this puzzle, they could stop the harassment. They arrived at Ian's hotel. Ian gave Jim the rental car keys. "Hopefully before I go back to New York, we will have a plan." Ian went to his room to check his messages. No one called. Sasha had not called back either which was disappointing.

Ian decided to call one of his old Jesuit professors, Father Samuels and asked him out for dinner.

The priest was startled to hear from Ian and said people inquired about him just a few days earlier.

"Those very people are the reason why I would like to see you."

"All right, why don't we meet at "the Tombs" at 12:30 tomorrow for lunch, instead?" Father Samuels suggested.

Ian agreed and hung up the phone. The phone immediately rang. It was Sasha.

"Hi stranger, How was your trip?"

"Good; I have a lot to report. When can I see you?"

"How about dinner?" She said.

"Great, when and where?"

Why don't you come over to my place?

"OK, tell me exactly where you live?"

"I live on the Pennsylvania Avenue circle in Foggy Bottom, the white faced apartment building across from the Hospital."

"Great, what time?"

"Can you be here in lets say an hour?"

"Sure, I'll see you then."

Ian hung up the phone and decided to get a nice bottle of wine. As he walked past his hotel coming back from the liquor store, Ian saw the same guys that were staking out Jim's car now parked in front of his hotel. Ian walked past them and headed down Pennsylvania Avenue.

He made it to the circle 20 minutes early. Ian arrived at Sasha's building in time to see more goons coming out of her apartment house. Ian was confused. *Was she in on this thing, maybe she is a government spy?* Ian sat on a bench next to the emergency room entrance to collect his thoughts and observe. The goon squad left but another car came in behind it and parked. The driver was on his cell phone as they parked around the corner out of sight. Four men were in the vehicle. Ian stayed on the bench and then an idea hit him. He called Sasha.

"Hi, I'm sorry but I have to change our plans and wondered if we could do it tomorrow night instead?"

She said, "Sure, tomorrow night would be fine. Call me in the morning and we will set it up."

"Great, sorry for the inconvenience, I will explain everything when I see you." Ian clicked off the phone and continued to watch from the bench.

No more than ten minutes passed when he saw the driver get a call. They drove off heading in the direction of Ian's hotel.

Damn, she's in on this. He had managed to keep a few things back from her but it was only a matter of time until she figured it out. *In any event, either way, I know she is involved in bringing me down.*

Ian crossed the street and then waited in front of Sasha's outside apartment door with his brown bags providing a good excuse for someone to let him in. A couple arrived with their keys. He held the door after they inserted their key. They all went in together and entered the elevator.

The couple pushed two and Ian pushed three on the control pad. Ian went to apartment 3C and rang the bell. Sasha opened the door dressed in a nightgown. Ian barged in and said, " I thought it would be all right for me to visit now since your friends have left." She didn't know what to say. Ian gave her an "I know everything" look and she fell apart. She began to sob and Ian thought, *she is a good actress, too.* Sasha told him she had been coerced into helping them. Ian patiently listened as he opened the wine. He poured both of them a glass and then asked her who "they" are and what do "they" know. She said, "They are government people and they know everything you told me. They know about Jim. They know you are meeting the priest for lunch tomorrow."

She didn't have to tell me that but maybe she said it just to get me thinking she is only a pawn and telling me all she knows. Ian asked her why they came to her in the first place.

She told him that her first job in Washington was working as a historical researcher for Department of Justice and her spiritual hobby interested some people who now work in the White House. Sasha confided in Ian that she also spent time at the Foxhall estate.

Ian thought she was lying. Her story was too pat. He played along, trying to hide his disappointment. Ian finished his glass of wine, abruptly got up and gave her an excuse that he had to get back to his hotel. He said he was very disappointed. He told her the truth that he had developed feelings for her and had hoped things would have worked out better between them. He knew she would counter with the "we can make it happen" stuff and that she felt the same way, and let's try again" crap. Ian tried to look encouraged and played the part as best he could, knowing she would be on the phone the instant he left.

He called off his lunch with Father Samuels and realized he had to get in touch with Jim to tell him he found out the identity of their mole. Ian went to the rental car desk inside the Ritz and got a car. He drove out Rt. 50 to Pussers in Annapolis. He found Jim at the bar.

"How do you do it?"

Ian said; "You are such a creature of habit. Once I figured out who your friend was, I knew where to find both of you. Ian looked behind the bar and said, "Hi Allison, long time, no see."

She said, "You are a piece of work, I haven't seen you in 16 years but who's counting and you look the same." She was being kind. At one time, they had a thing going. Ian remembered Allison was best friends with Jim's sister.

She said looking at Ian, "I will leave you two alone but don't leave before saying good bye."

Ian said, "OK, thanks."

Jim apologized for not calling.

Ian said, "That would have compromised us, both" and then Ian told him the story. Jim seemed confused about why White House officials were involved.

"I am developing a theory. Let's go back a couple of hundred years. John Carroll and his brother, Daniel were Jesuit trained and true

Catholics. Daniel Carroll gave up his farm to help make up the land needed for the District of Columbia. Who owned the land before Daniel? The title records show it was owned by a man named Pope who apparently called the farm, "Rome." Could there be a Vatican link?

Historical documents show Daniel Carroll and Ben Franklin were good friends and both were Freemasons. The Carroll's, Daniel and John were fiercely loyal to the new United States of America. Could there have been a pact between the founding fathers and the Vatican that exchanged the land needed for the country's new Capital and probably some money for quiet direct access to the new fledgling U.S. Government. The two Catholic brothers could have acted as power brokers to cement the deal which included using Georgetown as the main training center for high ranking bureaucrats to run the Government for the past two hundred plus years.

Look Jim, the message is in plain sight in the University's seal; written on the scroll "From Both Sides - Utraque (Church and Secular State) into Unum (One)." John Carroll only trusted the Society of Jesus as the Catholic representative. In 1805 after their Suppression ended and the Jesuits partially returned back into the Catholic fold, John Carroll gave the College over to them with the understanding by certain members of the Continental Congress that the Jesuit School, Georgetown would be the platform for the newly formed Government to operate various programs under everyone's' noses. Let's look at our alumni. Sure, there are high profile graduates that have run the CIA, State Department and even a President but look at the incredible number of alumni that run the bureaucratic part of government year after year who are not subject to the vagaries of election. This all operates under the radar screen. Jim, how come the University is the only institution in the world allowed to use the same seal as the official seal of the United States of America?"

Jim's eyes got as big as saucers. He didn't know what to say.

Ian continued. "Suppose the Georgetown Jesuits are indeed those responsible to shepherd this relationship but they start to have problems with the Vatican. They know, literally, where all the bodies are buried. Suppose these Jesuits started flexing their muscles with the Vatican.

If there is a covert connection between the Catholic Church and the U.S. Government, who would stand to lose the most if a scandal regarding the Church was revealed. The number of teaching Jesuits at the school has declined severely since the 1970's which is just after their rumored rift. Did the Vatican step in and tell the School to take on more lay teachers in favor of Jesuits so they could have more direct access to the Government, themselves or did the Jesuits decide to further complicate the relationship by reducing the Catholic influence?"

Jim was reeling with questions.

Ian told Jim they had to cover themselves against reprisals from those Government officials in the picture and the Church, if they were involved in any way.

Chapter 25 - Hide and Seek

Ian looked at Jim. "We need help! Who can we call to do some leg work for us?" Jim said he knew a Jesuit that might be interested, a Professor Martin who taught him sociology.

"Jim, he may not want to get involved with this thing." Ian said trying to be considerate. Jim wouldn't hear it. "He is perfect. In my junior year, I had dinner with the man. He is quite bizarre, brilliant and totally obsessed with the Catholic Church. He always said there were unresolved issues stemming back to the time of Peter. His frustration was never being able to prove any of his theories. This curiosity became an obsession and any free time he had was spent studying the Church's early history. If we could point him in the right direction and Martin thought he could prove something, he would help us in a heart beat."

Ian knew he was running out of time from another perspective. He was sure his adversaries would find out about his children and hold them over his head once they realized Ian was not going back to the hotel. "Whatever we're going to do, we must act fast and in a way to protect me and my children." Ian said. They called Father Martin and set up a meeting with him at New South Cafeteria at 2 PM.

Ian had a friend who he knew from Georgetown named Barbara Wilson. Her University mentor once served as the Vatican representative. Ian called her and after ten minutes of small talk got around to asking for a favor. She agreed to make the call and tell her mentor about a small alumni gathering later on in the day and asked if he would mind meeting some of the attendees. After her call, Barbara called Ian back telling him the plan was a go and that she would show up later to make sure everything went smoothly. The meeting was set at 5:00 PM in the student union.

Jim and Ian arrived at New South, got a cup of coffee and waited for Father Martin. He showed up wearing a black beret, tilted perfectly on his head and a freshly snuffed out cigar hanging out of his mouth. Father Martin got immediately down to business. Jim explained the keen interest some people in the Government and the Church had in their project and the possible exposure of a long time mutual relationship. Father Martin understood that time was of the essence and he promised to get back to them with any information he could confirm. As they waited for their next appointment with Father Bart, Ian thought of another connection that he had over looked. He called one of the most powerful law firms in Washington. He had done quite a bit of business with Mr. Lockhart, the managing partner over the years. The lawyer specialized in arranging meetings. The deal was the lawyer had to know exactly "the who" and "the why" someone wanted a meeting. He would then determine the value and charge accordingly. Ian gave Mr. Lockhart a complete briefing. The seasoned lawyer told Ian he would arrange it and get back to him regarding the time and location and of course, the cost.

It was time to meet Father Bart who was anticipating an alumni gathering in the hotel but instead was escorted by Jim and Ian to the Taco Bell in the student union. He was not amused at being duped into this meeting but was willing to carry a message if it were worthy of his time. Jim gave him a very detailed explanation of what they had uncovered. They told him he was their choice to first see the University administration and then to contact the proper authorities in Rome. Father Bart repeated the information and then asked a series of questions making sure he understood exactly what was being asked of him. Barbara came into the student union minutes after Ian left to smooth over the deception. Jim talked his way past her questions while Father Bart gawked at Barbara. After exchanging a few pleasantries, Jim saw an opportunity to leave and took it. If they were right, the Catholic hierarchy would get back to them with some type of confirmation of their story. If not, their bluff had failed.

Jim walked out of the University's front gate, meeting Ian at the "O" street bus stop. The two drove back to Annapolis to begin their wait. They stopped at the Annapolis public market for chowder and something to drink before walking up the road to the Inn.

One of the bartenders knew Jim from the old days and came up to him with a cordless phone telling him it was Allison with a message from

Jim's sister that a Father Martin had called and needs to get in touch right away. Jim called Martin who had the information they requested. He also had a bit more which was unbelievable since he had only been on the case for a few hours. Jim told Father Martin he would be by to pick it up. Jim and Ian did not finish their next drink before Allison called again to tell Jim that a Father Bart called to say that he had transmitted the information and would call him back no later than Friday. Ian was thinking that timetable was cutting it close. He had to go back to New York but Jim could probably handle it. They finished hearing the band's set and went to bed.

The next morning, Jim and Ian were back on campus picking up the file. Father Martin had found out a lot of information and confirmed that Bailey never actually gave the property to anyone. All the right innuendos were made but he still owned the estate. The second thing Martin reported was that he could not find any evidence of a Vatican sponsored military or Swiss Guard posted at the estate. Any appearances of a legitimate Church sponsored rectory were a hoax.

Ian picked up his voice mail messages and one of them was from his dealmaker lawyer. The meeting had been arranged and the bill would be paid by the government. Ian suspected a double cross but determined he didn't have much of a choice but to go through with this meeting. Jim went to the copy shop and duplicated all of the material. Lockhart had arranged for Ian to meet the White House Liaison to the Vatican at the Hay Adams lounge. Ian was hoping this person would have no idea of what was going on. As he watched the man coming toward him, Ian realized his guest was the White House Council.

He said that he had heard a lot about Ian and his friend and was certain they could come to some arrangement; "otherwise you two are going to have a very unpleasant end." Ian didn't flinch and gave him the copies of what he had gathered.

The elderly statesman tried to bluff and threaten, at which point Ian looked him in the eye and said: "Don't go there. You can trust your soul to the fact that the originals are sitting in a safe place waiting for the time I don't check in. I want a call from you telling me that your people have totally backed off. If you don't, Mr. New York Times will be putting your handsome face on the front page. Do you understand me?"

"What do we get in return?"

"You get the opportunity to be blackmailed like so many before you and like it."

"What do you want?"

"You will be told in time. What I want now is you and your associates off our case."

"I will get back to you." He got up and walked out. The waiter returned with the two drinks that were ordered and asked about Ian's friend. Ian said his guest had an urgent need for Imodium AD and would not be back but to please leave his drink.

Ian knew he couldn't go back to his hotel to pack. He wouldn't hear from the White House or Father Bart for some time and wondered if both parties were talking to each other, confirming the data that he and Jim had passed on. Jim drove Ian to the shuttle as Ian had a disturbing thought. *Maybe they are going to strong arm me in front of the children.* Ian had Jim call to introduce himself to their new friend at the White House and to say that if Ian saw anyone in New York, the deal was off. Apparently, that is exactly what was to go down but Jim's message got through.

Ian lived in a rented condominium. The kids loved to play hide and go seek in the large underground garage. Ian was always "It." The games lasted for hours so anyone trying to get in touch with him was guaranteed to get frustrated. By the time Ian got back to his condo after taking the girls home to their mother, he had a number of messages, one of them was from Jim saying, "The call we expected has come in and we need to meet."

Ian arrived at Reagan the next morning. Jim was waiting in the lounge. "What time did you get here?"

"About four hours ago. I didn't have any place else to go."

"The Government guys want a meeting to discuss terms and conditions."

Ian was not expecting that response: "who do we call?" Jim produced a number.

Ian dialed the number and the voice on the other end said, "Meet us at the St. Regis in 45 minutes?"

"Fine!" Ian asked Jim to be available across the street at Trader Vic's. The world-class bar at the St. Regis was beautifully wood paneled accented with tooled leather, everywhere. The Secret Service arrived in force. The White House men walked into the bar from the lobby. They sat down and were very direct. "You produce the originals or you will suffer a very bad accident resulting in your death and the rape and torture of your daughters." They got up and left. No talk; No discussion. Ian waited for the deadline to pass, went to the hotel pay phone, and called the Times. He asked for the sports editor. He got Lindsey and asked him to place a call. Ian was put on hold while Lindsey made the call using the number Ian had given him. He got the man at the White House and relayed the message and then reconnected with Ian telling him he had done exactly what Ian had asked.

Ian thanked him and said, "Someday I will tell you all about this."

Lindsey responded, "All I know is that you owe me big. I want five on the front side." Ian agreed and hung up. Then he went over to Trader Vic's, ordered a few Mai Tai's and then told Jim what had happened. "We called it."

The next thing they knew, ten huge Secret Service agents were standing all around them, which they also expected when the White House Counsel walked through the door alone.

"You weren't bluffing."

Ian said."My demands have changed. I want you to resign your position at the White House but stay on to finish this." The pompous ass was horrified. He didn't expect Ian would get so personal. Mr. White House Counsel swallowed hard and asked what else. Ian told him he wanted a letter stating their innocence in this whole affair and signed by him and witnessed by someone extremely credible.

"You can deliver it off to me at my hotel."

"What else?"

Ian said; "Nothing now, I will let you know in time."

The White House Council and his entourage left.

Jim then asked Ian what his friend at the Times said. Ian told him to say. "I have a picture of the White House Chief of Staff in what looks like a house mingling with beautiful nuns, talking with their martial arts trainers, and holding what looks like a cocktail with a very big smile on his face. Would you like me to start asking questions?"

Ian said to Jim, "If they didn't have anything to hide that move would have toasted us. Obviously there is some sort of a cover up."

Looking at Jim, Ian asked; "Have you found out anything more on the estate?"

"No. I am expecting to receive some information soon."

"Does the New York Times really have the pictures?"

"No, I couldn't stop their reporters if they did but my friend Lindsey can always say he was fishing for a story after he got a hot tip if he was ever called on it but I don't think the Chief of Staff wants to stir the pot, do you?"

Ian was back in his favorite hotel checking in when the realization of what they were doing hit him. The possibility of the Church reacting violently was now more probable than the White House. Ian was apprehensive as to the next wave of threats that would be coming their way.

If they could only get the information they needed. Ian turned off the phone and went to sleep. Jim and Ian agreed earlier to use defunct landmarks to establish meeting places.

Ian received a message from Jim to go to the CT Club. The CT Club had been turned into a gym years earlier. Ian got dressed and left. George was a Midwesterner who went to the University of Chicago and established a career in commercial real estate. Jim owed George money and apparently thought he could get George off his back by having Ian offer a form of barter arrangement to expunge the debt. Ian upon introducing himself to George asked if he knew Paul Bailey. George said that he had helped acquire certain properties for Mr. Bailey in the past. Ian told him that along with Jim, they were working on an expose about Mr. Bailey and that if they could tie him to a specific prostitution ring, the two would have a great story to sell the tabloids. George stiffened up and said his business was real estate and he didn't see how he could possibly help.

"Didn't you sell the Foxhall estate to him?"

"Yes, but I have had no further contact with the man."

Ian then pulled a picture from his jacket pocket and handed it to George. "Then could you tell me how you ended up in this picture with one of the nuns from the estate?"

"I don't know?"

"How would you like to explain that "I don't know" to your wife?"

"My memory is suddenly coming back."

George was like a school boy confessing his sins. He told Ian he was the advance man for Mr. Bailey in D.C. and that part of his pay was taken in trade.

"What does Bailey have to do with the Church?"

"I don't know?"

"Do you want to play this game again or are you going to tell me what I need to know?"

"Bailey has direct access to the Pope."

"Thank you! What does he have to do with the White House?"

"Nothing, I don't know of anything he does with the White House."

Ian showed him the picture of the Chief of Staff and said; "one more bad answer and I am going to call your wife. You will have the likes of Rauol Felder up your ass forever. Tell me everything you know."

"OK, OK, Bailey does under cover covert black operations work for the Vatican but has his own agenda to exacerbate the Church's sexual abuse problems which in all likelihood will give Bailey direct control of much of their real estate property worldwide, selling it off to pay settlements. I was going to get rich in the process. Are you satisfied, now?"

"Not quite! I will forget we ever had this meeting if you tell me one more item. Why are there White House Officials involved?"

"Some of these Officials want to offer defecting disillusioned parishioners an opportunity to join their secular way of life, a "plate substitute" if you will."

Ian couldn't help but to laugh as he asked; "How do you know that?"

"Because I was in the room when the plan was discussed and that is why everything must remain quiet."

"We never had this conversation. Oh George, what did Jim say to get you here?"

"He told me he had a solution for paying me and it could be worth a lot more money to me than what he owes."

"Well, don't you think he was right?" Ian asked.

George rolled his eyes as he went up the stairs. He did not look back.

Ian then called Jim. "We got the smoking gun. George knew the whole deal and told me everything."

"What did he say?"

"Do you remember the rendering plant? I'll meet you there."

Ian drove to K Street, got out at the parking lot across from Chadwick's and walked down and across the street toward Key Bridge. The plant had long since been converted into office space.

Jim was waiting.

"Ok, what's the news?"

"The news is that we are screwed. George told me what we didn't know, which is why the government guys were after us. Ian filled Jim in on his conversation with George.

"I also found out that our Mr. Bailey is ready to double cross the Church but until he does it, he can make us out to be the bad guys. We were very lucky to get Father Bart to go to bat for us because if we let the information slide without informing the Church, they might think we are the ones trying to discredit them."

Jim looked at Ian and said, "I don't know how to say this but it turns out Father Bart works for Bailey. I just got that information while I was waiting for you. Where do we go from here?"

This was not good news. Ian asked, "Who told you that? How do you know that? Maybe you're wrong?" "No, I was told that by Father Martin and shown a picture of Father Bart and Mr. Paul Bailey at the closing years ago when the estate was purchased. We are now going to need the same type of helpful material on the Church as we developed on the Government."

Chapter 26 - Duct Tape

Bailey knew everything. Father Bart told him the entire conversation. Jim heard through the grapevine that the Foxhall Estate henchmen that worked for Bailey were looking for them and that Ian and Jim would be portrayed as wayward Catholics caught up in a sinful sex fraud to discredit the Church. Ian asked Jim to be in touch, gave him some more cash saying, "Call me at the hotel, tomorrow."

Ian decided to go to Sasha's apartment. He got the super to let him in and made himself at home. He gazed out from her picture window at GW's emergency room entrance thinking this was the same angle used in covering President Reagan's assignation attempt. Sasha walked into her apartment to find her TV on and none of her lights working. The scene unnerved her, but nothing like the smurf ball that Ian inserted into her mouth followed by duct tape covering her mouth and hands and finally a nice gentle shove onto the couch with a tape finale applied to her ankles.

"It's nice to see you too, honey. I thought I would keep you company since you ratted me and my friends out, the least I could do was to be available to find out their next move. Double cross appears to be the order of the day, no "nun" intended. You knew Bailey all along and played both sides against the other with me in the middle so I had some Photoshop work done in putting together a little album of you two. Wait until the Chief of Staff gets the album of you sitting two places down from Bailey at the estate during a charity function. I got that one from the Post. The next shot is where you are dancing with Mr. Bailey, at the last inaugural ball. Everyone has that one too but the next five shots which I got off your computer earlier are far more interesting. The first is you in a nun's habit outside the Foxhall estate. The second is you sitting at a computer at the estate and then there is my handy work of you and Mr. Bailey spooning with follow ups of his nibs performing a little "coochdivus" and of course, your reciprocation. How do you like it so far? I would hate you to think it was just my derriere exposed.

I know your boss will ask you a lot of embarrassing questions especially after he sees your pretty face associated with a nun prostitution ring on the front page of one of the tabloid rags. Mr. Bailey will also continue to hold you in his highest confidence until he also sees the pictures. Finally, your bathroom privileges have been suspended until further notice, so that wonderful Moiré silk fabric on your sofa may require some stain remover. Sasha struggled to talk. Ian paid no attention to her. She was obviously frightened. Ian turned up the TV loud enough for her to get discouraged in making noise. The phone rang. The first message left was from an unknown man who said he would call back.

Ian finished watching an entertainment gossip show when the second call came in which was from Bailey, himself. To say that his voice shocked Ian was an understatement. He said he loved the get together they had two nights earlier and was making sure she got the flowers he sent. After he hung up, Ian couldn't help himself. "You really are quite the "Mata Hari" aren't you? That little coquette routine really has some legs. Have you spread them for everyone inside the loop or just the guys who have offices at the estate?"

Sasha tried to speak again but the smurf ball was totally water logged and even her tone was muffled. Ian put a crazed look in his eye, one that was way over the top. She calmed down. Ian, then, turned on the local news. The segment lasted about 10 minutes, after which a third call came in and second message from Mr. Unknown asking, "Where the hell are you, it's urgent you call me."

Ian thought this guy sounded crazed enough to come over. Ian had something very special planned for him so he did a little rearranging. Ian moved Sasha into the second bedroom and turned off the TV. He didn't want to disturb her smurf gag so he sound spliced her outgoing phone message greeting to say, "I will be __ as soon as I can."

The message was garbled enough where, Mr. Unknown would think she was in the bathroom and would be out in a minute. Ian turned on a hot shower to set the mood with steam; the vanity mirror light provided soft ambiance and the door was set slightly ajar to provide an invitation. He knew any red-blooded man would sneak a peak, and when he did, Ian would be there. Sure enough, a short time later, a skinny man walked from the elevator into the hall and rang her doorbell.

When she didn't come, he fumbled for his key. As soon as he put the key into the door, Ian hit the play button. "Skinny" entered the apartment and moved closer to the bathroom door to see if he could catch a glimpse of Sasha's naked figure. Ian was ready to "smurf ball" him but the man was trained. He had Ian on the floor in seconds and was about to beat him senseless when his jacket sleeve caught the edge of the wall sconce. The stuck sleeve hung him up long enough for Ian to duct tape his free hand and foot together. Ian, then, moved to tape up the other hand still caught. The man was beginning to yell at Ian when the smurf ball was inserted instantly producing "a calf caught in a hog tie event" look. Ian instinctively developed nervous laughter knowing full well that "Skinny's" eye language was threatening him within an inch of his life.

Ian turned him over and tidied up the job. When he was finished, Ian was out of duct tape but Mr. "Skinny" wasn't going anywhere for quite sometime. Ian took out the man's wallet and discovered him to be a lobbyist for a produce growers association. Ian then found a number of different ID cards. Ian didn't know what to make of it but decided to let everyone calm down a bit before attempting to find out more.

Ian was unsure of how to proceed since any discussion would allow Skinny's mouth to function, which Ian wasn't willing to risk, so he made the best out of the information found in the man's wallet. The beautifully made leather billfold had a few credit cards, business cards, and

300

a driver's license and then there were his own business cards. On the back of one of his cards was a name and number Ian recognized, Jim's. Ian hoped it was because the man was tracking him.

In the man's jacket pocket was his cell phone. Ian looked at the speed dial menu and sure enough, Jim's number was on it. That explained a few things. Ian was glad he hadn't shared everything. Where did the lies begin and where did they end? Ian then called Jim's sister and left a message that he had been shot and was in GW's emergency room.

By looking out of Sasha's window Ian could see who showed up at the ER and maybe find out who Jim was really working for. Bailey's muscle men showed up at the ER entrance 15 minutes later. While waiting outside, the driver used his cell phone. Skinny's cell began to ring. Ian ran into the bathroom and turned the water back on; the combination of the interior walls and water made a perfect static sound. Ian answered the phone. The man in front of the ER said, "MacAlester is nowhere to be found, instructions?"

Ian responded by saying, "go back, I'll call you later." The man clicked off his phone. Ian knew at a minimum he had one of Bailey's lieutenants duct taped in the next room.

This was beginning to make sense except that Ian's concocted romance between Sasha and Bailey turned out to be real with Jim being their inside man. *Why had they gone to the trouble of including me unless they were setting me up to be the fall guy all along? I would be the perfect patsy.* Ian had inadvertently upped the ante by getting his "Times" friend involved.

Ian camped out on the sofa and fell asleep until about five AM. His two guests were asleep and making quite a mess of their own. Ian went into Sasha's study, made his calls and left for his hotel. He walked into his room at about 6:30 AM. Everything was quiet. It would liven up shortly so Ian ordered breakfast and waited. As the room service waiter prepared his table, Ian turned on the TV to the local news when it started. The first video clip was of the "Foxhall" estate and the reporters waking up its women inhabitants with questions.

The police raided the place because someone had called in claiming that the Catholic Church was sponsoring a house of prostitution for monetary and political gain. Then a breaking news story involving the same estate featured a freelance reporter apparently uncovering a scandalous sexual connection between Mr. Paul Bailey, who allegedly gave the estate to The Church and Ms. Sasha Burnes, who, at one time, was reportedly a nun staying at the estate. The police were quoted as looking for the freelance reporter and if anyone knew of Mr. Jim Moriarty's whereabouts to please give them a call. Ian looked outside into the courtyard to see the two men stationed there drive away.

After the initial reports, there were TV updates every ten minutes on breaking news. Ian called his friend at the Enquirer to check if his tabloid person had found the open door to Sasha's apartment. He said yes and they were preparing the story for the front page. The guy Ian hogged tied was Bailey's first in command, who had a long-standing relationship in one of the Church's most honored military orders and had connections with some of the most important Vatican officials. The man had a wife of 17 years and three children. The pictures found in Sasha's apartment incriminated him of having an affair with Sasha simultaneously while Mr. Bailey was also having an affair with her. Sasha had already copped the victim bit and was willing to tell all for the right price, which would include Bailey's double cross of the Church and his elaborate preparations to extort and defraud the Church out of millions of dollars.

Chapter 27 - The Ratio

†††

Ian sat in his overstuffed chair in Fairchester looking through his sliding glass doors at the Chinese pavilion that edged Long Island Sound. He heard the small waves falling on shore as he took out his notes *These are instructions found in the Meditation Manuscripts that I bet would mirror the gospel according to Jesus.* Ian remembered researching the reference to this gospel as the one stolen from the University of Cairo in 1998. The story said it was never recovered and when Ian went back to research it again all references were no longer on the Internet. Ian organized this ancient information to make the case for a very different spiritual message, one that would give very different meanings behind these writings. His telephone rang. It was The D.C. Metropolitan Police. They found Ian's name on Debra Laurie's calendar and wanted Ian to come down to talk about Debra Laurie and her death. Ian hung up and redialed his phone connecting him to his favorite Georgetown hotel. The operator answered and Ian asked for the concierge.

"Concierge, how can I be of service?"

"Good evening Carl!"

"Good Evening Mr. MacAlester, Are you calling about the package?"

"Yes and to ask you to prepare my room for tomorrow night, do you have any information on who sent it?

"The package was picked up at "the Crypt" in Copley Hall on Georgetown's main campus. One of the students escorted the messenger into the chapel. He was told to take the plain white envelope found in the last row of chairs. The bill was paid in cash and there was no other information that I could find out, sir."

"Thank you Carl! I will see to it you find a little "joy" in your mail box."

"Thank you, I'll see you tomorrow, Good Night, sir!"

"Good Night!"

Ian felt validated that the Crypt figured into this mystery. The puzzle was getting more intricate and yet coming full circle.

The leather workmanship on both manuscripts was hand crafted by Samuel Tosh. It was amazing to see their mint condition for artifacts so old. Who was the keeper of this second manuscript? The second manuscript had ominous overtones where the first did not. He realized that indeed the same meditation methodology could be perverted, resulting in something far different from experiencing the beauty of the Kingdom. It also conveyed more information about Agrippa. Specifically referencing Agrippa's use of his own mystical knowledge in combination with what he learned from James and Mary to create what has been referred to in Freemasonry as the mysterious force. Agrippa's death did not intrigue Ian as much as the suggestion that he was transformed in some manner, existing in a different realm. Ian's thoughts went back to Tyson's lab and the ominous warning later delivered by Raven. The manuscript mentioned that there were secrets within secrets, a similar meaning found in the Bible.

Many of the spiritual milestones applied to Samuel Tosh, Agrippa and to Ian. They shared a common experience of simultaneously being of two natures connecting in the Kingdom; one, inside the Kingdom, part of the divine experience while the other remained outside and apart, in a void.

The next morning he drove to Washington and checked into his hotel and immediately headed for Georgetown's campus. Ian tagged along with some smart keyed Copley resident students. He entered Copley. The question of who was monitoring him filled Ian's mind. He sat down in the same seat he had once occupied when following his old roommate. The Chapel had been spruced up but with its low arched ceiling, it was still very much true to its name. Ian walked to the altar to find the secret lever to open the trap door. Once again, he had to stop searching when some students and their parents came in. Ian went outside, facing the science building when he thought he saw a man that looked like Father Cortez. Ian began walking fast to catch up to him but before he could even yell to the priest, the man was gone. *Is it even possible he's alive? Could the second manuscript be from Cortez? How could he know anything about this? We parted ways so long ago.*

Ian thought it was unlikely Father Cortez would have kept up with him after graduation but he could not imagine anyone else. He went into the alumni association headquarters to see if Cortez was still affiliated with the University. The alumni house was closed so he went to the Jesuit activities desk. The Jesuit staffing the desk was new but said he would look into Father Cortez's whereabouts.

Ian didn't want to wait for the information so instead went to Lauinger Library where he was directed to the Jesuit section. While looking for a current Jesuit roster, Ian found a book referencing the Jesuit teaching method called The Ratio Studiorum. The "Ratio" was a special method used to train individuals in spiritual development. The student was asked to determine why he or she was created. The process joined moral, spiritual and intellectual disciplines that shaped the student's skills and habits of thinking. At the core of the "Ratio's" teaching was the "eloguentia perfeca;" which was devoted to exercising the student into thinking critically. Drill him or her in speaking forcibly to all types of audiences and finally, train the student to write convincingly. Was there a connection between this Jesuit teaching method and some of the same tenants found in the Meditation Manuscripts? As he walked back to his hotel, Ian promised himself he would find Father Cortez and perhaps some answers to these questions.

Chapter 28 - Segovia

††

The sun was shining on a beautiful spring morning in Segovia, Spain. The City was crowded with visitors going to Alcazar Castle. A commotion was going on in one of the alleys just below the Castle. A large man was waving his hands yelling as he chased a young boy, "Hey, you, kid? Where did you get that bread? Come back here before I slit your throat." The young boy always out maneuvered this particular merchant who had far too often experienced this specific humiliation. The merchant stopped and said to all that would listen "Look how generous I am! Even if I catch him, I will not prosecute this boy."

Xavier Aloysius Cortez waited under the lace lady's table until it was safe for him to come out. His great aunt sat at its head. He knew she would never tell any of the family how he got the bread for them twice a week. He dusted himself off and walked down one alley across another and up to his home. He and his family lived close to the Catholic Cathedral. Xavier's parents, Juan and Celina Cortez could trace their origins back to Roman times. Juan's family had been devout Catholics in a primarily Protestant area.

The Jesuits had established schools hundreds of years earlier but none of Juan's family had any formal education. Celina's family, on the other hand, had extensive training in reading and writing. Her father's brother broke with their Protestant tradition and became a Jesuit.

Many said that Celina's grandmother had special psychic gifts and that she helped the rest of the family with her visions. Zyta Rodriguez was a very quiet woman. She was old and detached from almost everyone. The only person she let into her world was Xavier. She had a special spot for him in her heart. Many thought she favored him because he had contracted polio when he was four. His condition was not severe but it left him with a noticeable limp except when he was running.

The disease somehow seemed to have given him extra leg strength when he used his muscles for running but in a normal walk, his affliction was all too apparent. Zyta knew Xavier was going to have to learn to cope with much more than a mild case of Polio and she had to help him as best she could. During one family gathering, Zyta motioned for the boy to come closer to her chair while asking Juan to get his grandmother-in-law a drink.

"Listen to me, boy, I have wisdom to share with you and only you."

"What is it great grandmamma?" Xavier asked.

"You feel called to the priesthood? You have said so yourself."

"Yes, that is true."

"Yet you love to steal and make all sorts of mischief, isn't that also true."

"Yes!"

"What I am about to tell you, Xavier is very important and concerns a family duty. For two thousand years our family has kept a book containing God's wisdom. I did not give it to the last two generations in our family because I felt that none of them were worthy. I blame the book for making me live so long. I will wait for you to mature. I want you to take over for me. Do you understand?"

"No, great grandmamma, I don't."

"Your directness is one of the many reasons I have chosen you. The Jesuits must educate you, first. Go to your friends now and we will speak of this, later. Tell no one what I have told you, swear to me."

"I swear that I will tell no one of your secret, great grandmamma."

The spring turned into summer and one night as his family prepared for bed, Xavier was outside looking at the stars when a man rode up on the most beautiful black horse he had ever seen. The Jesuit had come to collect Xavier to begin his schooling. The priest was made comfortable for the night and the next morning, Xavier went with him to the island of Majorca where he would spend the next seventeen years under the most stringent learning regimen imaginable. During this time, the only visitor that regularly came to see him other than his mother and father was his great grandmamma. She spent years telling Xavier snippets of what the manuscript contained and how it interfaced with the Church of Rome and how it did not.

On her last visit she said, "Trust no one with this information." as she gave him the manuscript "and be vigilant in your maintenance of the manuscript. I am dying and will not make it back here again. I love you and hope that all will work out for you according to God's plan." They spent a few more hours together and that was the last time Xavier ever saw her.

He received many punishments from the Jesuits resulting from his bad temper. Xavier had fits of rage that made him lose all rationality. His fits were completely unmanageable. All who instructed him were fearful of his "moments". Xavier could also experience elements of joy. When this happened, his body shook with pure ecstasy. These moments often occurred when he was in deep prayer.

He remembered Zyta telling him the reason their family was entrusted with the book in the first place was their gift of intense emotionality. She said, "The last two generations suppressed their feelings and therefore didn't have the experience." She kept saying he will understand someday when he learns the meaning of the manuscript. Xavier had no idea what she was talking about most of the time. He humored her as much as he could, shaking his head "yes" in understanding while passive aggressively thinking of other things.

His academic passion of Physics in Spain was significantly behind that found in the United States. Xavier asked to be transferred to

Princeton University where he hoped to be taught and collaborate with the best minds in the field. He had developed many of his own theories about the structure and behavior of atomic particles and was very anxious to be in a community that would understand and critique his ideas. On a personal basis, Xavier would experience rage as he matured and quarantine himself when he felt it coming on. He would have liked the companionship of a wife and missed the experience of being married to a woman, but when he had his episodes, he was glad not to be with anyone.

His fellow priests admired him for his intellect but the idea of Xavier advancing in the Jesuit hierarchy was out of the question due his behavior problems. He was a true credit to the Society of Jesus in every other way. The transfer came through and Xavier found himself on a ship heading for New York. He was thirty years old when he first stepped onto Princeton's campus. The students were not accustomed to seeing a man of his age let alone a priest attending daily classes.

During the years with the Jesuits, Xavier's teaching included self-defense training the other students had not seen before. His hazing had a lot more to do with him being Catholic than being Spanish. During his first few months at Princeton, he had managed to keep his emotional torrents in check, but he knew there would be a day of reckoning if he did not get more proactive in tempering his behavior. Packed under his clothes in his steam ship trunk lay the old manuscript his great grandmother constantly referred too. During his years in Majorca after his great grandmother passed on, he never opened it. He was convinced the manuscript was just a fantasy of an old woman. Perhaps there could be some information about his ancestors but probably innocuous in nature. Also due to his extreme workload, he rationalized he didn't have the time for curiosity seeking.

In many ways, the day he opened the manuscript in Princeton was the first time he really ever looked at it. He turned to a page somewhere in the first third of the book just to see what was in it. In the left hand margin of the page was very neat writing that began a long side bar note with a sentence written in Spanish,

"Alfonso was overcome by rage to a point of being afraid." This information amazed Xavier. He scanned additional pages of the manuscript and realized that his ancestors truly experienced his same condition. It also discussed their feelings of joy.

The manuscript referenced that by using the family's affliction in concert with the meditation techniques described in the manuscript, some family members found a way to experience the Kingdom of God in visions. Xavier was very skeptical concerning many of the manuscripts statements, enough so that he put it back under his clothing.

Xavier worked tirelessly on his quantum theories. As the first semester came up to the Christmas vacation, Xavier longed to go back to Segovia to visit his parents but he received a letter from his parents that they and his two siblings were coming to New York City for the Holiday.

The reunion was held at the Waldorf Astoria Hotel.

"Ma Ma, you look so good." Xavier said as he smothered her with hugs and kisses. Juan was overjoyed to see his son and could not get over the size and grandeur of New York City.

"Xavier, it is so wonderful to see you."

"How was your trip, Father?"

"The trip was very nice, we had interior rooms on the ship but it was fine. We were very well treated and there were men from the U.S. government watching over us. They said that the war required them to be on many civilian ships. Xavier, I do not know that I believe them. They spent too much time with us and seemed to pay little attention to the other passengers but enough about our trip, tell me about you."

"Well, Father, I am working on a major project for the University and learning the essentials of atomic theory. This is what I have yearned for ever since I realized my passion for Physics." Xavier continued, "I am happy to be here in the United States and being so well treated. I, too, think someone else is behind our good fortune."

"Come Xavier; let's not look a gift horse in the mouth and go down to the beautiful lobby." The entire family took a tour of the City. After spending a few days with his family, Xavier went back to Princeton.

The same government men from the ship contacted Juan at his hotel. They asked him to come to Washington as their guest. They wanted to discuss an important matter with him. When he arrived in Union Station, they greeted him and escorted him to the State Department. Once Juan was made comfortable, he was met by Jose de la Campa, the senior official on the Cortez case. Jose attended Madrid University and welcomed Juan in perfect Castilian Spanish. He offered Juan coffee and something to eat.

"Mr. De la Campa, why have you asked me here?"

"You do get to the point quickly, Mr. Cortez. What I am about to tell you could come as somewhat of a surprise. Your son has become very important to our national defense effort. He is one of only a hand full of men that understand the nuclear makeup of enriched uranium. His work with advanced mathematics allows him to be part of a team that is working on a project so secret we have quietly limited access to the group. Since your son and your family are Spanish Nationals, we want to extend an invitation for your entire family to become U.S. citizens. We would help you relocate here in the States and establish you in or near a Spanish community in either New York or Philadelphia. We respect your customs and wanted to be formal in our approach befitting the head of the Cortez family. Xavier has no idea that we have been involved with overseeing his safety since he arrived. I know I have given you quite a bit to think about."

"And if I decide to decline?"

"You and your family will be given enough time to say good bye to Xavier and we will send you back to Mr. Franco, who as we speak, is murdering more civilians as he promotes his fascist regime. De La Campa regained his composure and said, "I am sorry for that out burst, Mr. Cortez. Many of my friends have been imprisoned or killed."

"What about the rest of my family? My wife's mother is still alive What about her?"

Jose did his level best to hide the fact that he might have a bite.

"Mr. Cortez, let me check into that. Could you excuse me for a moment?" Jose went down the hall and turned into the smoking lounge which was filled with big leather chairs and standing cigar/cigarette ashtrays. Jose sat down, lit up a cigar, and spent the next 15 minutes smoking it before returning to Juan with the great news. "We can accommodate your request, if you so chose."

Juan sat back and thought for a minute replaying all of the atrocities he had seen Franco perpetrate on the Spanish people including on his own family and friends. "Thank You, Mr. De La Campa for your kind invitation. I will need to talk this over with Xavier's mother. When can I get back to you?"

"Monday would be fine. If you come to a decision earlier, please do not hesitate to call."

"Before I leave, can you tell me more about the areas our countrymen have settled in and what kind of work we can find here?"

Jose looked at Juan and said; "Why don't we discuss all of this over a late lunch and then I will put you back on the train to New York. They went to the Brass Rail and then Juan was put back on the train.

Juan looked out the window at the beautiful countryside and thought "how could there even be a choice, all of Europe was in war. Franco was running the country into the ground. Spain was in the worst economic shape of any European country with not much hope for any future."

††

"Absolutely not, Juan, I don't want to talk about it anymore," Celina whimpered.

"Darling, this is an opportunity of a lifetime and our wonderful son is making it possible. Why wouldn't you want to stay here? After all, isn't this the land of opportunity?"

Juan, I have a secret to tell you that no one outside our family has ever spoken about and it weights heavily on my heart. Celina shared with Juan her family involvement with the ancient manuscript. Juan asked, "Does Xavier or the others know about this manuscript?" Celina answered truthfully that she did not know. Juan said he would discuss these things with Xavier and then call Washington. Juan then called Xavier and asked to meet with him.

Juan and Xavier sat just at the perimeter of Peacock Alley in the Waldorf's lobby.

"Xavier, I have just returned from Washington. Were you aware of this?"

"No, Father, what did you do there?"

"You are worth a great deal to the U.S. war effort and they are the ones taking such good care of us. They asked if your mother and I along with the rest of our family would like to start a new life here in the United States."

"Is this something that you and Mama would like to do?"

"That is the reason I wanted to meet with you. I was told today of a sacred book, a manuscript, your mother's family has been responsible for since shortly after the time of Christ. Your mother is afraid that this book is still back in Spain and she is worried sick about it."

"Why would she think the manuscript would be at the house?"

"Because she thinks that her grand mother willed it to her at death but neglected to tell her where it was before she died."

"Father, I have the manuscript. Great Grand Mama willed it to me. I have a letter from her confirming that fact. Mama does not have to worry about it. The manuscript is my responsibility now." Juan conferred with Celina. She was ecstatic at this news; they made their decision to stay and went out to dinner to celebrate.

‡‡

"Xavier?"

"Yes, Mama."

"What is in the book? I have been told about it my entire life?"

"The manuscript is a record of travelers that came from Jerusalem and about our family having intense emotional energy."

"That's it?"

"That's pretty much it!"

"Why was grand mother so secretive about its contents?"

"I think she didn't want you or any of the other children to worry about what seems to be a family affliction."

"Xavier, you wouldn't be hiding anything from your old mama, would you?"

"No, Mama, This book is of no concern, really. It speaks of our family's intense emotional make up and things that don't make much sense to me."

Celina looked down at her tea realizing her son was not telling her everything but she also knew he would take good care of the family treasure. She decided not to pursue it and was content with the idea that she did not have any unfinished business back in Spain. Xavier went back to work at Princeton but realized he had not checked in with his superiors since he arrived in the States and knew he was overdue in talking to someone. He asked the administrative secretary, "Could you please place a call to Loyola University in Chicago Illinois?"

"Hello, Loyola University, can I help you?"

"Yes, can you please connect me with Father Alberto De Mateo?"

"Whom shall I say is calling?"

"Xavier Cortez."

"Are you a priest or is this a lay matter?"

"I am a Jesuit."

"Thank you! Please hold!" the receptionist said.

Xavier found himself waiting for at least ten minutes when the receptionist returned saying; "Father, I am so sorry to make you wait but Father Alberto can not be found anywhere which is strange because I didn't see him leave today. Shall I have him return your call?"

"Yes, please have him contact me at Princeton University."

He went back into the laboratory and sometime later that day, Xavier received a call from Loyola University.

The secretary asked, "Father Xavier, where would you like to take this call?"

"Please put it into Mr. Oppenheimer's office, Gladys. Thank You!"

"Hello!" Xavier said.

"Is this Xavier Cortez?"

"Yes, who is this speaking?"

"This is Father Joseph Sullivan. I have some distressing news about your Father Alberto. While he was in his office, he passed away from an apparent heart attack. His body will be flown back to Brooklyn for burial. I am sorry to have to tell you this news, especially over the phone."

"Do you know if he had any information for me?"

"No, I am sorry. I thought it appropriate to call to tell you he would not personally be returning your call."

"Thank you, Father Joseph, Could you give me the particulars of where I could find his family as I should attend his funeral." Father Joseph gave Xavier the address and phone number of the family and then said good-bye.

Although Father Alberto was Xavier's superior, Xavier had never met him and thought out of respect he should call upon his family. Xavier made his call and Alberto's sister answered the phone.

"Hello, this is Xavier Cortez. I worked with your brother for a short period. I was wondering if you could tell me about his funeral arrangements. She introduced herself as Alberto's sister, Florence and invited Xavier to the wake. When she found out he was a Jesuit, she asked him to stay at their home. Xavier graciously accepted, took the train to New York and then a subway to High Street.

Florence met Xavier at the subway stop. She was the only person on the platform. As Xavier walked off the subway car, he saw Florence and immediately became flooded with carnal thoughts. For years, he had not been plagued by any serious sexual desire. He had always considered himself lucky yet in just a matter of seconds, all of that disappeared. He was in lust. Xavier could not look at her and she sensed it.

"Father, was your trip comfortable?"

"Oh yes, the train was very nice and the subway was convenient."

Xavier kept looking away.

"Is something wrong, do I offend you in some way, Father? You look away from me and we have only just met."

"Oh, no, you have done nothing wrong. I am shy and I believe it is more befitting my station if I do not have eye contact with you. You know the old saying the soul is seen through the eyes. I am very afraid that if I look long enough into your eyes, I may never be able to pull away." As soon as those words came out of his mouth, Xavier realized he had been too straightforward and should have left some things unsaid.

"We have just a short walk to my parent's home on Columbia Heights. They came upon a beautiful brown stone home with wide steps leading up into a very formal entrance. In truth, the outside staircase ended on the second floor with an English Basement first floor complete with kitchen and dinning room leading out onto a flagstone terrace overlooking New York's Harbor and lower Manhattan Island. Xavier was mesmerized by the views, the skyline and Florence.

"Are both of your parents alive?" asked Xavier.

"No, my father passed away five years ago. My mother is slightly handicapped and spends much of her time, upstairs. My brother has taken care of the family since my father's death and he will be sorely missed. Florence took Xavier to his room on the fourth floor. The room had the same gorgeous view as the garden below. It also had its own bathroom and was huge in its proportions.

Florence introduced him to her mother saying only that Xavier is a friend of Alberto's. Xavier noticed that her mother suffered from dementia as she began to ramble on about how the Russian Romanoff's would be coming to dinner and she was busy preparing for it.

Florence then brought him back to the staircase, gave him a house key saying that cocktails and dinner would be served at 7:30 and it would be formal. Xavier went up to his room, unpacked, lit up an Old Gold and gazed out his picture window overlooking Manhattan. He sat on the window seat for an hour just taking in the view. He looked forward to a nap and a walk leaving plenty of time to get ready for dinner. As soon as Xavier hit the pillow, he was out for two hours. When he awoke, he did not immediately remember where he was but it all came back to him as he thought of Florence.

He dressed in casual lay clothes and went out for a walk. He went along the promenade and strolled on Montague Street. Xavier admired the nice shops, restaurants and the Heights Casino. As he headed home, he noticed a man following him. He had also seen him at the train station. Xavier dismissed it as either Secret Service or coincidence. The house key Xavier felt in his pants made him think about what it would be like owning something like Florence's house with all of its stature and prestige. He rationalized he would be content in just having the experience and the freedom to move in its beautiful setting but he yearned for more time with Florence.

He bathed and prepared for dinner.

Xavier had brought dinner clothes with a formal shirt that accepted his cleric's collar. As he walked down the stairs into the living room, he noticed Florence in a beautiful sequined Retro gown tight enough for Xavier to get an idea of her physical attributes. *She is magnificent.* He thought. She was busy talking to one of her uncles. Alberto's mother was dressed elegantly; sitting in a high backed cane wheel chair with her embroidered lap cover draped over her legs. Xavier realized no one had told her mother about Alberto's passing. He played along, telling Alberto's mother how nice her dinner party was going.

Florence led the conversation into other small talk before asking her mother to be excused so that she could introduce Father Cortez to the rest of the family and friends that were attending tonight's dinner.

"Thank You for your astuteness, Father. Her heart could not take such bad news at this time and the whole family feels that it might be best never to tell her as she has not seen Alberto for so long that she may never miss him."

"I understand."

Florence was served a Dubonnet on the rocks from one of the butlers. Xavier counted twenty five people not including the houseguests which totaled five on the fourth floor alone. He found her family and friends to be very well educated and adept in all of the social graces. One of the guests was a professor of mathematics at Columbia and Xavier found him very engaging. The ringing of a small silver Dutch girl bell announced that dinner was served. As the guests descended down the stairs, Xavier noticed the dining room had been transformed into a cabaret, complete with an upright piano. His dinner partners were two of Florence's friends. The lady to his right was the wife of a distinguished lawyer and the woman to Xavier's left was the secretary to the President of Macy's department store. She was a single woman and somehow had a connection to Alberto. He would have to wait for an opportune moment to find out more. As they all sat down, Xavier became aware that Florence had been starring at him since he sat down at the table. The eye contact was intense. Florence wanted Xavier to know she was interested. Xavier could not stop answering her look. He was aware of his behavior but could not help himself. By the time the filet loaf arrived, Xavier was engaged in conversation with the lawyer's wife trying to avoid Florence's gaze. It was no use, by the time the flan was served with its thin caramel sauce, the two were completely eye locked but for some strange reason no one else seemed to notice. The meal ended and the group gathered around the piano. The butler served after-dinner drinks and Xavier received a glass of Remy Martin that could have easily been the best cognac he had ever tasted. The playing of songs only strengthened the storm of their sexual tension. When the party ended, all of the guests filed out into the street, good-byes were said and then the houseguests went up to their rooms. Xavier went into his room, undressed and took a bath. As he enjoyed the warm water, he heard something in his room but dismissed it as house settling. As he got up, he realized he was not alone. He put on his robe. As he entered his room, he saw Florence still in her dress looking at him with a puzzled expression.

"I am very perplexed Father. I am extremely attracted to you. It's beyond my control!"

"And I with you, we must be strong and not succumb to our fleshly desires."

As they told each other about their thoughts, the grandfather clock on the second landing struck one and Florence said she had to go.

Xavier walked her to the door and made sure no one was in the hall.

Florence slipped out but heard one of the other guests on the stairs so she flew back into Xavier's room. As she twirled around with her back to the closed door, they kissed. His lustful passion exploded right there. His emotional state of carnal lust caused him to experience an orgasm without any physical stimulation. It was accompanied with a full emotional vision of what it would be like to make love to her. This emotion and physical release was every bit the extreme experience in a carnal way as his rages were in anger or his meditation created utter joy and fulfillment. Florence had no idea of what just had happened. They shared another kiss before Xavier sent her on her way.

The next morning Xavier found himself at the breakfast table, unable to focus. His thoughts were filled with guilt, anxiety and questions about his dedication to the Church. The funeral parlor was just a few blocks away and he decided to walk. Out of the corner of his eye he spotted the same man he remembered seeing at the train station, standing a block down the street. Xavier was headed in that direction and was thinking of approaching the man when the man turned and walked toward the funeral parlor. Xavier watched as he went in and dismissed it as coincidence. Once inside Xavier read the marquee listing and found the viewing room for Father Alberto.

He saw many of the same people in the room that attended the previous night's dinner party. He said hello to them as he approached the casket. He knelt down to pray when he realized the man in the coffin was not the man in the picture he was given with the transfer papers he received in Spain. Xavier did not know what to do as he saw Florence coming into the funeral parlor from the street. The mysterious man from the street waved him into the anteroom and introduced himself as Special Agent Jones of the Secret Service.

"I don't know what to say except that I am very confused."

"Father, that is why I am here, to tell you that the man you knew as Father Alberto worked for the Secret Service. The reason for the deception was to protect you against foreign agents that may try to abduct you or members of your family. The man in the coffin is the real Father Alberto and he was aware of our involvement. Now you are exposed to the very element we tried to keep you away from and it would be to your best interest to leave shortly after this wake and skip the funeral. We will escort you back to Princeton."

"This is all very irregular, why would my Jesuit superiors allow this, much less condone it?"

"Because they are afraid for your safety and they are helping us with the war effort."

Xavier thought for a moment. *The fact that this is the real Father Alberto does not make that much of a difference since I did not know either of the men and the man in the casket was my real supervisor, which is the main reason for my attendance in the first place.*

"I would like to stay here for awhile and then I will go back with you."

"I will be waiting in the foyer when you are ready to go."

Going back inside the main salon, Xavier went up to Florence giving her his sincerest sympathies and then sat down in the back of the room. After an hour, Xavier approached Florence and thanked her for the family's kind hospitality but said he had to return to Princeton this afternoon. "Circumstances are such that we should not tempt the situation any farther."

"I agree, Good-bye Father, I hope to see you again someday."

"I hope so, too."

Xavier put on his coat and went with the two Secret Service men.

They stopped to pick up Xavier's belongings. After going over the George Washington Bridge, they headed up the Palisades. They were going in the wrong direction. Xavier became suspicious these men were not who they said they were when he was hit in the back of the head and lost consciousness. Xavier woke up to find himself in a cell located in a stone walled cellar. The cell had a small adjacent bathroom and was really quite nice. He had fresh fruit and cheese placed on a side table. A man came in to inquire if there was any thing he could get for Xavier.

"Who are you and why am I here?"

"All in due time."

"I have a right to know now!"

"You have no rights."

"Why are you doing this to me?"

"All in due time, Father."

The man left and Xavier was once again alone. He could hear voices.

A disagreement ensued on the floor above with one of the voices being female. Xavier tried to listen but could only make out every third or fourth word and it made no sense. A third person came into the conversation and quieted everything down to the point that Xavier could no longer hear anything. He looked around the cell for anything that might help him escape. He saw a belt strap that held up a pipefitting. He undid it and began working the belt buckles tongue into the cell door's key hole.

Xavier had no idea what he was doing but the lock was poorly designed and after a time Xavier managed to get it to move and after a few more minutes Xavier opened the door and went down the hall. No one was guarding the rooms. He made it to the lower basement storm door and went up the staircase, opened the exterior hurricane doors, and saw that his prison was a luxurious mansion. He climbed the perimeter wall and was picked up by a farmer heading toward the Hunts Point market to rid himself of a load of somewhat spoiled produce. Xavier made a deal with the farmer that he would pay a price equal to what his harvest would yield if he could be dropped off at the bus station. After paying the farmer, Xavier got on the next bus heading toward Pittsburgh. When Xavier first arrived in the States his superiors told him that if there were any type of emergency to contact Jesuit House in Washington, D.C. He arrived there at eight the next morning. It had been a long convoluted trip and Xavier was in need of a soothing bath. He walked into Jesuit House and was escorted into a small waiting room. He was greeted by two men.

"I am Bishop John Branigan and this is Peter Maxwell of the Secret Service."

Peter Maxwell said; "We know that you were abducted. We could not get to you fast enough. The people who took you were Nazi spies. We caught one of them who told us they wanted information concerning the project at Princeton and to talk to you about some sort of family diary.

These spies are after ancient religious relics and your great grandmother seemed to have something of value they wanted. Do you know what we are talking about?"

"Yes, my great grandmother gave me a diary that she kept. I have only skimmed through it but believe me when I tell you it is no relic."

"May we examine it?" asked Maxwell.

"Of course, whenever it would be convenient."

"Actually Father we would like to bring you back to Princeton now where we will keep guard over you and your colleagues and perhaps then we could look at your great grandmother's diary."

"Of course and thank you"

"Don't mention it."

"Now Mr. Maxwell, would you please excuse us? Xavier and I have some Church business to discuss." asked Father Branigan.

"I will be waiting outside."

"Father Xavier, is there anything to this diary?"

"No, your grace, it primarily pertains to a family malady and what our family did to control it."

"Xavier, I am leaving you in Mr. Maxwell's hands. We are anxious for you to help the project along as it is also to the Order's benefit. If there is anything you need, please don't hesitate to call."

"Well, there is one question, why did you let me be deceived about Father Alberto?"

"What are you talking about? Who is Father Alberto?"

"He was my direct superior according to my transfer papers."

"I am sorry Xavier. I have no knowledge of any Father Alberto. You were given your transfer from Spain directly by the Vatican and we here at Jesuit House are your U.S. superiors. We felt you were in good hands in having the U.S. government watching over you with us getting periodic reports every few months. I will look into this Father Alberto personally and call you with my findings. Obviously something has fallen in between the cracks."

"Thank you your grace."

Xavier left the room very confused. The Secret Service escorted him back to Princeton. Once he arrived, he went to his room and handed over his great grandmother's diary. The agents took it and left. Xavier saw their car leave his parking lot some 30 minutes later. He knew they looked at the diary to see if it was authentic before actually heading back on the highway. Xavier's great grandmother anticipated that people would find out about the real manuscript. She painstakingly prepared and kept an alternate personal diary starting some 50 years earlier. Xavier pulled out the real ancient manuscript and looked at it with a newfound respect. Xavier read the Spanish portions of the manuscript cover to cover. He had to translate the Aramaic without being discovered.

The next morning there was a knock at the door. Xavier had put the manuscript away minutes earlier so he answered the knock straight away. The Secret Service agent inquired as to why he had not gone to the lab and asked if something was wrong.

"No, I didn't sleep well last night, just catching a cat nap before starting my day."

"Sorry to disturb you Father, I will be outside."

"Thank You!"

Xavier spent the next four days in the lab and surfaced only to eat and bathe. He was engrossed in his work. Xavier had succeeded in finishing his calculations and now could take a few days off. He was not in his room ten minutes when there was a knock at his door, "Sorry Father, I know you just got back but my superiors wondered if you would come with me to Washington. They have questions about the diary."

"Sure give me a minute and I will get ready. He jumped into the shower and while still drying off, he checked under the floorboards, the manuscript's new home. It was safe.

Xavier entered the D.C. office where ten people were in attendance.

"Father, my name is Nicolas Jomaninsky and these are my colleagues. We have been asked to comment on this diary and its relevance regarding the Nazi's most recent attempt to steal items of national security. The diary was written over a period of 50 years and indeed has some information as to your family's emotional problems but offers very little about Jesus or anything to do with God, so we were wondering why these relic hunters would be so interested in it."

Xavier acted in a manner consistent with confirming his earlier statements. An older woman at the table waited for Xavier to finish and then asked "Father, your great grand mother wrote incessantly about the love of her family and the emotional curse that all of them suffered. Could you comment further on this?

"Yes, she was obsessed with our family's emotional behavioral problems and was afraid for them. She knew that any of us were capable of murder or worse if provoked and our capacity to love is equally intense. These intense emotions can also vacillate from rage one minute to tears of joy the next." Xavier masterfully answered other questions but the elderly woman was not convinced Xavier was telling the entire story but she remained silent. After the questioning was over, Xavier was driven to Jesuit House. He met with the Bishop.

"Hello, Xavier, how goes the inquisition?"

"They really seem quite nice."

"Don't kid yourself my son, they're vultures especially Cecily McCormack. She is an old bird who I swear is psychic. She's like a Jack

Russell dog. She never lets go. Xavier, stay away from her. She will run you down if she has any thought that you have not been entirely forthright. By the way, I looked into your Father Alberto. He was in Chicago but never assigned as your superior. I and the Secret Service are looking into finding out what your Brooklyn experience was really all about. This is a real mystery to us and I'm sure to you as well."

Finishing, the Bishop gave Xavier keys to a room upstairs and said, "I understand you could use a good sleep. Please enjoy yourself. There are clothes and money for you up stairs. I will see you before you go."

Xavier went upstairs and found a fresh set of clothing and one hundred dollars on the night table. After bathing, Xavier went to sleep. When he got up, an attendant brought him a light breakfast and gave him directions to the monuments in the city.

Xavier walked around Washington and found it to be a most beautiful place. He thought he would like to make D.C. his home when he was through in Princeton. He walked through Georgetown's Campus. A feeling came over him as if he was part of the School's fabric. He went into Healy and wandered up to Riggs library. He felt something immediately. Due to his heightened senses, he realized something was different. He sat at one of the many tables, and watched the students study. He knew they were oblivious to the energy he felt. Xavier stayed on for a few more days and then returned to Princeton. His work was progressively getting more into specific problem solving which gave him an idea as to what the group was really trying to do. FBI agents were with them at all times.

In September of 1945, Xavier was offered a chance to move to New Mexico. The bomb was dropped in Japan a month earlier and Xavier was conflicted as to his role in the killing of so many people. He became moody and very difficult. He was under very close watch from the government especially Cecily McCormack. She had strong ties to the more clandestine branches of government and on more than one occasion mentioned to him that she was convinced Xavier knew more than he let on about the diary. Xavier knew she was personally responsible for at least three shakedowns of his living quarters. He never touched the floorboards. He applied to be transferred to Jesuit House and wished to teach Physics at Georgetown. He continued his work at Princeton and used his collaboration as his thesis for his doctorate degree. Since most of the professors reviewing his work knew less about the subject than Xavier did, his degree was conferred quickly. After graduation, he received his transfer to Washington but there was no mention of a teaching position.

Once in Washington, Xavier was evaluated. The Order was well aware of his special problems and there was an interest in ascertaining how serious the behavior disorder was before letting him teach students. The Princeton collaboration enabled Xavier to enrich the Order's coffers but had not allowed him to interact with many people. Xavier was given a series of tests. He was then asked to wait at his parent's home for the results.

Juan and Celina had adjusted quite well into the American way of life and very much appreciated that their family was safe from Franco. They could not wait to have their son home with them.

"Xavier, how long will you be with us?" asked his mother.

"At least three weeks, maybe longer."

As they sat in their small living room, Xavier wanted to complete some unfinished business.

"Mother would you like me to show you the book that great grand mother gave me?"

"Oh yes, Xavier, I wanted you to show it to me many times but I felt you would do it at a time of your own choosing."

"Here it is."

Celina first saw the cloth covering which when undone revealed the most beautiful leather coverlet she had ever seen. The smell of the leather was so fresh and yet she was certain it had to be very old.

"Xavier, how old is this book?"

"The manuscript is more than nineteen hundred years old and contains some very interesting information about our family, Jesus Christ and Mary Magdalene. Our family was one of five chosen to keep the manuscripts safe from extinction and has been the keeper of this manuscript all of this time. It was originally given to us because of our special emotional make up. This emotional intensity has always been a curse to our family but it can also be a blessing acting like a catalyst to bring on what is referred to in this manuscript as "the Kingdom state of consciousness." Our ancestors exhibited their high intensity emotions under a meditative trance referred to as "the Light and Calm." This practice allowed our ancestors to gain access to the Kingdom of God in their mind's eye; they were the best students of Philip, the Apostle. Are you aware of any of this?" asked Xavier. Both parents shook their heads no, as they were trying to grasp what Xavier was saying.

"There is no human intermediary needed to be in God's presence and no payment of money needed to obtain entry to the Kingdom as the Catholic Church would have its parishioners believe."

"Xavier, this is all very hard for your mother and me to believe. Are you suggesting that the message of Jesus was not the doctrine of our religion but instead a practice that the average person could perform to gain access to the Kingdom of Heaven?"

"Precisely, Father and our family has played a great part in the preservation of that knowledge."

"Xavier, you are a Jesuit. What makes you think that any of this is true?"

Xavier was sitting on a love seat across from his father and his mother. He pushed it back and said; "Please prepare to see the light of the Kingdom." With that, a white light vortex appeared over the coffee table, it had a golden hue. He then closed it.

His father said; "Xavier we are old people who do not know about such things."

"I just wanted you and mama to see what our family ancestors have been able to do in preserving the true message of Jesus. As the keeper of the book, I wanted you to know its contents and its power."

His mother said. "Xavier, let us never speak of this again. Grandmother was correct in leaving this information under your control as we are afraid and too old now to want anything to do with this."

Xavier's tests came back normal and he received his next assignment, to teach at Georgetown. He was thrilled and told his parents who seemed relieved that he would be involved in a school. Xavier studied the manuscript and learned Aramaic. He researched all the references made in the margins.

Xavier's first days at Georgetown were spent adjusting to the schedules of teaching and prayer. Many students were international. They kept him informed about his native Spain and other European countries. Xavier was not political but many Jesuits in Washington were and again he found himself having to be very resourceful in answering and dodging questions. He would excuse himself from the dinner table to avoid conversations that would force him to engage in personal philosophy with his other Jesuits. Xavier was well aware all Jesuits were trained in observation. He was concerned that his secret could be discovered by their ability to probe. The slightest variation in expected behavior would be noticed.

During the early sixties, Xavier spent many hours in Riggs Library and had a favorite spot on the fourth stack. It was another beginning of a school year with Xavier sitting in Riggs Library. He became utterly spell bound as he saw a woman mysteriously appear in the third stack. She was the most beautiful woman he had ever seen but unlike his experience with Florence, Xavier had no lustful feelings and was incredibly intent on just beholding such a true vision of beauty.

She looked directly at him and motioned for him to come to her. As he approached, she placed her thoughts directly into his brain. He was stunned. Xavier thought she must be an angel of some sort. He began conveying his deep appreciation for being allowed to experience this fabulous encounter. She cut him off and was very direct in her message; "Do not be afraid. I am here to tell you of coming events. Look for a student who will attend this school. He is arrogant, prideful and shares a similar fate to yours but unlike you, does not have any background to help him with discernment and wisdom. I am asking you to help this boy when he comes across your path but you can never let him know you are watching him or stand ready to help him until he asks for it. Together we can pave the way for the rest of the story to unfold." Xavier absorbed her message. Any lingering doubt that existed about the Kingdom and his role disappeared.

He fought the notion of just accepting the apparition's word for everything and began thinking, "All of this is just a figment of my imagination." She thought back instantly, "No Xavier, it is not; you have been under our watchful eye for many, many years. I must go. Is there anything you want to ask?"

"How will I recognize this student?"

"At dinner one night, you will know."

As soon as those words were conveyed, she disappeared and Xavier was standing alone on the third stack. As he walked back up to his seat, he noticed his limp had utterly disappeared. He felt better than he had in years. He was amazed at his high energy level and renewed sense of vitality. He had so many questions.

Years passed with no student, Xavier thought he missed him some how. The only consolation was that whenever Xavier spent time in the Library, he felt her energy and was comforted by that fact. Finally, during one of the freshman orientation dinners he heard Ian talking at the next table and knew he was the one.

Xavier became despondent when Ian exhibited no interest in learning about the knowledge. Xavier would go to the Library in the middle of the night and talk to the stacks of books hoping the beautiful woman would return so he could ask her what to do. There was never an answer.

Xavier was sure Ian was the student yet time passed with no further contact. One night while Xavier was again up in the fourth floor stack, he noticed Ian on the first floor. Suddenly, the beautiful woman appeared looking at Ian then over to Xavier acknowledging Ian was the student and then disappeared.

Xavier stood silent thinking *that was an interesting way of delivering a message. What am I to do but wait!* Every library encounter Ian had with his

Raven, Xavier was the witness. Although not privy to Ian's visions, Xavier

was aware that something significant was taking place. He knew somehow

that his beautiful lady was instructing Ian. There was a tinge of jealousy

on Xavier's part. He also realized Ian was prevented from detecting

his presence during the encounters with her. On one such encounter,

the stairway light shown directly on Xavier yet Ian was oblivious to his

presence. Xavier found his interests changing. He became an expert on

time and worked with its every aspect. The timing of events, speeches,

wars, anything related to actions and reactions. Xavier became convinced

that timing was the most important ingredient to any event and that there

are no coincidences in life.

Chapter 29 - Otto Grumman

Years after Ian's graduation, Xavier was attending a fundraiser in the President's Office of the University. A young woman latched onto him and was very curious about the old Riggs library. She wanted to know everything about it and began by saying that she was a student of Physics but formally educated in Judaism. Xavier skeptically thought he might be detecting a gentle mental massage being given him by this inquisitive young woman but he wasn't sure.

"Father Cortez, are you aware that Riggs Library could contain an artifact of monumental importance?"

"No, what kind of an artifact?" Xavier responded.

"One that has only been referred to in fantasy stories."

"Now, you have my interest Miss ...."

"Cohen, Sandra Cohen."

Xavier extended his hand and said; "It is a pleasure to meet you. Now tell me more about this artifact."

"Well it appears a priest at Rennes le Chateau in Southern France discovered certain information and a number of relics important to mainstream Christianity. After executing his extortion plan against Rome, the priest became paranoid that his life was in danger. He contacted his closest friend who happened to be a teaching Jesuit here. My research leads me to believe that at a meeting between the two men, information and/or relics were passed from the Priest to the Jesuit who supposedly hid them in Riggs Library. Have you ever heard a story like that?"

"No but it is a fascinating tale." said Xavier. "Did you learn who Béranger Saunière's friend was?"

"Only that he was a Jesuit here. A grounds keeper in France kept a diary of all of Saunière's contacts. He was on the Vatican payroll. I was just one of many researchers who went to that region originally to look into my Jewish heritage only to find out that the local town's people made their living by telling these stories."

"So you don't really have anything to back the story up?"

"No, just a few French people entertaining us in a wonderful restaurant."

"Well, Miss Cohen, thank you for sharing such a story with me."

"You do seem to know something about this."

"Yes and No, I grew up in neighboring Spain and have heard many stories about that priest and his hold over the Vatican but never anything about him having friends at Georgetown and nothing about hidden relics."

The function ended and Father Cortez walked back to his quarters. As he was walking, Xavier began thinking how everything was falling into place. During the last ten years, his aging had slowed almost to a stop and his limp had disappeared since his first encounter with the beautiful angel in the library.

Once in his room, Xavier undressed for bed and crawled under the covers. He was not there two minutes before the phone rang.

"Hello?"

A telephone operator inquired, "Is this Father Xavier Cortez?"

"Yes, who is this?"

"Please hold!"

"Father Cortez?"

"Yes!"

"I am calling you about an Ian MacAlester. Do you remember him?"

"Who is this?"

"Let's just say I am someone you will meet and take very seriously."

Click.

Xavier did not know what to make of the call. He went back to bed. The next day he attended Mass and then went to breakfast. He opened the Post to see that the previous night's event at the School received some coverage. Miss Cohen got great billing as one of the foremost Judaic Relic investigators in the world. The article mentioned her latest trip to Israel and the Sinai. The article also said she was part of one of the translating teams allowed to work on the Dead Sea scrolls. Xavier found her humility refreshing. Then his thoughts went to the previous night's phone call.

Who would even know about MacAlester and why would anyone associate him with me unless the person knew something about our common connection?

Xavier called the Alumni Office. "Hello, this is Father Xavier Cortez. I am trying to locate a student who graduated from here some years ago. I would like to find out where he is today."

"What's his name, Father?"

"Ian MacAlester!"

"Did you say Ian MacAlester?"

"Yes, is there some problem?"

"No, it just seems he is a very popular person this week. The strangest sounding man called earlier saying that we should have Ian MacAlester's information ready when someone calls for it, then hung up the phone and here you are asking about him, Father."

"Do you have the information available?"

"No, we thought it was a crank call. I will get on it immediately and call you back."

"Thank You!" Xavier hung up and started correcting homework. At day's end, Xavier got a call.

"Father Cortez, this is Jennifer at the alumni office. I have the information you requested. Ian MacAlester lives in New York. He is married to another graduate and together they have four children. That is all we have on him."

"Thank You, Jennifer. Can you give me his address?"

Xavier took down the information and called Jesuit House. He asked to speak to a man he used before on personal business.

"John, this is Xavier. How are you?"

"I am fine my old friend. How are you?"

"Well, Thank You! I need a favor."

"What is the name?"

Xavier gave John all of the information and John responded; "The fee will be the same. I will get back to you in a few days."

"Thank You, John." As Xavier hung up, he remembered the last time he used his services to find out about the Father Alberto affair. Xavier sat back lighting up a first level Monte Cristo number 2 as he looked over the city remembering how he handled that situation thanks to John's work. The phone rang interrupting his train of thought.

"Xavier, this is John. Your package is ready."

"John, we just spoke, how did you do this so fast?"

"I love my work and this guy was easy. Come to my apartment anytime and I will have it waiting in the box. If you need more, it is available but I have synopsized all of what I think you want to know. I feel comfortable with the abridged version."

"Thank You!"

"Are you planning a next step?"

"No, my friend, just a "little look see" at the moment."

Xavier got dressed. After Mass, he called a cab and had the driver wait while Xavier went into John's apartment lobby and retrieved his package from the concierge desk. He was disappointed at how light it was. *John has done a poor job this time.* He stuffed it in his coat pocket and went back to campus. Xavier opened the envelope and was amazed; John had printed on both sides of each page and filled them with photos and newspaper articles.

Hmm, Ian has been busy. Beautiful girls! I recognize the wife. I might have had her in one of my classes. Xavier finished reading the analysis John provided and was in complete agreement as to John's well done short version of Ian's life. After finishing the dossier, Xavier put on his gym clothes for his usual workout routine. He had maintained his physical condition and had actually increased his stamina.

A voice called out. "Hey, Father Cortez, do you ever spar? Do you know how to fight?"

Xavier saw a young man coming toward him aggressively.

"No, I am too old for that but I try to keep in shape."

For some unknown reason Xavier became suspicious about the boy and decided to go along with it. The boy threw the first punch and missed. He threw another punch and missed again. Xavier saw the boy's eyes flash in a very unusual way.

"Are you all right, young man?"

"Shut up old man and fight!"

He looked to see the young man coming after him as Xavier ran into the middle of the basketball floor where the girls' team was practicing. One of the girls saw him and ran over to see what was happening when the boy rounded the corner to strike Xavier. The girl attacked the boy and called for the rest of the squad to come to her rescue. They managed to hold the boy until security arrived.

"Are you all right, Father?"

"How do you know me, my dear?" Xavier asked, playing the fatherly priest role.

"I was in your Philosophy class last year, professor. Do you remember me?"

"I will from now on. Thank you for your helpful intercession. I don't know what I would have done had it not been for you and your friends."

"We were glad to be there for you." said one of the other girls.

"Thank you again, very much."

As Xavier walked off the floor, he noticed his old limp had returned.

The Campus police called, "Father, this is Peter Bahls of Campus Security. We have a boy here who reportedly went crazy at the gym and tried to hit you. Is that correct? Would you like us to turn this matter over to Metro Police?"

"Have you spoken to the boy," Xavier asked.

"No, I haven't personally. Why do you ask?"

"Peter, please do me a favor. Talk to him and call me back after he has had an opportunity to tell his side of the story."

"Are you sure this is the way you want to proceed? From what I understand, this boy tried to really hurt you. Pardon me for saying so Father but you should throw the book at this kid."

"Peter, please do as I ask and call me back."

"Ok!" Peter hung up the phone.

Xavier had finished getting dressed when the phone rang.

"Father, it's Peter Bahls, I have talked to the boy. Either he is the best liar I have ever met or he has some form of amnesia. He claims not to remember anything about today. What do you want me to do?"

"I want you to take all of his information and let him go."

"Ok, Father."

Xavier hung up the phone and called John to start surveillance on Ian and also look into the identity of student who assaulted him. The student's name was Owen Walters.

††

"Mrs. Walters, this is Father Cortez from Georgetown University."

"Is Owen hurt or something, Father?"

"No, Mrs. Walters, he is just fine. I do not want to alarm you but I would like to talk to you for a few minutes. Is this a good time?"

"Well, I wish Owen's father was here but please go ahead."

"Thank You, Owen appears to be a very nice boy. His record shows him to have been the valedictorian of his class and to have been the President of his National Honor Society Chapter. Is that correct?"

"Yes, Father, we raised him to be very hard working and studious."

"Has Owen ever exhibited aggressive or violent behavior?"

"No, as far back as I can remember Owen has never been in a fight."

"I was working out in the gym when Owen, whom I had never met, invited me to go a few rounds in the boxing ring."

"That doesn't sound like our Owen at all."

"After reviewing his file, I came to the same conclusion."

"Do you know if he has new friends or people that could cause him to act out this type of behavior?"

"No, Father, Owen is a loner."

"Mrs. Walters, if you don't mind I would like you to keep this between us. You can certainly tell your husband."

"Whatever you feel is correct, Father, will you get back to us?"

"Yes, of course, I will call you in let's say ten days and give you an update. Would that be all right?"

"Yes, that would be fine."

Xavier gave her his telephone numbers should her husband have any questions and called back campus security.

"Peter, this is Father Cortez. I have taken the liberty of looking into this boy's background and think it was a one-time thing but I would like your people to keep an eye on him. Is that possible? Can you do it very discretely?"

"Yes, Father we will watch him. When would you like us to report back to you?"

"Let's say a week."

Xavier went about his business as usual. The week passed quickly and Owen's routine included the library, the cafeteria, the Tombs and studying in his room. He was a loner and appeared to have few friends. After Xavier received Peter's report, he walked over to Owens's dorm and waited for the boy to return from class. Owen walked in the front lobby, stared directly at Xavier and seemed to have no recollection of the previous week.

"Owen, My name is Father Cortez. Do you know me?"

"I don't think so Father, can I help you? Do you teach here at the University?"

"Yes, but that's not why I wish to speak with you. Do you have a minute? Maybe we could sit here and chat. I have some questions for you."

"Sure, Father what is it that you want to know?"

"Do you remember being in McDonough Gymnasium last week?"

"Why no, Father I don't. I know I was there because the campus security police took me to their offices alleging that I was harassing someone at the gym but I don't remember anything about it."

"I was that someone. Does that help?"

"You were the person I was harassing. What did I do? I just don't remember a thing. I was in my room and then I was in the campus guardhouse. It was the strangest thing that has ever happened to me."

"That's why I am here. I sensed you were not yourself. I took the liberty of calling your parents who validated everything you just told me. Could I ask you some questions about your personal life over the past few months?"

"Sure!"

"Have you met or spent anytime with a person or people that could have influenced you in this type of behavior?"

"No!"

"Have you read or studied something that could shed some light on this?"

"No!"

"Have you been exposed to any sort of group hypnosis or other activity that could have influenced you?"

"No! Not that I am aware of."

The intense questioning created a high anxiety within Owen. The boy's demeanor changed. Xavier was ready.

"I command you to reveal yourself."

Owen looked at Xavier and said, "You know who I am and I am coming for you." Owen's facial expression changed back to normal. The boy was petrified.

"Owen lets go up to your room. Do you have a roommate?"

"No!"

"Good!"

"I think we can fix this condition. Everything will be all right."
Owen looked at Xavier with complete confidence and was willing to do
whatever it took.

"Father, what just happened to me? I have no idea what I did. I feel
disgusting."

"Owen, I will explain everything to you after my friends have
examined you. Just know you will be fine. Xavier went down the hall and
made a few calls. When he came back to Owen's room, it was empty.
Xavier was in a panic. He ran up and down the hall calling Owen's name.
No response, he ran into the bathroom. Owen had just finished slitting
his wrists. Blood was everywhere. Xavier applied tourniquets above both
wrists. Less than ten minutes went by before a doctor and Father Quail
were in Owen's room. After examining him, the doctor called Xavier aside.

"Father, this young man could have a number of medical disorders
that could account for this type of behavior. Let's admit him into the
hospital for tests."

The two Jesuits packed some clothes and the boy's dopp kit in a
gym bag and walked him over to the hospital. Xavier thanked Father Quail
for his observation of Owen; "I can't thank you enough. I will call Owen's
parents and let them know his condition."

Father Quail said. "You're welcome; Call me in half an hour for an
update."

Xavier walked back to his quarters and relayed the recent events to Owen' parents. Xavier then called Quail as instructed.

Xavier opened with, "Well, what's with the boy?"

"Only time will tell, Xavier. Do you know more than you're telling me?"

"Yes, but I am afraid to share it. I don't want to get you involved with something that may already be out of control."

"Xavier, I am already involved. We better sit down and go over what you know and soon. How about getting something to eat in lets say an hour?

"Ok!"

"See you in the dining room tonight at 5."

Xavier suspected Quail of having his own agenda which was troubling but unavoidable.

"Ok, Xavier, what gives with the boy? Do you know?"

"I think the boy could be experiencing a form of remote mind control. I learned about this condition from a family heirloom. I have things to tell you but not here."

"When?"

"After dinner, let's walk down by the canal. I will tell you there."

"OK!"

They had a few glasses of wine and ate their meal. They left the dinning room and began walking down the library steps to Prospect Street.

"Ok, Xavier what's so secret?"

"I am going to tell you a different story about Jesus."

Xavier told John about his ancestors and the relationship they had with many of Christianity's main characters but the story was quite different from the one told by the Catholic Church. They walked along the canal heading up river.

"Xavier this is too fantastic to believe."

Xavier understood the dilemma and seemed to change the subject by asking if he had a near death experience or knew someone that did?"

"No!"

"I have something to show you."

Both men walked on a much smaller trail leading to the water's edge. Quail turned to face Xavier when he saw Xavier create a small light vortex in front of his chest.

"You have my attention, Xavier!"

"This vortex signifies the beginning of a process that is beyond your current belief structure." Xavier said as he closed it down.

"What was that?"

"An entry way."

"To what?"

"To the Kingdom."

"What Kingdom?"

"The Kingdom of God."

Quail looked at Xavier and even though he had just seen something quite fantastic, said "Look Xavier you just showed me something very impressive but I don't know what that was, suppose it was just a figment of my imagination. You are brilliant! How do I know that you didn't somehow hypnotize me? You expect me to believe that was a portal to God's heaven. That would be truly unbelievable!"

"It is the gateway to God's heaven and it was conjured up in my mind."

"And what that was has something to do with the boy? That somehow he has become attached to the dark part of this reality?" Quail asked.

Xavier responded, "As always, eloquently put."

"Xavier, you know all of this from a family diary, pardon my skepticism but this story rivals anything I have ever heard."

"You know more about the scrolls found at Nag Hammadi than anyone on this campus. Think about it. I will prove my point reciting one verse found in the gospel of Thomas. Verse 50, Have I not just shown you the light? "

"What is it you would have me do?"

"I need you to help me find out what is happening to the Walter's boy and who is behind his torment."

"You think there is a manipulator who can tie into the boy's psyche?"

Xavier looked down river, lost in thought and then begrudgingly said "yes, I do!"

"I will look into it."

"Please be very discreet and be careful."

"I will be careful. Don't expect to hear from me anytime soon. I am going to research your outrageous claims. I will also keep an eye on the boy."

"Thank you, I am sorry to bring you into this mess but it has clearly gotten bigger than one man can handle."

As they walked back to campus, Xavier could not help think about MacAlester. He was aware that Ian was embroiled in legal nightmares including a messy divorce.

††††

"Hello, my name is Father Cortez. I am a professor at Georgetown University. I wonder if I could talk to Mr. Carole Julius."

"Does he know you, professor?"

"No but he graduated from Georgetown a number of years ago."

"I see, please wait."

"Julius here, can I help you?"

"Mr. Julius, you never met me but I need some assistance with a small investigation and wondered if you could help me?"

"Who is it?"

"His name is Ian MacAlester."

"He is a neighbor!" Julius said and continued, "Father what is it you would like to know about him?"

"Background, he is going through a difficult time, could you look into it for me?"

"Easy, not cheap, do you have the means to pay for this information?"

"Yes, I do!"

"I will be in touch."

†††

One night as Xavier was finishing dinner, a call came into the dining room from the University administration office.

"Father Cortez, you have an overseas phone call. Where would you like to take it?"

"Please put it in the front office. I'm sure no one is there this time of night."

"I will wait for a minute and put it through."

The phone was ringing as Xavier walked through the door.

"Hello?"

"Hello, is this Xavier Cortez?"

"Who is this?"

"I am distantly related to your great grandmother's closest friend. I have spent some time tracking you down. I am coming to the United States in a few weeks and would like to set up a meeting with you to discuss some topics that both my relative and yours had in common. This would pertain to some very rare manuscripts that both of them enjoyed. Would this interest you?"

"Yes, it would. I would very much like to meet you. I will make myself available. I teach almost every day but my nights are free. Are you able to set a time now or do you want to call me when you arrive in the States?"

"I will call you then if I may. I need to firm up a few commitments that are still in flux."

Xavier asked, "What is your name?"

"My name is Otto Grumman. I am sorry for not introducing myself earlier."

"Well, Otto, if I may call you that, I look forward to seeing you soon."

"Yes, you may and I look forward to it as well."

Chapter 30 - Meditation Manuscripts

Otto Grumman came down into the hotel lobby to meet Xavier. He was a good-looking man, older but hard to age define. His hair was bright white with a well-honed athletic build. His gait and posture was that of a man considerably younger. Xavier had not seen this type of elegant style since he lived in Spain.

"You must be Father Cortez."

"Yes, it is a pleasure to meet you, Mr. Grumman, ah, Otto."

They made small talk for about 20 minutes recalling Xavier's time spent in Spain and side trips to Germany and France. The conversation lent itself to exposing Otto's large life style. Xavier was made very aware that Otto had a distinguished career in the Nazi SS and along with his brother, was a relic hunter. They enjoyed special favor with Hitler, himself. As the conversation progressed, Xavier was getting very nervous.

"I must get down to business. Father Cortez, have you ever heard of the Meditation Manuscripts?"

"Tell me about them?"

Otto smirked knowing full well Xavier knew everything. "They reportedly give the recipe to gain entry into the Kingdom of God through meditation."

Xavier responded, "That is a far cry from what has been taught for the past two thousand years."

"Yes, isn't it? Let me go on. During the war, my brother and I were sent into southern France on a mission to find evidence of the existence of any relic that could give the Third Reich an advantage. Hitler was convinced there were such relics and therefore it became our duty to find out about such items as the Holy Grail, the Arc of the Covenant and the Meditation Manuscripts.

I was getting very close to uncovering significant information about the Manuscripts when my brother met a woman named Ruth Tosh. She was an attractive woman in her late fifties and my brother married her. She knew every move I made before I made it and successfully threw me off track in my search. I was totally unaware of her manipulation. The only reason I even became suspicious was that I watched as both my brother and I aged but this woman seemed to get younger. She never lost her white hair but her body was in better tone than mine, even when I was in peak condition.

I had done well after the war and started to amass some real wealth. I could afford to have my sister-in-law followed. I found out she was the connection to these manuscripts. My brother was reluctant but acquiesced to my snooping. I felt she became aware of my brother's betrayal. She vanished, and with her the knowledge of the Mediation Manuscripts and any proof I had concerning them. I became obsessed with gaining access to these manuscripts and after twenty years of study became aware that there were a few such manuscripts sprinkled throughout Europe and now, the world, each covering a different aspect of the Kingdom and its power. One day, I invited my brother to my chateau. I gave him a spectacular lunch and some "treated" wine. I learned about Ruth's only friend, your great grandmother. She had no other friends that I could find and thus the trail has led me to you.

"You, Xavier, have had quite an interesting life and I know that you know exactly what I am referring too so I will not beat around the bush. Here is my proposition. I want to read and study these manuscripts before I die. I believe Ruth did go to the Kingdom and will return when she has found the right person to give the responsibility of keeping her manuscript as incredible as this all may seem. I think you are in possession of your great grandmother's manuscript. I have the money and the power to take it from you, but I have found out the entrusted tenders of the manuscripts have certain powers to put a curse against anyone who violates them or the manuscript. I do not want what happened to Agrippa to happen to me. I will deposit $50 million in a bank account of your choice. I will trust you to censor your manuscript, within reason but I must have access to its core information.

You can use the money in any way you wish. There will be another $50 million deposited after you have delivered Ruth's censored copy to me. Do we have a deal?"

"What do you want to accomplish by having the information contained in these manuscripts?"

"I am getting old. I want to right the many wrongs I have committed. I want to gain access to the Kingdom of Heaven when the time comes. Cheat the grim reaper if you will."

Xavier knew he was dealing with a very shrewd man.

"Mr. Grumman, I will look into this further and get back to you."

"I leave in a few days, Father; I want to gain an understanding before then if possible."

Xavier nervously answered, "I will take your wishes into consideration and call you with my answer."

Otto said good night and left. Xavier sat finishing his coffee suffering deep consternation as to what to do, next.

Chapter 31 - A Meeting of the Minds

Xavier had the hotel doorman hail a cab and, as he climbed into the back seat, directing the driver, "Please take me to 36th and P Street North West."

"Main Campus?"

"Yes, Thank You!"

Xavier gazed out the window as they proceeded down Pennsylvania Ave, crossed the Rock Creek Parkway Bridge and ran into traffic on "M Street." Xavier's mind was racing. He became very nervous over what he was considering. *I have never explored this power. I will use it to find out who this character Grumman is and what he really wants. My great grandmother was right. There are people out in the world who somehow are aware of these most sacred manuscripts and I must protect them at all costs. Timing is everything. There are no coincidences."*

As he walked into his quarters, he locked his door and sat in a straight-backed wooden chair that he placed in the middle of his spartan bedroom. He began to meditate. He had practiced this same meditation for years but never completed the full exercise because he never felt worthy of what his manuscript promised but now, under the circumstances he needed to find out who Otto Grumman was and his motives. Xavier began going into a deep calm.

As he, for the first time, started to enter the portal, the beautiful woman of the library came to him in his vision and said, "Stop, go to Riggs library!"

Xavier was immediately back in his bedroom. He put on a pullover and went to Riggs. He found the door locked. Xavier looked in amazement as the lock gently turned and the door opened. She was waiting for him on the third level stack.

"Hello, Xavier!" She thought.

"Hello!"

"You want to know about Grumman!"

"Yes!"

"You are afraid of this man?"

"Yes!"

"You have good instincts. Mentor Ian MacAlester. Give him your manuscript. He will get Ruth's. MacAlester will be meeting Grumman very shortly. He will come to find you and when he does, show him everything you know to imprint his mind. I know you understand my meaning. You must also get him to talk about his experience to expose what he has most assuredly suppressed. He is unaware as to the great strides he has made in discovering The Cypher. His experience will enlighten you and together the two of you will continue on this journey."

Xavier left the library and headed toward the Tombs. *Why should I have to give up my manuscript? Who was this MacAlester and why is it my job to baby sit him?*

He pondered his jealousy over a merlot and resigned himself to his new position of mentor. *After all, any part in this play will be a privilege to perform.*

Months passed. Cortez called Grumman to say he needed time to consider his proposal without admitting or denying his allegations. Julius gave him information on Ian but nothing he didn't already know. While Xavier was on his way out of Nathan's one night after having dinner, he looked to his left and saw Ian MacAlester talking with someone at the bar. He could not believe it. *What are the odds of this happening?* He waited at the Riggs bank across the street as it looked like MacAlester and his friend were paying the bill. When Ian and Rosco left and walked down M street, Xavier followed MacAlester to his hotel. Xavier then went back to his quarters and called his friends to keep track of Ian. When Ian came back into town next, Xavier would be waiting.

†††

"Xavier, this is John. Ian is back at his favorite hotel." Is there anything that you would like me to do?"

"Yes, I have a package to deliver to MacAlester. Can you arrange that for me?"

"Consider it done and I will keep an eye on him."

"Thank You, John!"

††††

Ian had just arrived back in Washington to follow up with The Metropolitan Police about Debra Laurie. He had a wonderful night and was ready to start his day. Ian dialed the concierge desk, "Good morning! Carl, what is a stay here without me calling you asking for some unusual help? I have another request. Could you find out about a Father Cortez? He's a Jesuit Priest that used to teach at Georgetown. I can't believe he would still be there but we might find a thread too track him down. I don't want anyone to know that I am looking for him."

"Mr. MacAlester, I am happy to oblige."

The phone call was put on hold for an instant.

"Hello, Ian, I hear you are looking for me!"

"Father Cortez?"

"The very same."

"How did you know?"

"Why don't you meet me down stairs in the dining room and we will discuss everything over breakfast."

Ian walked directly into the dining room and saw Cortez, sitting at a table with his back to him, looking out into Rock Creek Park.

"Father Cortez, it is so go…."

Ian stopped in mid sentence and just stared at Father Cortez.

Ian blurted out, "This is impossible, simply impossible!"

"I must admit, seeing me for the first time in so long could unnerve even the most open minded of people. Yes, it is really me. Why don't you sit down?"

Father Cortez hadn't aged a day since Ian was in college. They exchanged their experiences and how time had treated them when Father Cortez, having some fun mixed with a tinge of jealousy, asked, "Ian, tell me of your experience with the manuscript. Our beautiful lady of the library has assured me that your story will enlighten and entertain."

Ian was astonished at the question; "You have seen her? You are the only other person who has ever seen her. I really thought I was losing my mind. Is there something specific you are interested in knowing?"

"Tell me about the True Believers."

"You never did waste any time, Professor. My interpretation of the True Believers is that they did not think Jesus died for people's sins but for the people's laws, to absolve people for not following the Torah's laws and for allowing gentiles to be a part of the Kingdom of God without having to be Jewish and for all those people not educated in Jewish tradition. This is why he told his disciples to follow James because James was of the Jewish Law and kept the Jewish tradition. It would be James that would keep the laws for all True Believers and they would incorporate Jesus' message into a more accepting practice of spirituality not religion." Ian continued; "Mary Magdalene, Thomas, Phillip, Lazarus and many others spread the word of God in its spiritual message and left the laws for James to sort out. That was the original plan. The Sadducees and Pharisees hated this notion of accepting gentiles into any part of their faith. They labeled Jesus, a heretic. What ever happened at His crucifixion must have been memorable because twenty years after the event, the rolls of the True Believers were swelling.

The rift between Peter and Paul against James deepened and forged different messages. There has been significant success in ethnically cleansing The True Believers message by the Catholic Church. The True Believers believed that prayer, meditation and mind over matter brought them closer to the Creator. They learned from Mary's message that they could in fact have Heaven on Earth by practicing certain meditative techniques, sharing their blessings and avoid getting caught up in the material world. They had a tremendous reverence for nature and placed a strong emphasis on personal responsibility and accountability. It's not just the will of God but the will of the individual; something the soul feels is needed to advance. Innocent III was petrified his "flock" would learn the real message spread by Jesus' wife and that this information would eventually destroy his church so he killed all the Cathars, who adopted a form of True Believer ideals. It started the 800 year inquisition to exterminate the last remnants of a philosophy that in all likelihood Jesus actually handed down."

Ian stopped for a minute and ate his food. Although Xavier knew the history, he did not organize the information in the way Ian presented it. Ian continued, "Jesus could be well within Jewish tradition and preach the message of the Kingdom of God."

Xavier asked, "That's quite an accusation about the Church ethnically cleansing this idea out of existence."

"Father, our lady of the library showed me a vision of how it began and why. The Pope got rid of the spread of this spiritual virus and the French King got money and lands. King John of England was too busy getting excommunicated. The net result was another thousand years of passing the plate and the elimination of a compelling competing idea that was very bad for Church business. Father, by no means am I claiming to know the answers. I'm just a guy who has stumbled onto what looks like some very interesting questions and I have had visions that suggest some very ugly answers. It is up to you academics to connect the dots.

The two men finished their breakfast and sat in the hotel lobby talking. Xavier began telling Ian his most current pressing information about the Walter's boy and his experiences with emotional intensity but he quickly realized they would need years to share all their knowledge. The two agreed to work together to find the other Meditation Manuscripts and to piece together information their current manuscripts held. Ian left to meet the police detective and Xavier sat a while longer thinking that their work would take them both away from the things they loved and life would most likely get very dangerous going forward.

✟✟✟

Tucked in the heart of the Dolomites is the village of San Cassiano with its population of just over 700. This location is considered one of the most tranquil places on earth and perhaps one of the best for practicing meditation. The language is Ladino or Rhaeto and has been spoken since the Roman occupation. On the outskirts of the village is a magnificent castle perched high on a mountain top overlooking its neighboring pastel colored peaks. In the castle's Brazilian rosewood study sat its owner and oldest resident, Otto Grumman. If he had to speak, Ladino was preferred but thought transfer was so much more efficient. He briefly thought of Owen Walters and instantly saw out of the boy's eyes, surveying the hospital room where the boy has been quarantined since his suicide attempt.

"Good and Evil is so passé. *Wait until they see what comes next.*"

Epilog

Chapter 32 - Epilog - A Little History

After finding the Gnostic scrolls in Nag Hammadi, Egypt in 1945, why did it take 50 years to translate them? My research began in 2001. At that time, there were fantastic stories of smuggling, intrigue and theft as to how the Nag Hammadi scrolls finally became available for translation. It was reported that some were stolen and that others were split up and sold, never to be seen by the public. I found a reference regarding a Gospel of Jesus stolen from the University of Cairo in 1998. Eight years later, in going back to see if the stolen scrolls were ever recovered, I couldn't find any reference to the events or even a meaningful account as to what actually happened. The gospel of Mary has less speculation to its existence but it too is mired in controversy. A large number of pages were never translated. The reasons cited were dilapidation and disintegration. In actuality few pages were ever translated and even those had key words missing.

The controversy doesn't end with the documents themselves. There is debate as to the accuracy of their translation. Who translated them and why were those particular scholars chosen to translate and publish the scrolls' meaning? Was the Council of Nicaea in 325AD influenced by the "Dove" vision Jesus had during his own baptism in adopting the concept of The Holy Trinity? This mystery is far from being solved.